Praise for Jennifer Erin Valent's
Fireflies in December

"Valent's debut is both heartwarming and hand-wringing . . . [and] the cast of characters is rich."
—*Publishers Weekly*, starred review

"Winner of the Christian Writers Guild's 2007 Operation First Novel contest, Valent has created a darkly evocative historical novel that boldly explores the divisive effects of unreasoning hatred, greed, and fear on a community . . ."
—*Booklist*

"With expressive descriptions and credible characters . . . Valent shines an awareness on the racial tensions in the South in the 1930s and its impact on innocent children."
—*Romantic Times*, 4-star review

"An impressive book . . . a great story with interesting, credible characters . . . [that] will keep readers turning pages."
—Crosswalk.com

"I found this book difficult to put down and it stayed in my heart well after reading the last page."
—*Christian Women Online*

"A tight, finely crafted novel that challenges us to root out any hint of prejudice in our own hearts . . ."

—Titletrakk.com

"We're proud of Jennifer, and you're about to learn why. I envy your first look at this new talent. You won't be disappointed."

—Jerry B. Jenkins, *New York Times* best-selling author
and owner of the Christian Writers Guild

"Jennifer Erin Valent's debut novel is as sweet and salty as the South itself."

—Jan Watson, award-winning author
of the Troublesome Creek series

"*Fireflies in December* is an extraordinary first novel—a pure joy to read."

—Maureen Lang, award-winning author of *Look to the East*

"I love this book! And I cannot wait to see what comes next from Jennifer Erin Valent!"

—Eva Marie Everson, coauthor of the best-selling
The Potluck Club series

COTTONWOOD
WHISPERS

Jennifer Erin Valent

AWARD-WINNING AUTHOR

TYNDALE HOUSE PUBLISHERS, INC.

Carol Stream, Illinois

Visit Tyndale's exciting Web site at www.tyndale.com

Visit Jennifer Erin Valent's Web site at www.jennifervalent.com

TYNDALE and Tyndale's quill logo are registered trademarks of Tyndale House Publishers, Inc.

Cottonwood Whispers

Designed by Dean H. Renninger

Edited by Sarah Mason

Published in association with the Books & Such Literary Agency, 52 Mission Circle, Suite 122, PMB 170, Santa Rosa, CA 95409-5370, www.booksandsuch.biz.

This novel is a work of fiction. Names, characters, places, and incidents either are the product of the author's imagination or are used fictitiously. Any resemblance to actual events, locales, organizations, or persons living or dead is entirely coincidental and beyond the intent of either the author or the publisher.

Library of Congress Cataloging-in-Publication Data

Valent, Jennifer Erin.
  Cottonwood whispers / Jennifer Erin Valent.
    p. cm.
  ISBN 978-1-4143-3326-7 (pbk.)
  I. Title.
  PS3622.A4257C67 2009
  813'.6—dc22
                                                                   2009016462

Printed in the United States of America

15 14 13 12 11 10 09
7 6 5 4 3 2 1

TO MY PARENTS, JOE AND BARBARA VALENT,
for their faith in me.

AND TO MY SAVIOR
for blessing my faith in Him.

Acknowledgments

I'm blessed to have too many people to thank, but I'll do my best to remember all those who have created a web of support around me. My sincere appreciation goes out to everyone at Tyndale House Publishers for continuing to believe in my work; to Karen Watson for making me feel so welcome at Tyndale; to Stephanie Broene, my gifted acquisitions editor, for caring so much about my characters and stories; to Sarah Mason, my hardworking editor, who never fails to provide the missing pieces to my plotline puzzles; to Babette Rea, my marketing manager, for beautifully displaying my work to the public; to Maggie Rowe, my publicist, for rescuing me from my horrible bios and encouraging America to read my books; to my agent, Wendy Lawton, for guiding me so smoothly through the maze of publishing and giving me so much of her time and wisdom; to Jerry Jenkins and everyone at the Christian Writers Guild for their continued support of my writing; to meteorologist Jim Duncan for answering my spur-of-the-moment weather questions; to my parents for never doubting me no matter how crazy my plans sound; to Trish for being more than a sister, for being a friend; to my family for their love and encouragement, especially Ethan, Micah, and Cady—my biggest fans; to Aunt Jan and Rosemary for their tireless prayers; to Grandma and Aunt Donna for so proudly spreading the word about my books; to Corinne and Michelle being my unofficial publicists; to Cristi, Missi, Mel, Amy, Ginny, Lori, Joan, and Karen—my friends and encouragers; to Brian and Stephanie for working with me as I learn to balance two careers at once; and to Austin and Sarah for reminding me how fun life can be.

Chapter 1

I've heard the dead whisper.

Every time I tell my best friend Gemma that, she frowns at me, says, "There ain't no such thing as ghosts," and then tells me I'm crazy. But I'm not crazy. The dead really can whisper, only it isn't their ghosts that do it. It's the memory of them.

There's a place around the bend from my momma and daddy's house where a stone cross rests beneath a cotton-wood tree. That cross is where I first heard the whisper. It's not really a grave so much, but a marker to remind people of what we lost that day. I was only seventeen when we placed that marker there, but it still looks pristine, like it was made just yesterday. Only yesterday was a long time ago, and time has brought a whole lot of changes since—some good and some bad.

And that's just what I was looking for in that summer of 1936 . . . changes.

The last day of the school year saw me and Gemma meeting up at the pharmacy for a soda to celebrate another year of my surviving school. When I got there, she was standing outside the building, swinging her purse by one hand.

"Where you been?" Gemma asked when she caught sight of me. "I've been waitin' ten minutes."

"Teacher took a long time givin' her end-of-year speech. She sure does like to talk."

"Sounds a lot like you."

I wrinkled my nose and gave her a shove, but she was the only person who could talk sharp to me and not get an earful back. We were like sisters, Gemma and me, and the way I figured it, sisters should be able to say near about anything to each other.

We sat down at the pharmacy counter with confidence because Mr. Poppleberry, who ran the place, didn't have a thing against colored people, and he welcomed Gemma in all the time.

"I'm gettin' a job this year," I said determinedly once we were settled with our chocolate sodas. "I'm tired of not havin' money to do things with."

"Where you gonna work? Ain't much open around here these days."

"I'll find somethin'. Everyone in Calloway knows I'm a good worker."

She shook her head. "Work ain't so fun as you think. It

ain't all independence and extra pocket change. It gives you backaches and weary bones, too."

"You've only been workin' at the Hadleys' for two months, and you sound like you're old hat at it." I took a long sip of my soda and sighed. "Heck, you get to spend your days in that big old mansion of theirs." I rested my chin on my hand and gave her a sideways glance. "All the same, you won't catch me workin' for no Hadleys. They're just a bunch of uppity do-nothin's."

Gemma shushed me with a kick on my shin, and I gasped, pointing an angry glare her way.

"What'd you do that for?"

She didn't say anything, but I saw her straighten up in her chair a little bit and look up past my head.

"You girls gettin' somethin' cool to drink?" a man's voice asked from behind me. "Sure is a fine day for coolin' off any which way you can."

I spun around in my seat and turned back just as quickly when I saw it was Joel Hadley walking our way. Joel was the youngest son of the Hadley family, but his dangerous reputation belied his twenty-one years. I knew Joel Hadley for a charming scoundrel, and I was disgusted that my end-of-school celebration would be marred by his presence.

Gemma smiled at him with an extra twinkle in her eye. "Just givin' Jessie somethin' special. She finished school today."

"Good ol' days," Joel said with a sideways smile. "Seems

a long time ago, all that school stuff. Seem long to you, Gemma?"

"Not so much, Mr. Hadley. I'm not too long out."

Joel patted my head as though I were a five-year-old instead of the almost-seventeen-year-old that I was. I sat up a bit straighter. "You got some business we're keepin' you from, Joel? We don't mean to hold you up or nothin'."

Gemma glared at me so quickly that I barely noticed it between the dumb smiles she kept giving that boy, but I knew it was there all the same.

"Well now, I was just takin' a break from my work. I came on over for some cigarettes and lo and behold, I got an extra treat, seein' such pretty faces."

Charm oozed from his pores far too easily to be natural, and I couldn't believe for the life of me that my wise Gemma could be taken in by such nonsense.

I fingered my straw and avoided looking at either of them. "Guess you'd better get back to the bank, then. Seein' how it's your daddy's bank and all, we'd best not keep you from your work."

Joel eyed me for a minute, slowly rolling a toothpick back and forth in his mouth.

After several seconds, I met that gaze with a forthright one of my own. "You got need of somethin', Joel?" I asked innocently.

"Nope." He stared at me for a minute longer, and I didn't like his look one bit, all narrow-eyed like a rabid fox. I just looked casually back down at my soda, stabbing the cherry at the bottom of the glass. I fished it out and popped it in my mouth like nobody was even there.

Gemma cleared her throat. "Tell Mrs. Hadley we're right grateful for the tub of strawberries she sent home with me yesterday. We all appreciate it, I'm sure." With those words, she turned to me for agreement, nudging me beneath the counter.

As it was, I knew nothing about a tub of strawberries, so I shrugged and said, "S'pose we are. I ain't tried one yet to tell."

I could see by Gemma's face that she thought me rude and undignified, but I was of no mind to give notice to men who put on faces that didn't match their insides. Pretty pictures were all well and good, but if there wasn't a good story behind the picture, it meant nothing. And that's what I thought the whole lot of Hadleys were: just pretty pictures with no meanings.

Joel finally took his eyes off me to reply to Gemma, but his manner toward me remained charmingly hostile, and I was surprised that Gemma didn't notice the coldness he showed me. Or maybe she did, I thought, and she just didn't care. No matter what she thought, she was now giving all her attention to Joel.

He tipped his hat at her and smiled. "Plants are full this year. Don't see any need in lettin' them rot."

Gemma nodded in reply, her docile mood making me doubt her true identity. The Gemma Teague I knew didn't get flutters over men and strike fancy poses like she was doing now.

"Well," Joel said, "best get goin'. Time and money wait for no man." He tipped his hat at Gemma again, flashed me a wry sort of grin, and walked off to buy his cigarettes, leaving us to sit in a moment of tense silence.

It was only after Gemma had stirred her soda for about a minute that she looked up at me with chagrin and said, "Jessie, what'd you have to go and do that for?"

"Do what?" I asked, though I knew full well what she meant.

"You was downright rude to Joel Hadley. Downright rude!"

"Me?" I argued. "Did you see the looks he was givin' me? He could've near burned a hole in my skull."

"He had every right to after the way you talked to him. Sakes alive, Jessie, he's a Hadley."

"That make him the king of England or somethin'? I ain't got to bow to Hadleys no more'n I have to bow to Peeboe the milkman. Since when do I got to give people extra respect just for bein' richer than me?"

"That ain't got nothin' to do with it," Gemma said in exasperation, though I could see she wasn't quite sure herself what she meant. "It's just . . . well, I work for them and everythin'."

"Don't mean you gotta worship them."

"I don't!"

"Way you looked at him, a body would think you did."

"I don't want to talk about it," she said in a huff. "I just don't want to talk about it."

We sat there for a bit in an uncomfortable silence while Gemma slowly sipped her soda, and I wished I hadn't finished mine already so I'd have something to do. I leaned on the counter and tapped a rhythm on it until another thought came to my mind. "He smokes cigarettes too."

"So?"

"So? It's a smelly old habit. And Momma always says it's a stumblin' block."

"There ain't no commandment about smokin'."

"There ain't no commandment about tippin' cows, neither," I said abruptly, "but we ain't supposed to do it."

"Luke Talley himself works in the tobacco factory, and you want to marry him."

"But he ain't smokin' it!"

"What's the difference between smokin' it and makin' it for other folks to smoke? Besides, your daddy don't smoke hay in that pipe of his."

I glared at her, not sure which way to go in this argument since I'd only brought it up by fishing for something else to blame Joel Hadley for. I went back to tapping my fingers and avoided looking at her.

Gemma tossed her napkin down and grabbed up her purse. "I don't want to talk about work today," she announced. "I don't want to talk about nothin'."

That's exactly what we did as we walked home. We talked about nothing. We didn't talk about her job or school or anything else. To avoid the tension, I tried thinking of other things, like what I was going to wear to church that Sunday. I thought about asking Gemma if I could borrow her red hair bow, but I wasn't sure I should speak to her about anything just then, much less about something so trivial as a red hair bow.

We often borrowed each other's things for church seeing as how we went to different congregations and the people there wouldn't realize we were swapping. Gemma went to a colored church a few miles down the road. It was a sticking point with me that four years after her momma and daddy died, Gemma still had to stay away from certain places we went to even though she lived with us. But the way Gemma saw it, we weren't going to cure all the world's ills in her lifetime, and the fact that we were at least untouched by violent prejudice lately was advancement enough for her.

"A body's got to wait for change sometimes, Jessie," she said to me once. "We done gone to hell and back just to get rid of the violence, and it's a miracle itself for us to see Calloway at peace with me still livin' at your place, even if some do turn a cold shoulder. I'll take that to my heart and be happy we got this far."

I'd assumed she was likely right, but I still had parts of me tied up in knots over people's strangeness. Nonetheless, I'd had to get used to the fact that Gemma had gone to a different school and a different church and couldn't freely walk into any store in town she wanted to.

I glanced over at her and studied her face, thinking it

didn't look so angry as it had before, so I cleared my throat to get her attention and said, "You wearin' your red hair bow on Sunday?"

"Probably not," she murmured.

"I was thinkin' I'd wear my white dress."

She swung her purse by her side and continued to watch her feet as we walked along, kicking up the dry dust. "Guess you want to wear my bow."

"I was thinkin' on it."

"You can wear it."

We walked on for a couple of minutes in silence before Gemma seemed to decide there weren't any real good reasons for us to keep fighting. She kept looking down at the ground, but her voice got a little lighter when she said, "Guess you think Luke will think you look right pretty in that red bow."

I snapped my head up. "No ma'am, I don't! I just like lookin' nice on Sundays, is all."

Her eyes glittered. "You talk a big talk, but come Sunday, you'll stew over how to wear your hair and whatnot. Just like you always do. And you'll swoon over Luke like always."

"Don't matter none, I told you." I took my own turn to watch the ground, since looking at Gemma only told me she knew how I truly felt despite the lying words I was saying. "Anyhow, Luke wouldn't notice me in a month of Sundays."

"If he did show you attention right now, your daddy'd kill him. You best be happy he don't see you as more than a sister yet."

"I'm nearly seventeen," I argued. "I'm enough of a woman to be courtin'."

"Not courtin' a man of twenty-three. The minute Luke were to show you some attention, your daddy would be loadin' the shotgun."

"Oh, he would not. Daddy wouldn't kill Luke."

Gemma waved a hand in front of her face to dismiss the subject. "If it's meant to be, Jessie, it'll be. That's all there is to it. It just ain't meant to be *yet*."

I shrugged, guessing she was probably right, though I hated to admit it. Gemma went on inside, but I stood on the porch steps for a minute giving a little thought to her idea that Daddy would have the shotgun on Luke if he came courting. I shook my head at the notion and sighed. It seemed every other day I heard my momma moan about how fast time was flying, but the way it seemed to me, I couldn't get old fast enough.

Chapter 2

"Wasn't it just yesterday you turned thirteen, Jessilyn?" my momma asked me as she scrambled some eggs. "And here you are turnin' seventeen today. I declare, time flies faster'n a body can keep up."

I had no reply. I could hear her like her voice was in the background, but I was too busy wondering about Gemma's ways with Joel Hadley the day before.

"You got any special hopes for this birthday? any big plans you didn't let me in on?" Momma tried again.

When I didn't answer, she stopped beating the eggs and glanced at me. I was sitting at the kitchen table, thoughtlessly buttering biscuits.

"Jessilyn," Momma said. And then she repeated, "Jessilyn!" a bit louder to get my attention.

I finally snapped out of it enough to say, "Yes'm?"

"You butter them biscuits any more, you'll have nothin' left but butter with a little biscuit attached." She laid her whisk on the counter and put both hands on her hips. "You got your head on today?"

"Think so."

"You sure?"

I dropped my head down onto my arms and wailed, "I don't know, Momma."

Daddy walked past the kitchen door, stopped, and poked his head into the room. "What's wrong with Jessilyn?"

"Just confused, I think," Momma said, talking about me like I wasn't in the room. Momma just about always attributed my anxiety to teenage girl things.

"Well, what's got her confused?"

"Seventeen, I think."

"Sadie, how's seventeen make a girl confused?"

"Ain't seventeen; it's the things that come along with seventeen."

Daddy lowered his voice even though I was only six feet away from him. "Ain't she already been confused at thirteen, fourteen, fifteen, and sixteen?"

"Daddy!" I cried.

He ducked his head a little and held his hat out in front of him in a placating gesture. "Honey, I was just wonderin' out loud. I didn't mean nothin' by it."

"You meant somethin', all right." I stood up quickly with a squeal of my chair. "I must be the worst person in the world to live with, I guess, seein' as I'm always confused and all."

I let my butter knife drop onto the table with a clatter and ran out of the room. Now, I knew I was being crazy, and I felt bad knowing that I'd left my daddy shaking his head at Momma. But I also knew that Momma would say, "She's just a growin' girl, Harley," and he'd accept that and head out to the fields. I knew that because it had happened a hundred times already in my young life.

I made my way through the fields to do some thinking, even though thinking was probably the last thing I needed to do. As usual, I ended up walking past Luke's house. I pretty much had a homing instinct toward that little cottage in the woods, and I knew I'd find him home on this Saturday morning. He was out back leaning over his old worktable, fully engrossed in his chore, but when he caught sight of me, he dropped his tool and stepped in front of the table with one quick movement.

"Jessilyn!" he said nervously. "What're you doin' sneakin' up on me like that?"

"I ain't sneakin'. I'm just walkin'."

"Well, I can't really talk right now, you hear? I got things to finish up."

He was standing there strangely, his cheeks all red, and I leaned over slightly trying to see what he was obviously trying to keep me from seeing. He kept moving in different directions, first to the right and then to the left, whichever way was necessary to keep me from catching a glance at his project.

I was far too curious to leave without finding out what he

was hiding, so I ambled a little closer to him. "You got some-thin' to hide, Luke Talley?" I asked with a sly smile.

"I don't hide things."

"You are too hidin' somethin'," I insisted.

"Now, Jessie, just stay back. You're dreamin' things up."

"Why should I stay back if I'm just dreamin' things?"

I walked a little farther toward him, but he made a sud-den move and stumbled backward over something. When he landed on his backside, I caught sight of what he'd hidden from me, and I forgot all about asking him if he was all right. Rushing to his side, I said nothing of his unfortunate position and just stared at the beautiful jewelry box that sat on that rickety old wooden table in Luke's backyard.

It was incomplete—one of the doors hung half-attached and the wood was bare and unfinished—but it was quaint and charming nonetheless.

"Did you do this?" I asked him in awe.

"Doggone it!" he said, slapping his leg with his hat to dis-lodge the dust on his pants. "Why don't you listen?"

"I asked you a question. Did you make this?"

He ran a hand through his sandy hair, tugged his hat down onto his head in a frustrated sort of way, and sighed. "Yes, ma'am, I did make it. And now if you ain't up and ruined the whole thing."

"Ruined it?" I argued, still fascinated that he had done such fine craftsmanship. I had seen Luke make many a chair and table, but never something so fine as that jewelry box.

"I ain't even touched it, and you're sayin' I ruined it? I didn't break a thing."

"I didn't say you broke it, Jessilyn," he mumbled. "Just never you mind and let me get to work."

"Well, why can't I watch? I ain't never seen you make somethin' so fine before. I'd like to see how you do it."

"I'm almost done, anyhow. Ain't nothin' to watch but me tightenin' some screws and paintin' some wood."

Seeing as he seemed to be in a fine and nasty mood, I said nothing more. Instead, I moved back a few yards and settled into the crook of a tree to watch from a distance.

Thinking I'd left, Luke fiddled with the jewelry box door. "Sneakin' around like that," he muttered under his breath, bending over to pick up the screwdriver that had rolled under the worktable. "That girl's always comin' round when she shouldn't. I swear it!"

I bristled at his comments. "If you don't want me comin' round no more, then you just say so."

My exclamation caught him by surprise, and he stood too quickly, slamming his head on the table. "Dagnabbit!" he yelled, rubbing his head. "Would you let a body know you're around before you scare 'em half to death?"

"What're you yappin' about? I was just talkin' to you no more'n a minute ago."

"Well, I thought you'd gone."

"Well, maybe I will go."

The two of us squared off like sparring partners, our eyes

narrowed at each other. Then he just shook his head and said, "Girls!"

Now, I'd known Luke for four glorious years, and the way I figured it, he could say just about anything to me and get away with it, even if I did fuss at him for show. But he couldn't have done much worse that day than to call me a girl. I'd loved Luke since the day I'd met him, and I didn't want him thinking of me as just some girl. The rage in my voice made that point loud and clear.

"Girl! Don't you dare call me a girl."

Luke raised an eyebrow and said with a clenched jaw, "If I'm talkin' to a girl, I call her a girl. You want me callin' you a boy?"

"I'm a woman!"

He tossed his screwdriver onto the table with a clatter and took a few steps. "Now, Jessie, don't get started with all that again. Every time I say the word *girl*, you go gettin' angry. It ain't like I'm callin' you a baby or nothin'."

"You may as well have," I cried. "Callin' me a girl! I'm seventeen today, case you didn't know it, and I ain't no girl."

"I know all about you bein' seventeen," he yelled. "You're gettin' sore over nothin'."

"Well, I ain't no little girl."

"I never said you was. You think I'd go through all the trouble to make a fancy jewelry box for some little girl? No sir!"

I stood ramrod straight, ready to fire back, but his words

suddenly took root in my brain. "For me?" I squeaked out. "You didn't tell me that was for me."

His cheeks started to take on that red flush again, and he studied the ground. "Well, what'd you think I was hidin' it for?"

"I thought you just didn't want me knowin' you did it, like you were embarrassed to let me see."

"I didn't want the surprise ruined, is all. I was runnin' late with it, anyhow, and now all this arguin' set me back even more."

I walked slowly back over to the intricate box. Nobody had ever made anything like that for me in my life, and to have it come from Luke was like a dream come true. I studied its every curve and swoop, running my hand lightly across the grain of the wood.

Luke came to stand beside me and watched my face with a mixture of embarrassment and satisfaction. "Now that the cat's out of the bag," he said at length, "d'you like it?"

"Do I like it?" I murmured. Filled with that surge of anxious emotion that could come over me when I was with Luke, I stumbled for words.

"Well, do you?"

"I . . . I . . . ," I stuttered, taking short, wobbly steps backward away from him. "I . . . love it, Luke," I finally managed to say. "It's the prettiest thing anybody ever gave me."

He swallowed hard. "I ain't no good at givin' presents to *young ladies*," he said, putting emphasis on his new title for me. "I wasn't sure what you'd be thinkin'."

"Well . . . I like it. Are you bringin' it by tonight?"

"I've been invited for cake, ain't I?"

"You've been invited for the whole supper."

"So I'll bring it with me then."

I stumbled backward a little more, said, "Guess I'd better be gettin' home," and ran off with shaky legs.

I was fairly bursting with pride when I got home, but I wasn't about to tell anyone. The way I figured it, no one would think Luke's gift as special as I did, and I wanted to enjoy every bit of it without someone putting a damper on my enthusiasm. They could just see it tonight at my birthday dinner.

I took extra care at making myself look pretty for that evening, but I was a poor hand at dressing my hair. I was just starting to lose my patience when Gemma came up behind me, taking the iron from my hand to make perfect ringlets.

"You should wear it up today. It's the way a woman should wear it for a special occasion."

I could always depend on Gemma.

A dozen hairpins later, Luke arrived, the sound of his voice making my toes tingle.

"He's here!"

Gemma added one more hairpin and stepped back to admire her work. "There! You look like a real lady."

I kissed her cheek, scurried out into the hall, and then skidded to a stop before reaching the top of the steps. That was where I straightened my skirt and took a deep breath so I could descend the stairs as casually as possible.

Luke greeted me with a low whistle. "If you don't look a perfect lady, I don't know who does." He glanced at my daddy. "You must be mighty proud havin' a pretty lady like that under your roof."

"Sure enough, I am. Problem is, I'm gettin' worried about all them boys my pretty lady might start attractin'. I ain't cut out for seein' boys lined up at my door."

"That ain't gonna happen," I said adamantly.

"And why not?" Momma asked. "Matter of fact, Buddy Pernell was askin' about you just the other day when I was gettin' my groceries. Think he's maybe a little sweet on you."

"Ain't no boys who need to get sweet on me," I said. "I won't pay them any mind, anyhow."

"Oh, you're just sayin' that now," Momma said. "Come on and eat, everybody, before the supper cools."

Gemma and I hung back behind the rest, and I exchanged a glance with her.

"Ain't no boys for me," I reiterated.

"I know, Jessie," she said. "Ain't nobody but Luke."

I smiled and took her hand. She understood me better than I understood myself, and I loved her for it.

After supper I opened my gifts, my hands still shaking as I undid Luke's awkwardly wrapped package even though I knew what it was. A lifetime's worth of worries couldn't have wiped the smile off my face that evening, and it was stretched near to breaking point as I pulled the bow off. My cheeks were sore as could be.

When I pulled that jewelry box out, Gemma and Momma made all sorts of exclamations about how pretty and fancy it was.

"Ain't that just the nicest thing you ever owned?" Momma asked me.

"Luke made it," I announced proudly.

"Why, Luke Talley, you done outshined yourself. I didn't know you could do such things."

Gemma ran her hand down the side of it and sighed. "It's really somethin', that it is. We'll need to find a nice place for it in our room, Jessie. A right nice place."

Daddy, however . . . he didn't say a word. He just stared at it and cleared his throat a few times. "That's an awful grown-up gift," he said when the excitement died down. "The kind of gift a real lady gets."

We all looked at him strangely, wondering about his meaning.

"Sure enough it is," Momma said. "Which makes it fittin' for a girl of seventeen." She tugged at one of the perfect curls Gemma had made on my head.

Daddy nodded slowly and stared at that box.

"What've you got to say about that craftsmanship, Harley?" Momma asked as she fingered one of the spindles. "Mighty fine piece of work, don't you think?"

Daddy paused before he spoke. "Sure enough. The boy knows how to handle a chisel."

Luke nodded at Daddy and said a nervous word of thanks, but he looked uncomfortable all the same, and I could feel the good excitement just dripping away under Daddy's hard stare. I saw Momma give him a little look of warning.

"Well, I think it's the best thing I ever seen," I said in an attempt to break the tension.

"You just need more jewelry now," Momma said with a laugh. "You know, I got me a pearl necklace I been meaning to pass on to you since Daddy got me those fancy ones for our anniversary last year."

"Pearls, Momma?" I asked, clapping my hands together. "Real pearls?"

"Near about as you can get, I guess. And now you'll have a right nice place to put them, too."

"Now, who done said a thing about the girl wearin' pearls?" Daddy asked suddenly. "One minute she's gettin' fancy gifts from boys, and now you're talkin' about her wearin' fancy pearls."

"Harley," Momma cautioned, "what in the world . . . ?"

"I'm just wonderin' when turnin' seventeen meant a daddy ain't got no say no more."

"No one said you ain't got no say. We're just talkin' a little jewelry."

"Seems to me we're talkin' about the girl like she's twenty-five and marryin' age."

I stared at him with pleading eyes. "Daddy, you're ruinin' my birthday."

"I ain't ruinin' a thing. I'm askin' a question, is all. When did my baby girl become a woman of the world?"

"Harley!" Momma exclaimed. "You and me need to talk on the porch. Right now!"

Daddy sighed long and hard. Though my momma wasn't known to push him around, there were times when she meant to have her way, and this was one of those times. Her whole demeanor said so.

"All right, Sadie," Daddy finally said. He pushed his chair back swiftly, sending a squeal throughout the silent kitchen, and followed Momma out the front door.

Luke was sitting back in his chair with his thumbs stuck under his suspenders, his head hung low. "I didn't mean to upset him none with my gift."

"There ain't nothin' wrong with that gift. It's perfect. He's just bein' ornery." I looked at Gemma, and she gave me a weak, sympathetic smile. "You don't think there's anythin' wrong with my jewelry box, do you?"

"I think it's right nice," she said with a bigger smile this time. "You did a real nice job, Luke."

"I sure didn't mean to upset anyone. . . ."

His words tugged at my heart, but I couldn't think of a single thing to say to make him feel better.

Sitting as quietly as we were, we could hear Momma's and Daddy's voices as they argued on the porch. It was hard to hear particulars, but Momma and Daddy always paced when they fought, and I knew it would take only a minute or two for them to move up the porch toward the kitchen.

Sure enough, it didn't take long for us to hear my momma say, "Harley, she ain't a little girl no more."

"That girl's my baby," Daddy replied. "Always has been."

My cheeks grew even hotter, and I lowered my forehead into my hand so Luke wouldn't see.

"She ain't no baby," Momma continued adamantly. "You best start realizin' it now."

"She ain't no grown woman, neither. I don't want her gettin' fancy gifts and wearin' fancy things. It's trouble, I'm tellin' you."

Poor Luke looked mortified, and he hopped up from his chair, saying he needed to visit the bathroom.

Even through the window, I could hear Momma sigh. "Honey, listen. If you go actin' crazylike over natural things, Jessilyn is gonna feel all tied up inside. She ain't doin' nothin' wrong. She's just growin' up. And our job as her momma and daddy is to help her do it, not keep her from doin' it. You hear?"

It was Daddy's turn to sigh, and though I couldn't see him, I could picture him rubbing the back of his neck and staring at his feet during the long silence that followed. That was what he always did when he was thinking about something he didn't like to think about. Especially when he thought he might be wrong.

I didn't hear either of them say another word. Instead, I heard their footsteps go across the porch, heard the screen door clatter as it closed behind them. Luke wasn't back by the time they came in. Momma gave me a soft smile when she caught my sad expression.

Daddy just looked around the room sheepishly. "Where's the boy?"

"The bathroom," Gemma answered for me.

"I'm right here," Luke corrected as he came back into the kitchen. "You need me, sir?"

"Well now, I . . . I got me some explainin' to do. I s'pose I just ain't used to my girl growin' up. I didn't mean to make nobody feel bad." Daddy came to me and placed his big hand on my head. "I didn't mean nothin' by it, baby. Don't you go lettin' my worryin' bother you none. It's just somethin' daddies do sometimes."

"I didn't mean to go upsettin' nobody," Luke explained. "I hope you don't think that."

"Son, don't go makin' me feel worse than I already do. I got me a belly full of crow as it is, and you feelin' bad will only make me feel fuller. You didn't do nothin' wrong, and I'm sorry I made you feel you did."

Daddy held out his hand for a solid shake, but even though the air had lightened a bit, some damage had already been done. We were all a little on edge for the rest of that evening, and it wasn't any less awkward when I walked Luke to the edge of the road.

"Sorry 'bout all that," I told him. "You know Daddy. . . ."

"Oh, sure . . . I know. He didn't mean nothin'."

But I could see by his face, and by the distance he kept between us, that Luke was feeling strange being with me now. Whether Daddy had meant to or not, he had brought to life a situation that hadn't existed before. Luke had never seemed to see me as more than a kid sister, but Daddy's reaction to his gift had, for the first time, identified me as something else entirely. Now the whole possibility hung in the air like the wet heat of that June evening, and there was a wall between us that I'd never known before.

"Well," I began tentatively, "thanks, anyway. I really like it."

He nodded at me and tipped his hat. "I'll see you later, Jessie," he said, and then he moved off with that loping gait of his.

I watched him until he rounded the corner out of sight, then went back up the walk and plopped down on the porch steps, burying my face in my hands. I heard the screen door open, and I could tell by the pace of the footsteps that it was Gemma.

"He ain't gonna be the same around me no more," I said, my voice muffled.

She sat down next to me. "Thought you'd like that. Ain't you always wanted him to see you different?"

"Not like this. Now he feels all funny, like he can't be himself around me or nothin'. I can't believe my daddy."

"Didn't matter if your daddy did it or not, Jessie," she said. "It was bound to come up someday."

"But I don't want things to change for me and Luke."

"Yes, you do. You always have." She nudged my knee with her own. "Ain't no changes that ever come easy. But changin's got to happen, no matter."

I knew she was right, but it didn't make that funny feeling

in my stomach go away. I laid my head on her shoulder and tried not to think about it. But that wasn't any good. Nearly everything I thought about in those days had at least a little piece to do with Luke.

Chapter 3

Sunday afternoon I was lying on my bed reading a book, so engrossed in it that I only realized Gemma was changing her clothes when she asked me to button her up.

"Where are you headin'?" I asked as I tossed the book aside and reached to help her.

"Work, of course. Where else do I wear this old muslin?"

"You don't work on Sundays."

"I do today. It's the Hadleys' anniversary, and they're havin' a big party."

"Momma know about this? She don't like nobody workin' on the Lord's Day."

"She says it's okay just this once."

"How late are you gonna be there?"

"Till around eight, I guess."

"You're gonna miss fried chicken night," I told her solemnly.

"I'll get somethin' from the kitchen at the Hadleys'."

I promised Gemma I'd save her a chicken wing, but I wasn't the least bit happy that she wouldn't be eating it with me. "I'm gonna go pack you up a snack to take with you. Them Hadleys got to be too stingy to give food to the help. You're lookin' skinnier'n usual these days."

"They feed us well enough, Jessie."

"Well, I'm packin' it anyways," I said over my shoulder on my way out. "Things are liable to get busy there and I don't want you forgettin' to eat, you hear?"

I packed Gemma a sack with muffins and two boiled eggs, then went outside to sit on the porch and wait for her, setting the sack on the swing beside me. It had been five minutes of waiting and wondering what in tarnation Gemma could be doing to dawdle so long when a fancy black car sped up into our driveway.

"Joel Hadley!" I spat out like a curse word. "What's he doin' here?"

"Hey there, Jessilyn," he called through the open window without any true kindness in his words. "Gemma ready for work?"

I wrinkled my nose. Since when did Joel Hadley start keeping tabs on Gemma?

I got up from my seat on the porch and ambled over to his car with my hands in my pockets, inspecting his expression.

"What d'you want to know for? She'll make it to work on time, if that's what you're worried about."

"I'm sure she will," he said with exaggerated charm, though he was having to put on a better show than usual, I could see. Joel Hadley didn't like me any better than he liked a toothache, and his eyes confirmed it even if his smile didn't. "Gemma's always on time, no doubt."

"Well then, what do you want to know for?"

"I figured on givin' her a ride, is all. Ain't no reason for her to walk the whole long way with me passin' by here anyhow."

I eyed him up one side and down the other, and my inspection did nothing but reaffirm the fact that I didn't trust him one bit. There wasn't one single Hadley who would give a ride to a colored girl.

"Joel Hadley, you got somethin' funny up your sleeve?" I asked him bluntly.

"What are you talkin' about?"

"There ain't never been no time before when you've asked to give Gemma a ride. Seems to me most times you're up to somethin', anyway. Ain't no reason for this time to be different."

His face got a little red, and his charm began to melt away to reveal the Joel Hadley I knew. "Now, Jessilyn, why don't you just go on in and tell Gemma I'm here for her?" he asked, his tone restrained. "I ain't got time to sit here chitchattin' with you. Go do somethin' useful for a change."

"I ain't lettin' Gemma in no automobile with you. No sir. You're about as trustworthy as a snake."

"You got a tongue on you, Jessilyn," he barked. "Somebody's gonna clip it out one day, you keep that up."

"Jessie," Gemma called from the porch, "you go on back inside."

I bristled at her tone and turned to stare at her in defiance. I took several steps toward the porch. "Since when did you become my momma? You ain't got no right to order me around."

"And you ain't got no right to go makin' nasty comments to my boss. You want to get me fired?"

"Way I figure it, that ain't such a bad idea. I don't trust them Hadleys. Not a one. And definitely not that one."

She started to skirt past me, but I grabbed her arm. "You can't be thinkin' of gettin' in there with him."

"Ain't nothin' wrong with savin' my feet from the walk."

"There is if you put yourself in trouble for it."

"There ain't no trouble," she hissed back at me. "He's just givin' me a ride."

"Since when do rich white men give rides to colored girls, Gemma? You tell me that."

She stood there for a long moment, her eyes averted from mine, before she yanked her arm free. "I'm gonna be late," she muttered.

"I'm gettin' Daddy. He'll never let you go."

"Your momma and daddy are on their Sunday drive, and you know it."

I stood there on that porch helplessly and watched Joel nod at Gemma as she approached him. He got out and, like a perfect Southern gentleman, opened the door for her.

Only it was the back door, not the front.

Gemma paused for a minute, and I could tell by her body language that Joel's actions had taken her by surprise and cut her to the quick. But after a moment's hesitation she forced a smile and climbed quickly inside.

My cheeks blazed at the idea of Joel Hadley shoving my Gemma in the backseat like we shoved our dog, Duke, into the truck bed. "At least she's further away from him back there," I growled to myself as they drove off.

I was still stewing when Luke Talley walked up a few minutes later, minus his usual cheerful whistle. The absence of those tunes made the air between us seem heavy, just as it had the night before, but the thought of Gemma sitting in Joel Hadley's backseat pushed my worries about Luke aside.

When he caught sight of me and my sour face, he must've known right off there was trouble. "You look snakebit, Jessilyn. What's wrong?"

"Gemma! You know she got picked up in a fancy automobile by Joel Hadley?"

"Joel Hadley? What in the world for?"

"He says he was drivin' by and stopped to give her a ride to save her the walk to his house."

Luke leaned his back against the porch rail and frowned. "Ain't no way a Hadley would go givin' rides to colored girls."

"That's just what I said."

"What'd your daddy say about that?"

"He ain't home. Nobody's home but me."

Luke looked off down the road like he could see Joel and Gemma even though they were out of sight. "I don't like it. Somethin' ain't right about that."

"I'm glad to hear I ain't the only one seein' sense." I crossed my arms. "You know what I'm goin' to do? I'm goin' to ring them up in a few minutes and make sure Gemma got there; that's what I'm goin' to do."

"That's a fine idea, Jessie. We ought to check up on her." He sat down in the porch swing and chomped a piece of tall grass. "I don't like that Joel Hadley. He ain't to be trusted, so I see it."

Now that I had some peace about Gemma, my butterflies from last night woke up and started flying around their home in the pit of my stomach. I sat gingerly next to Luke, leaving plenty of space between us. "You see? It's no wonder we're friends, seein' as how we look at things the same way most times."

Luke tapped me on my nose. "There you go, Jessie. We've got somethin' special, you and me."

My heart started racing, and suddenly I wasn't thinking about Gemma at all anymore. "You think we got somethin' special?" I asked wonderingly.

He looked away quickly, clearing his throat like he wished he could swallow those words back up. "Well, Jessie . . . what

I mean is . . . seems to me I remember savin' your life in the swimmin' hole first day we met."

"I remember."

"So the way I figure it, when a man saves a girl's life . . . well then, they got a special kinship, like. Ain't nothin' gonna change that."

There was that word *girl* again. It seemed these days I could go from girl to woman and back to girl again faster than I could blink. We sat there for a minute before I ventured to speak. "Luke?"

"Hmm?"

"You sayin' we'll be together forever?"

"Well . . ." He gave the porch rail a shove with his feet and set us swinging. "That depends. Who's to say you won't fall in love with some passerby, and he'll marry you and take you off–"

"I ain't marryin' no passerby," I spluttered, figuring Luke Talley ought to know by now that I was marrying him someday.

"All right," he said with a chuckle. "Don't go gettin' your dander up. I was just sayin' . . ."

"Well, don't say it. I ain't leavin' to marry some stranger."

"Yes ma'am!" My familiar temper was a balm for our discomfort, and Luke's mask of indifference slipped off his face just a bit. "That suits me just fine, Jessilyn. I ain't gonna complain one bit about you stickin' around."

I looked away from him so he wouldn't see me trying not

to smile and sat there in silence for some minutes, wallowing in the joy of his words. He'd been through enough with my family in the past four years to become like one of our own, and I meant to make it official before I turned twenty-one. I already had it all planned out. All I needed now was to convince Luke and my daddy of the same thing. I was mulling over names for our first child when I remembered my promise to phone the Hadleys', and I hopped up quickly, setting the swing to wobbling. "Gotta call Gemma," I called over my shoulder on the way inside.

"Gemma Teague?" the woman on the other end repeated when I asked to speak to her. "I ain't seen her all day."

I knew it was Miss Taffy I was talking to. She was a large colored woman who had a bold tongue and an impatient nature. People didn't push Miss Taffy's buttons without getting their ears boxed, and I didn't feel like hearing her yell at me just then. But I pressed her a little bit more.

"She wasn't supposed to be there until now, though, Miss Taffy. I was just makin' sure she got there safe."

"Makin' sure she got here safe?" she repeated. "Land's sake, ain't you white folk got better things to do than checkin' up on people every time they leave the house?" Without warning, I heard her drop the telephone and walk off with loud, clomping footsteps. "You seen Gemma Teague?" I heard her ask someone. "What d'you mean, 'huh'? I said, you seen Gemma Teague? . . . Speak up louder, girl! Ain't a body two inches away from you could hear what you're sayin' in that little mouse voice of yours." Then I heard her say, "Uh-huh. Well, get on back to work. You waitin' for me to give you a trophy or somethin'?"

Luke pushed the door open and looked at me questioningly.

I shrugged in response. "I'm waitin' on Miss Taffy," I whispered. "I think she near about beat information out of one of her kitchen help."

He smiled widely and leaned against the doorjamb.

"You there, Jessilyn Lassiter?" Miss Taffy called into the phone. I leaped back a little as her booming voice bounced off my ear.

"Yes'm."

"Winnie says she done seen her get in no more'n a minute ago. Makes me wonder why she ain't checked in with me yet, then. Don't everybody know they's supposed to check in with Miss Taffy first thing they get here? Lord, give me patience with these ornery workers I got to put up with day in and day out."

That was the last thing I heard from Miss Taffy because she hung up the phone then without so much as a "good evenin'."

I hung up and ambled toward Luke, chewing my lip thoughtfully. "She says Gemma's there. Though she ain't seen her herself, and she'll probably lay into Gemma for not lookin' in on her right off. Hope I didn't get her in trouble."

"You was just checkin' in 'cause you were concerned, is all. Ain't no reason to worry."

I looked at the clock and sighed. "Guess I'll get some

supper started. Ain't got no idea what's keepin' Momma and Daddy."

I sent Luke out to pick some tomatoes, and I watched through the kitchen window as he walked by, thinking of a day when I'd be making dinner for him every evening.

"Someday," I murmured. "Someday, Luke Talley. You just wait."

Momma and Daddy came home a few minutes later, and Momma was full of apologies about running late.

"I'll tell you, Miss Jessilyn," she rattled on as she pulled pans out of the cabinets. "Bart Tatum passed us on the road to home, and don't you know he had to stop us to say hey? That man can talk a body's ear off. Here I am thinkin' I've got to get this chicken on, so I tell him so, and what do you think he does? He decides it's a fine time to tell us about his eatin' habits, every detail. 'Ain't no way to eat chicken but boiled,' he says. Boiled! And you can't have chicken without potatoes, of course, so he proceeds to give me his wife's recipes for hashed potatoes, mashed potatoes, fried potatoes . . . Ain't got enough hours in a day for all the ways that man eats his potatoes. And as if I don't know such things. I been cookin' since I could reach a stove."

All the while, I stood at the kitchen window, mindlessly mixing up the corn bread batter.

"You're awfully quiet, Jessilyn," Momma said, though she hadn't left me much room to fit any words in. "You got things on your mind?"

"Just thinkin' about Gemma," I murmured.

"What about her?"

I shrugged, deciding I didn't want to say much about Joel Hadley just then. "I was wonderin' how she likes her work."

"She ain't said much about it, it seems. I s'pose she likes it fine." Momma plopped some chicken into the hot oil and let the popping and crackling settle down before she asked, "You wonderin' for some particular reason?"

"I've been thinkin' about takin' a job myself, is all."

"Is that so? Whereabouts?"

"Don't know. I just got to thinkin' about it lately. Thought I'd make a little extra money this summer so I can buy some things when I want to. That's all. Maybe I could get a little work at the grocery store or somethin'."

Momma just said, "Huh!" and then pushed the chicken around with some tongs, softly humming a hymn.

Luke stayed for supper that night as always, and I was a little disappointed that most of the conversation was between him and Daddy and was all about the economy, something I had no interest in whatsoever. Of course, I wanted more of Luke's attention to be on me.

A little while later I got my wish.

"I'm gonna run on down to the Hadleys'," Daddy said. "See if Gemma's ready to come on home. I don't want her walkin' home this late by herself."

Luke stretched and got up from his place on the gold sofa in the den. "I can run on down for ya. If you don't think

Gemma will mind walkin', I'll fetch her and walk her back. I could use a little exercise after that big dinner."

"I'll go too," I volunteered quickly.

The three of them snapped their heads around to stare at me after my loud pronouncement.

"It'll look more proper, anyhow," I said as an excuse for my hastiness. "Instead of just Luke and Gemma walkin' alone."

"It'll just be you and Luke walkin' alone on the way," Momma clarified.

"I know, but . . . everyone round here's used to seein' me and Luke together. Ain't no surprise there."

Daddy sat quietly, puffing a bit of smoke out of his pipe, his knee bouncing nervously. I was waiting for him to turn me down flat, but Momma spoke up before he got the chance.

"All right, Jessilyn," she said. "You can go if Luke will have you."

Daddy shot up straight in his chair, but she put a calming hand on his arm.

"Why wouldn't Luke have me?" I demanded.

Daddy's face left no questions about his feelings, and Luke looked uncertainly at my momma, but she gave him an exaggerated nod to get him moving.

He grabbed his hat and went to the front door. "'Course I want you to come, Jessie," he said to head off my temper. "Come on now, and let's get. We don't want her decidin' to set off on her own."

On my way out of the house, I saw Momma standing there

with a secret smile on her face, and I knew she thought my crush on Luke was just the cutest thing in the South. I only hoped that smile would get her through the words she and my daddy were sure to have as soon as we were out of earshot.

I was in a little piece of heaven as I walked down that road beside Luke. He was whistling a tune I didn't know and shuffling along to make sure I kept up with him. Despite the fact that I was taller than most of the girls in town, my five-foot-seven couldn't even come close to Luke's six-foot-three, and he had long ago gotten used to slowing his pace for me.

"You happy school's out?" he asked after he had finished his tune.

"'Course I'm happy school's out. It's near to killin' me waitin' for graduation next year."

"It'll be here before you know it, I figure. Time has a way of flyin' by. Just think . . . we've known each other a good piece now, and it seems like only yesterday we first met at that swimmin' hole."

My mind did a little traveling back, and I remembered what a knight in shining armor he had seemed to me when he'd saved me from drowning. To this day, the gleam on his armor hadn't faded for me. I smiled at him. "Seems you've always been savin' me from somethin'."

He returned my smile. "My pleasure."

We walked in silence for a good quarter mile, and that was just fine with me because it wasn't the awkward silence we'd discovered last night. It was the same comfortable quiet we'd shared over the years, the one I treasured because only we shared it. Luke and I could enjoy each other as much quiet as we could talking.

As we neared the Hadleys', Luke let out a long, low whistle. "Take a look at all them automobiles. Must be *some* party."

"Usually is at the Hadleys'."

"Will you take a gander at that blue one?" Luke said in awe. "That's like somethin' out of a magazine."

"Don't get so close to it," I scolded as he leaned down to peer inside. "You'll get smudges on it or somethin'. The thing's clean as a whistle."

Luke spent the whole walk up to the house gazing at one automobile after another. It was true we didn't see too many automobiles in Calloway, Virginia, much less shiny nice ones. But the Hadleys had brought high society to our part of the world. The only reason they were here at all, we figured, was because Mr. Hadley owned a bank and a paper mill that he wanted to be nearby to oversee.

Despite the fact that I thought their house was amazing, I wasn't too impressed by the family. They all seemed haughty and proud, and that paper mill had stunk up all of the east side of the county.

Luke took a sweeping look at the house. "Swanky stuff."

"That's rich folks for you."

We went to the back of the house, because the country folk certainly weren't welcome at the front door during parties, and rapped at the door.

"What you want?" someone yelled from inside. "You askin' for scraps, you come to the wrong place. Get on with you!"

"No, Miss Taffy. It's Jessilyn Lassiter," I called through the screen door. "You know, Gemma's friend."

The heavyset colored woman walked to the door and looked sideways at me, her hand set on her hip. "Jessilyn Lassiter," she repeated. "You taller these days?"

I shook my head slowly. "Ain't grown much in the two weeks since I seen you last . . . that I know of."

"Uh-huh . . ." She studied Luke with one eyebrow cocked. "Who's that? Your daddy?"

Luke's head shot around when he heard that.

I stifled a giggle. "No, ma'am, Miss Taffy. That's not my daddy. That's Luke Talley. He's a friend of ours, come to make sure me and Gemma get home safe."

"Well, you needin' Gemma now?"

"We just figured she'd be through, so we'd walk her home."

She stared at Luke for a few seconds more, making him squirm a bit, and then turned away from us. "I'll give a holler out for her. But I ain't promisin' I'll find her right off, and I'm too busy to go lookin' for her."

"Yes'm."

I glanced at Luke and grinned widely at his flushed cheeks.

"What's she starin' at me for?" he asked.

"Maybe she thinks you look suspicious."

"Ain't nothin' suspicious about this face," he argued. "I'm as innocent as the day is long."

"I know it. Don't need to argue the point with me none . . . Daddy."

"Very funny!" he snapped. "Who does she think she is? Callin' me your daddy? I don't look old enough to be nobody's daddy."

"Ain't me who said it," I said with a laugh. "What're you arguin' with me about?"

"I'm just sayin', is all," he grumbled. "Callin' me your daddy. That's crazy talk!"

"She certainly got your dander up."

"Well, she's got nerve, is all I'm sayin'. And then she goes eyein' me like I was here to steal china and silver or some-thin'. . . ."

Luke shut up quickly because the woman came back and shook her head at us. "She ain't around here, seems. She might be out gettin' things from the summerhouse, but I ain't got time to go checkin' around for her."

"Can we go see if she's there then?"

Miss Taffy waved a hand as though she was done wasting her time with us. "Get on, then, and see for yourself. I got work to do."

Luke and I treaded across the perfectly manicured lawn, being careful not to step on anything important.

"Too much work takin' care of all these plants," Luke muttered. "Ain't a body got enough to do without foolin' with flowers?"

"They ain't got to do it themselves," I countered quietly. "They pay somebody to do it. Ain't no big deal when you ain't got to do the work and you have enough money to pay for anythin'."

"Bein' rich don't guarantee an easy life, Jessie."

"I didn't say it did." I took another long look around the grounds and sighed. "Sure would make it a sight nicer, though."

"Depends on who's got it. Money in a good person's hands can be a good thing, but money in a bad person's hands can do no end of evil."

"I s'pose. But look at these," I said, holding my hands out for inspection. "These are the hands of a good person. I think I could do some good with it."

He smiled and tugged at a lock of my hair. "Sure enough, Jessie. They're good hands. Now, whether or not they'll be filled with money someday, we'll have to see."

We came upon a short, sprawling brick building, and I peeked into one of the low windows. "Don't see nobody. You see anybody?"

Luke moved around the other side of the building, and I waited a minute for him to come back.

"Don't see anybody back there," he told me.

The window was slightly open, so I leaned close to it and hollered for Gemma. There was no answer.

"Guess we'd better head on back to the road and wait for her there," Luke suggested.

"If she ain't already started for home before we got here."

"We'd have passed her on the way. Come on. Let's get on out front before we do miss her."

We had just started walking back when we heard a door slam behind us. I turned around and waited a few seconds before I saw someone come walking quickly around the corner of the summerhouse. Dusk was settling in, but I identified her right off.

"Gemma?" I called. "Gemma, over here!"

She glanced up at me with color in her cheeks. "What're you two doin' here?"

"Come to carry you home, is all. There somethin' wrong?"

"No," she muttered, though she didn't look at us as she walked on past. "Just been busy. Too much to do around here."

"Well, Daddy said you were supposed to be done by now, so we came to walk with you."

"Ain't ready to go home yet." She still hadn't taken the time to look me in the eye and was twisting her hands in front of her. "There's more work to do, and I got to stay to see it done."

"But how will you get home?"

"I got two legs, ain't I?"

I was frustrated with her tone, and I made a move to say so, but Luke's hand on my shoulder stopped me.

"Mr. Lassiter don't want you walkin' home alone so late, Gemma," Luke said in a nice, easy tone. "If you got to stay late, why don't you ring him up when you're ready, and he can come by and get you in the truck."

Gemma didn't say anything; she just stared at her feet,

still holding her hands tightly together. I heard someone rustling across the grass toward us and looked past Gemma to see Joel Hadley coming from the direction of the summerhouse. I watched him stride across the lawn with that arrogant bounce of his and felt my body break out in a chill. There was no mistaking where he'd been, and I pulled my gaze from him to Gemma in one quick motion.

But she couldn't look at me, and I wasn't too young to figure out why. "I think you best come on with us now," I said quietly but sternly. I knew my Gemma, and I knew Joel Hadley. If there was trouble, I knew where it came from, and I wanted nothing more than to get her away from the whole lot of them. "I bet they got lots of help in there anyway. Miss Taffy's got her hands full of workers."

"Well now, what's the problem?" Joel asked. "Did I hear you sayin' Gemma's got to go now?"

"I ain't got to go," Gemma said quickly.

"We came to carry her home," I told him sharply. "My daddy sent us to, and I don't have no plans on leavin' till I do what my daddy sent me to do."

"That right, Gemma?" Joel asked, his gaze searing through her. When she didn't answer, he reached out and raised her chin. "I said, that right, Gemma? 'Cause we sure could use your help around here a while longer."

Now it was Luke who was getting upset. I could feel it just by standing next to him. He was angry the very first time I ever saw him, and I'd grown to know his anger well. It radiated off of him like heat waves.

"Seems her daddy wants her fetched home," Luke told Joel in no uncertain terms. "So I suppose that's what we'll do."

"I got work to do, Luke Talley," Gemma barked, her eyes meeting ours for the first time. "I got work, and I intend to finish it."

"Then how'll you get home?" I argued.

"I ain't no baby, Jessie. I ain't got to have a keeper always."

"We ain't got time to argue, and your daddy ought to know what's best for you." Luke reached out to take her arm. "Come on. I'm takin' you home before your daddy worries."

Gemma wrenched her arm free, her face painted with an anger I'd never seen aimed at any of us before. "I ain't got no daddy," she snapped. "Now get on home and let me do my work."

Her smart tone and harsh words made me cringe inside. Gemma had always loved my father, even before he'd taken her in as his own. I'd never heard her say such things about him.

Luke was about to lay into her; I could tell by the way his jaw tensed up and he hunched his shoulders like an angry cat. But he was interrupted by Joel Hadley.

"Now, if all this arguin's about gettin' Gemma home safe, then I'll ride her home in my car. Ain't no sense fussin' over a problem when it's so easy to fix."

"She ain't ridin' home with you, Joel Hadley," I said. "No sir! I ain't gonna sit by while you shove my Gemma into no backseat again."

Horror spread across Gemma's face. "You ain't got no call

to be sayin' those things to my boss, Jessie," she said, seething resentment turning her voice into a near whisper. "You ain't got no call to go humiliatin' me, neither."

"I wasn't humiliatin' you. I was defendin' you."

"You wasn't doin' nothin' good. I'll get my ride home with Mr. Hadley, and you can get on out, both of you." Gemma turned away from us, pausing to say over her shoulder, "I got work to do. You done slowed me up long enough as it is."

Joel stayed where he was, a tidy little smirk painted on his face, no doubt finding great satisfaction in our dismay. Then he nodded at us both, tugged the bottom of his dressy jacket down to straighten it, and said, "Y'all have a good evenin', you hear?"

Luke's fists were fixed to his sides, and he had his mouth clenched so tightly I thought his jawbone would pop out of his skin. "You best keep your filthy hands off that girl, Hadley. I swear if I find out you hurt her in some way, I'll break your scrawny neck with my own two hands."

Joel's hands were in his pockets, and I was sure he had them crammed there to keep us from seeing them shake. He shrugged nonchalantly and forced his eyes to square up with Luke's. "I don't know what you're talkin' about."

Luke made a quick jerking motion as though he was about to pounce, and Joel jumped back, leaving no doubt of his true fears. It was Luke's turn to smirk, and he watched Joel with a wicked glare as he turned and followed in Gemma's path, veering off only to go around to the front door, where Gemma would never have been welcomed.

My whole body shook from the anger and fear that filled me up to my ears, and I grasped Luke's tensed arm for support. "She's in trouble, Luke," I whispered. "We've got to help her."

He pulled my arm up and tucked it between his arm and his ribs, squeezing it tightly. "She needs help, sure enough. Problem is, I ain't so sure she'll let us give it. I ain't so sure she'll let anyone give it."

I walked home with heavy feet because I knew he was right. I'd seen a side of Gemma I didn't know, and I had no tricks up my sleeve for solving problems I'd never faced in my life.

Chapter 4

Daddy was sore when Luke and I told him about Joel Hadley driving Gemma home, but he didn't storm off to fetch her. Instead, he spent the next hour pacing the porch.

"Ain't he gonna do nothin'?" I asked Momma when the clock chimed nine thirty.

She looked up from her needlework and watched Daddy through the window. "Ain't much he can do, honey," she said quietly so Daddy wouldn't hear. "We told her she could work tonight, and parties run late sometimes."

"But she's drivin' home with Joel Hadley."

Momma took my hand and gave me a weak smile. "Honey, I don't like it any more'n you. Neither does your daddy. But Gemma's nineteen and near about full grown. Your daddy and me, we got to think hard about how to handle this. Okay?"

I nodded, understanding but unhappy all the same. I trudged upstairs and tossed myself into bed, staring at the circle of lamplight on the ceiling until the heat radiating from it forced me to turn it out.

When I heard Momma and Daddy's bedroom door shut behind them, I turned my light back on to check the time. Ten thirty, and still no Gemma. I grabbed my book and tried to read for distraction, but I had to repeat every sentence so many times before it sank in, I gave up.

It was near midnight when Gemma got home. I flicked the lamp out quickly and rolled over to face away from the door. I lay still and quiet, straining to hear if my daddy would have a few words for her. But all I heard was the click of his lamp being turned out now that he knew she was home.

I peeked over my shoulder when she tiptoed in. The moonlight cast a shadow on her form and revealed her slumped shoulders, her labored gait. I didn't know if it was work fatigue or sadness, but I was too angry to ask. Before she got into bed, she paused over me, but I closed my eyes, pretending to sleep, and she turned to her bed with a sigh.

It was hours before I managed to drift off, and when I woke up late the next morning, Gemma had already slipped out, leaving her bed uncharacteristically messy.

The heat of that morning made my head fuzzy, and I moved at a snail's pace, spending extra time washing up after a sweaty night's sleep. I'd lived in the South my whole life, so I knew an awful lot about summer heat. But that summer of 1936 brought a heat the likes of which I'd never seen. It nearly crackled in the air. Going barefoot across the grass was like walking on needles, and I was forced to wear shoes everywhere, which only served to make me even more irritable.

After I had some breakfast, I wandered up to the back fields and found Daddy standing there, staring into the distance, his hand shielding his eyes from the brightening sun.

"Lookin' at somethin' particular?" I asked, my tone subdued because I hadn't quite gotten over his display at dinner Saturday night.

He turned around suddenly. "Oh, mornin', baby." He paused a minute, seemingly contemplating the wisdom of keeping that nickname for me, but he smiled at me wanly. "I'm just thinkin'."

"Gemma at work already?"

"Yep."

"Did you say anythin' to her about last night?"

Daddy took his time answering my question. "I don't much like talkin' about you girls to each other, Jessilyn. You know that."

"Yes'r. But this time's different. She's got me worried."

"Baby, you ain't got to worry none." He paused again and then reached out to tug my ear affectionately. "I spoke with Gemma. We got an agreement between us so this don't happen again. Okay? Now that's all I want to say on the matter."

"Okay." I followed Daddy's gaze out to the fields where some dried brown leaves had begun to dot the crops. "In town the other day, I heard Mr. Poe talkin' about how we ain't gonna get much rain. He could feel it in his bones, he said."

"Well, let's hope Mr. Poe's bones are wrong." He pushed his hat back and leaned down to kiss my cheek. "I'll see you at dinnertime, Jessilyn."

"Yes'r." I watched him go, his shoulders low. My daddy always walked tall and proud, and when he didn't, I knew there was trouble around the bend. Hot and dry was a bad prescription for growing crops, and bad crops meant bad earnings for my daddy. I was starting to think hard about that job I'd talked about getting, only this time I was thinking the money might need to be used for family matters instead of for my own.

My heart was heavy and my face was already dripping with sweat, so I decided to head over to Miss Cleta's house down the road. She always had sweet tea at the ready, and she'd toss some fruit in it for extra taste. Not to mention that she liked to bake and I could count on getting treats at her house. If I was going to be hot, I might as well be hot and full.

I found her sitting on her porch, and she clapped her hands the minute she saw me. "I was just tellin' the Lord I could use some company today," she hollered. "And here some comes."

"Hey there, Miss Cleta," I called with a wave. "How've you been?"

"Oh, I always get by, Jessilyn Lassiter. You know me." She waved for me to come into the house, and I followed her inside. To my disappointment, the house didn't smell like something just out of the oven as it usually did.

"I'll tell you, this heat is just the end," Miss Cleta said as she pulled two glasses from her cupboard. "And don't you know, I had Elmer Poe stop in yesterday, and he said he sees a drought ahead."

"I know. He feels it in his bones."

"That's right. And long as I've known that man, he's never been wrong about the weather. He's like a walkin' almanac." She waved off my attempts to help her and pushed me into one of the kitchen chairs. As she poured the sweet tea, she continued talking. "Now then, that Elmer Poe . . . he ain't never been quite right since the day he was born. I remember seein' him a few days after he came into the world. I was only ten years old then, but I could see he weren't like other babies. Slow, the doctor called him. But that boy's got a sixth sense, I'm tellin' you. He knows things other people don't know. Even gettin' old and gray as he is, he's still got more instinct than any of the smart folk in town."

"I know he does. That's why I'm worried. Drought means bad things for my family, you know."

She set a glass in front of me and then put one of her blue-veined hands on my shoulder. "Jessilyn, God's got you in the palm of His hand. Every one of you. He has His eyes on everythin'. You have faith in that, now."

I smiled at her, but I wasn't so sure about what she said. Faith was something my momma and daddy shared. It was something I saw in Gemma and in Miss Cleta. But it wasn't something I had yet come to know for myself.

I watched her continue to chatter on about this and that while she pulled a tray of small round balls out of the ice-box.

"No-bake cookies," she told me as she set them in the center of the kitchen table. "It's the only way I can dabble in the kitchen on days like this."

I ate quietly for a minute before I said, "Think my daddy's pretty worried about a drought."

I could always talk easily to Miss Cleta, and I watched her while she took a long sip of sweet tea, contemplating what she would say.

"Well now," she began, "seems to me your daddy's known adversity before and got through it just fine."

"I s'pose."

"Not to mention that we don't know for sure that Elmer Poe's right with his predictin'. Besides, you remember what I said about bein' in God's hand. He'll watch out for you all right."

"Maybe so, but I got to find me some work. It ain't right to be sittin' around doin' nothin' all summer when my daddy's workin' so hard."

"Your daddy won't like you takin' work in town, Jessilyn. I can near about guarantee that."

"But we need money."

"You think he'd have your momma go out and get work?"

"No, ma'am!"

"Well then, he ain't gonna want you goin' out for work, neither."

"But he let Gemma."

"Gemma's a woman of nineteen. And besides that, no matter how much you feel like family, Gemma's not blood kin. He likely figures she's got a right to make her own choice."

I stirred my sweet tea with a spoon to corral a berry and plop it in my mouth. "Momma's got all sorts of things to do around the house. I ain't got nothin' to do all summer. And Gemma, she's workin' so much I barely ever see her. She didn't get home last night until midnight. My daddy was near fit to be tied. I swear I won't see her this summer at all, and I'll be bored as can be."

"You help your momma, don't you?"

"Yes'm. But that don't fill my time up much. She insists on doin' most of it. I expect she thinks I can't do some things as well as she can."

"Just stuck in her ways, I reckon. A body can get that way after years of doin' things themselves." She refilled my glass. "You know, I don't think your daddy would take money from you, anyhow. Even if he did let you get work . . . which he wouldn't."

"Well, I want some work. Even if Daddy won't let me give him the money I make, I can at least buy things that I need so he won't feel like he needs to buy them for me."

Miss Cleta just sat there in her chair, tapping the table, deep in thought. I ate two more cookies to fill the silence before she spoke up.

"What would you say to workin' for me?"

"What's that?"

"I said you might like to work for me. I ain't no spring chicken anymore. Could use some help with chores. Dustin' and gardenin' and such. You know how my arthritis has been actin' up lately. I could use an extra pair of hands maybe two or three days a week. My dear husband left me settled for a long life, and I could pay you the same as you would make moppin' floors at the grocery or some other such work."

"Do you mean that, Miss Cleta?" I exclaimed. "I could work for you?"

"So long as your daddy and momma agree it's fine." She folded her hands, a self-satisfied grin spreading across her face. "Yes ma'am. I do believe I've come up with a fine idea. I can say it's been too quiet around here these days. This place could use some livenin' up. And Lord knows you can liven a place up, Miss Jessilyn."

"I don't know I'd feel right takin' money from you, Miss Cleta. Bein' neighbors, I ought to be lendin' you a hand without expectin' a return for it. I figure Daddy'll feel the same."

Miss Cleta set her glass down so hard my iced tea spoon clattered from the vibration. "Now you see here, Jessilyn Lassiter, I ain't accustomed to takin' work for nothin'. A neighborly favor is borrowin' sugar now and again. It ain't cleanin' dusty tables and pullin' weeds." She crossed her arms emphatically. "No ma'am. If I want some help around this here house, I'm payin' for it. And you can tell your daddy that if need be. I'm his elder, after all, so he'll have to take notice of what I'm sayin'."

My eyebrows were arched high in surprise, and I sat dead still, not sure how to react.

Miss Cleta took a good look at my face and broke out in that hooting laugh of hers. "Land's sake, child, you look as if you'd seen a ghost. I don't think I've ever seen you speechless before in your life."

"I don't suppose I've seen you so determined before, is all."

"Posh! I'm an ornery old thing six days out of seven, and you know it." She used her napkin to wipe up a drop of tea that had spilled when she slammed her glass down. "But I still mean what I say. If you're workin' for me, you work for pay. You hear?"

"Yes'm."

"Well then," she said with a wave of her hand, "get! Ask your daddy so's I don't sit here in suspense all day."

I hopped up, nearly spilling my leftover iced tea.

"Slow down, now," she cautioned. "A lady doesn't go galumphin' around like that. You just take a slow pace."

"Yes'm." I took the last few sips of my iced tea to be polite, placed my empty glass in her sink, and thanked her kindly for her hospitality.

"You just come on down to tell me what they say," Miss Cleta told me, nodding in response to all the words of thanks I gave her as I made my way to the door. "I'll look for you, and when you come by, we'll talk about a work schedule if you get the okay."

By the time I reached the road, I was about to burst with excitement, and I wanted nothing more than to shoot off like a polecat. But I knew Miss Cleta would be watching me from the porch, and she'd be sure to holler after me to be a lady if she saw me tearing down the road. Instead, I waited until I turned the corner out of sight before I set off at a brisk run. I was breathless and dripping with sweat when I got home.

My heart sank when I saw that the truck was gone. I was stir-crazy, knowing I'd have to wait until Momma came back from wherever she'd gone to ask her about my job. At least it was getting near dinnertime, and she'd be back in time to fix something for Daddy and the field hands. I decided I'd head into the kitchen and get some food started. It couldn't but help butter Momma up, anyway.

Momma came in while I was putting slices of cold ham onto some of her homemade biscuits.

"Oh, good," she said when she spotted me working at the counter. "I'm runnin' late. I was visitin' with Mrs. Tinker and lost track of the time."

The mention of Mrs. Tinker made my spine tingle as it did every time. It didn't matter that Mr. Tinker had been executed for murder four years ago. It was still fresh in my mind, that summer of threats, violence, and betrayal; that summer when my daddy found out his best friend, Mr. Tinker, had betrayed us as a member of the Ku Klux Klan.

"You know," Momma continued, "there's somethin' goin' on over at the Colbys' jammin' up the road."

"What?"

"Don't know, and it was too crowded for me to stop and find out. But the sheriff was there."

"Maybe I'll run down and find out."

"Yes, you do that, Jessilyn," she said. "I'd like to find out if Mae's all right. You know, she's awful far along."

Mae and Nate Colby lived right past Miss Cleta, and I sometimes watched their little girl, Callie, while they stepped out for an evening walk or trip into town. Mae was as pregnant as could be with their second child, one that Miss Cleta insisted was a boy because of how low the baby was set in Mae's belly. In fact, the last time I had seen her, I stopped to help her dig up a few weeds since she could barely bend enough to grasp them.

There was no mistaking the trouble that surrounded that house today. Once I rounded the corner, I saw vehicles for the sheriff and two of his deputies. I marveled at how drastically things had changed since I'd left Miss Cleta's only a short time earlier. I spotted Miss Cleta on her porch, twisting a handkerchief in her hands, straining to see the Colby house.

"What's goin' on, Miss Cleta?" I called. "Mae all right?"

"Heavens, child, it's a sorry thing," she cried tearfully. "A sorry thing!"

Her voice and expression frightened the life out of me, and I ran as fast as I could up to the porch, taking the steps in one leap.

"What's happened?" I asked breathlessly. "Is somebody hurt?"

"It's the little one," she said in a voice that was shaken.

"The baby?"

"No, honey. It's Callie."

"Callie? What's happened to Callie, Miss Cleta?"

"She's gone missin'," she said with a sob. "She's up and gone missin' and they don't know where she's at."

My heart froze, and I stumbled down the porch steps, determined to find out more.

"There's a lot of commotion over there, Jessilyn," Miss Cleta called after me. "You be careful, and come on by to give me news when you find out."

"Yes'm," I hollered back. "I will." As I ran across the dried grass, I lost my footing here and there, fear making my legs go numb. I had spent enough time with the little girl in her three years on this earth to make me as fond of her as of a baby sister. I couldn't bear to think of her lost or stolen.

On my way inside the Colby house, I ran into Sheriff Clancy.

"Whoa there, Jessilyn," he said calmly. "Where you gettin' yourself to?"

"What's happened to Callie, Sheriff?" I pleaded. "Miss Cleta says she's gone missin'."

"Now why don't you just calm down. You look like a wild rabbit."

"But if she's gone missin', I want to help. Maybe I can find her. I know where she likes to play."

He took me by the shoulders and made to steer me down the porch steps. I didn't like Sheriff Clancy so much, and I certainly didn't like being manhandled by him. I crouched down to get out from under his grasp and turned to face him.

"Miss Jessilyn, it's bein' took care of," he said. "I done got four of my men out roundin' up a search party, and Callie's daddy is already out with some of the men in his family lookin' round. We ain't got need of your help just now."

"How long's she been missin'?"

"Can't quite figure on it. Seems maybe she gone off durin' the night. For all we know, she's just up and fallen asleep somewhere where we ain't seen her. Could be all this worryin' is for nothin'."

I heard his words, but they didn't make me feel much better. "I got to do somethin'. Can't I at least go look?"

He moved his chaw around in his cheek a bit and turned aside to spit. "I reckon you can go on and look anywheres you think a good idea, if that's what you want. There ain't no rules about it."

Through the screen door I saw Mae Colby sitting on the sofa, her face in her hands, shaking with sobs. Her momma was on the sofa beside her, trying to comfort her.

"Jessilyn Lassiter," Mae's momma called out. "That you?"

"Yes'm."

"You come on in here if you please."

I was as uncomfortable as could be when I entered that house, but the minute Mae saw me walk up in front of her, she took my hands in hers and said one thing. "Help me find my baby, Jessie."

The way she looked at me gave me chills. I was utterly compelled to help her, and the conviction in her eyes filled me with determination.

"You seen our Callie, Jessilyn?" Mae's momma asked through tears. "You seen her at all?"

I shook my head slowly, hating the words I had to say, knowing that they'd steal away some hope. "No, ma'am. I ain't seen her in three days."

Mae's momma put a hand over her mouth to hold back a sob and gripped her daughter more tightly.

"What happened, Mae?" I asked quietly, my voice shaking. "When did you find her missin'?"

"I didn't find her in her bed this mornin'," she said in what was more of a moan than anything, her words coming out in hiccups. "I thought she'd gone into the fields with Nate like she does sometimes. We didn't know till he came back an hour ago without her that she was . . ."

"She's gone wanderin' before, Mae." I peered out the window like I'd see Callie coming up the walk. "Maybe she went to the berry patch like last time."

"We already looked there," Mae's momma said, her voice catching. "We looked near about everywhere. Ain't nobody seen her since she went to bed last night."

Mae looked at her momma with desperation in her eyes. "I should've checked in on her last night," she wailed. "What kind of momma don't check on her baby girl?"

Her momma wrapped her up and rocked her like a child. I looked away, unable to bear the sight of them. "She's got to be somewhere," I said to myself. "I'll go look some of the places we like to play."

Mae pulled away from her momma's grasp, gasping for breath. "You do that, Jessilyn Lassiter," she said determinedly, her fists grinding into the sofa on either side of her. "You go find my baby girl and bring her back to me."

I stepped back awkwardly as she began to sob again. The sadness of that room was making my feet itch, and I knew I had to do something . . . anything. I turned and ran out past the sheriff, leaping off the porch without using the steps.

I stopped by Miss Cleta's and told her what I knew, then left quickly to set out on my quest to find Callie. Just after I left Miss Cleta's, I saw Luke running down the road. He slowed down and stared at the melee in front of the Colbys' house.

"Jessie!" he called. "A deputy came by the factory gatherin' some men to look for the Colby girl. They find her yet?"

"Ain't found a thing. I'm goin' to help find her."

He slapped his hat back onto his head. "Well, let's get!"

We stopped by my house first so I could fill Momma in, and we left her praying at the kitchen table with a half-peeled potato in her hand. When Momma felt prayer was needed, she stopped and did it, no matter where she was or what she was doing.

The first place we looked was Squalers Pond because I often took Callie there to let her toss stones in. It wasn't a big pond by any means. It was more like a big puddle, really, and not very deep. Luke and I rolled up our pants and walked through it, petrified the whole time that we might come upon a little one facedown in the murky water.

But we left that pond without seeing a sign of her and headed off to Clem Barrett's field, where he had a tree fort he let kids play in. There was still no sign of Callie, and as Luke and I wandered the county looking for her, my heart became more and more heavy.

We'd been searching for hours when Luke suddenly stopped dead in the middle of the road. "We need to go down Duncan Pass," he told me with certainty.

"But that takes us out of our way."

"I know. But we got to go down there anyhow."

"Why would Callie wander down there? There ain't nothin' there for her to do."

"That ain't no reason not to check. The girl's only three. Could be she got herself lost." He took his hat off and ran his fingers through his blond hair. "All's I know is we got to go check. I can feel it in my gut."

That was enough for me. I headed in the direction of Duncan Pass, struggling to keep up with Luke as we made our way down the road. He didn't slow his stride for me on this day. He just kept his head on a swivel, searching the sides of the roads for Callie, and walked with efficient speed.

Duncan Pass was well-known as a bit of a hazard. The road there curved sharply around a corner, leaving drivers to blindly wonder what they might meet around the bend. A sign at the side of the road warned people to go slowly, and though most regular residents wisely slowed down in those parts, some people just didn't heed the warning.

There was an eerie heaviness in the air as we rounded that vicious corner. I cast a nervous glance at the warning sign. I didn't need Luke's special instincts to feel that something was wrong. The late afternoon sun cast odd shadows across the roadway. No breeze stirred the trees; no squirrels skittered through the brush. There wasn't even a single bird singing a tune. It was as still and quiet as a graveyard, and as Luke slowed his pace to take a good look around, I instinctively reached out to grasp his hand.

He turned his head to look at me, his eyes solemn and worried, but even though his face frightened me, the firm grasp of his hand calmed my spirit a bit.

Together, we paced the road for the next ten minutes. I scanned the ground around us while Luke, with his heightened vantage point, scanned the surrounding brush. Even as I searched, there was a part of me that wanted nothing more than to close my eyes for fear of what I might see. But I could not look away, for Callie's sake.

We had just reached the old wooden bridge across Duncan Creek when I stopped dead in my tracks, pulling Luke to a halt along with me.

"What is it, Jessie?" he whispered.

I didn't say anything. My mouth was like cotton. Instead, I lifted one shaking hand and pointed toward the side of the bridge along the creek bank.

Luke dropped my hand and took off like a shot, leaving me frozen in place, my legs too weak to run. I ambled over with an awkward gait, my stomach swirling. I didn't want to see death, especially not untimely death, and yet I knew Luke needed someone by his side. I forced myself toward the bridge and found him kneeling on the ground, his breath coming in gasps.

"Luke," I whispered in a voice hoarse with fear. "Luke, is she dead?"

He lifted his bowed head and gave me a nervous look. "No, she ain't dead. But she's near enough. We need to get her help right now."

Knowing Callie wasn't dead gave me the courage to look at her, but my heart sank into my stomach when I saw her broken body lying there, blood tinting her clothes and hair. I stumbled backward a bit and then bent over to put my head between my legs.

Luke stood and rubbed my back with one hand, steadying me with his other. "Jessilyn, I know you're all tore up inside, but we need to get her help, and I'm afraid to move her without the doctor tellin' me I can. She's awful broke up. You need to stay here with her while I go get help."

"No! Let *me* go," I said desperately. It was getting late, and I didn't want to stay there with darkness and death so nearby. "I can get help and you can stay with her."

"Jessie, you can barely stand. Anyways, I can go faster no matter how you're feelin'. You got to let me go. The Colbys' is just a short ways down the road, and I'll get somebody to call for help. Then I'll head right back to you, okay?"

I wanted like anything to be strong for him, but my hands shook like leaves and my heart beat so hard I could hear it in my ears. Even though I wasn't able to calm my nerves, I nodded in agreement. I knew I had no choice but to stay behind with Callie.

Luke leaned over and kissed my forehead. "You'll be fine, Jessie girl," he whispered. "I have all kinds of faith in you."

Then he ran off faster than I'd ever seen him go, leaving me alone in the stillness. There was a slight early summer nip in the air as evening began to fall, and I noticed it for the first time, wrapping my arms tightly around my waist. But it was no use trying to warm myself. My blood was chilled inside me.

I knew I needed to go to Callie. My steps were agonizingly slow as I forced myself to her unmoving body, but at length I reached her side and dropped to my knees. Against my will, I was driven to measure her up, every last bruise and scrape. One of her legs was twisted to the side, making her foot point in the wrong direction. A bone on her right arm poked through her skin. And along her forehead was a patch of scrapes that I knew well as thorn marks, telling me she had passed through the nearby thorny brush. But I had no idea how she had gotten this way. For all I knew, some evil person had harmed her on purpose and left her here to die. And for all I knew, that same person could have come back to make sure the job was done.

I peered around the woods, but they were still eerily silent. At that moment, I would have given anything to hear just one bird singing or see one chipmunk dashing across the pass. The only movement I saw was that of a buzzard circling high above us, his hungry eyes watching and waiting for death to claim its prey. I said a quick prayer like I would have heard my momma pray, even though I wasn't very good at it.

As I bent my head again to look at Callie's swollen, unrecognizable face, my fear became overwhelmed by compassion. With renewed boldness, I reached out to lightly grasp her tiny, bloodied fingers.

And then I waited.

It seemed ages before Luke returned, but it really wasn't long at all. I can't imagine how fast he must have run. Fortunately, Dr. Mabley had been at Mae's side, so Luke was able to get him to come quickly. The sheriff drove Luke while the doctor drove his truck, and they sped up in a flurry of dirt and debris no more than fifteen feet away from where I crouched with Callie.

The doctor's face was painted with shock when he saw the girl, but he spoke gently to me as he tried to pry my fingers away from hers. "It's all right, Jessilyn. I'll take good care of her now. You go on over with Luke."

Although it had taken me a good bit of time to even look at Callie, I was now feeling compelled to stay by her side.

Luke came over and took me by the shoulders. "Come on away, Jessie. Doc needs to work."

I took Callie's hand out of mine and laid it gently on the ground. "She's just a baby," I murmured. "That's all she is."

Luke took me back to the sheriff's automobile and pulled a jacket out of the backseat, tossing it around my shoulders. "Sheriff says you can use this."

"Why didn't Mae come?"

"She ain't doin' too well," he said sadly. "When she heard how bad the girl is, she just went to pieces. Doc had to give her somethin' to calm her down."

I sat on a stump and put my head into my hands. "How'd it happen?" I asked, not expecting him to know. "How's a girl get to lookin' like that?"

"I'm sure the doc will have a good idea."

Within a few minutes, we were called over to help. The doctor had rigged Callie up so she'd stay still while being taken home, and the four of us carried her carefully to the bed of the truck. Luke and I rode in the back with her, holding her as still as we could while we drove back to the Colbys'. Nate Colby was home by then, having gotten the information about Callie being found. He was beside himself with worry and rushed to the truck when we pulled up.

There was all sorts of shouting and all sorts of questioning, but the only thing anyone really cared about was that Callie got on into Laurel Springs to the hospital. Luke walked me home, where we found Momma and Daddy waiting for us on the porch.

"You okay, baby?" Daddy asked me before we even reached the house. "We heard about the Colby girl."

"Harley was just gettin' ready to go out on a second round of lookin' when we heard how bad off she is." Momma's grip on her handkerchief tightened, lifted to swipe at her wet face. "Lord knows everyone must be all broke up, poor things."

"They're right upset," Luke said, respectfully pulling his hat from his head. "They've gone off to Laurel Springs. No doubt she'll be in the hospital for a while."

I listened to their conversation much like I'd listened to everything that day, with ears that felt stuffed with cotton. It was as though I was still sitting on that dim roadside alone with Callie's broken body, watching everyone else from a distance. I couldn't get the sight of her off my mind.

"Jessilyn," Momma said. "Baby, you ain't said one word. You all right?"

Luke put a hand to my back. "It's been hard on her, is all, seein' the little girl that way. And I had to leave her alone with Callie while I got help."

Momma moved to comfort me, but I didn't really want to be comforted right then. I took a step back and asked, "Where's Gemma at?"

"She ain't home yet. Seems the Hadleys asked her to stay on late again tonight."

"She didn't get home until midnight last night. What've they got goin' on over there that makes them need so much help?"

"Gets her a little extra money, anyhow, Jessilyn," Momma

said, trying to settle my nerves. "She don't seem to mind none."

That wasn't the way I saw it, but I didn't say anything. To my mind, Gemma had been strange since not long after she started that job, and I didn't like things that interfered with my and Gemma's friendship.

Momma and Daddy asked Luke to come in for supper, but he said he didn't feel much like eating, and I felt the same way.

"I'll take you by the hospital sometime, maybe," Luke said to me, tapping me under the chin with his finger. "Maybe day after tomorrow?"

I just nodded. Once he disappeared around the corner, I turned to Daddy. "Gemma not home yet?"

"Not yet. But she agreed to be home before dark. Ought to be here soon."

I slid down onto the porch steps. "I'll wait out here for her."

"Why don't you come on in for supper, Jessilyn?" Momma asked.

"I'm not hungry, Momma."

"A bite might make you feel some better, honey."

"I'll wait anyways."

They watched me for a minute and then walked reluctantly inside. While I waited, Momma and Daddy took turns poking their heads out the door, trying to get me to eat something, but I just kept shaking my head and sat on the porch waiting for Gemma. When I saw her round the bend,

I straightened up and stiffened my shoulders, determined to tell her just how I felt about that job taking up all of her time.

"Hey there, Jessie," was all she said when she saw me.

"I been waitin' here for you awhile now."

"Got a lot to do at the Hadleys'," she said quietly. "I'm tired. I'm goin' to bed."

I stood up to block her way. "I ain't waited out here all this time just to say good night to you."

Gemma never did like anyone trying to restrain her, and she bristled the minute I got in her way. "You move on out of my way, Jessie," she said through clenched teeth. "I said I'm tired, and I want to go to bed."

"Not till I say my piece."

"What you got to say that's so important it can't wait?"

"I can't figure you out. You ain't the same Gemma no more. You just work and wallow, that's all. Ain't no in-between."

"It ain't wallowin' to be tired after a hard day's work. Maybe you don't see it as so, Jessilyn Lassiter, but life ain't always about you."

"Maybe I should be tellin' *you* that. You ain't given me the time of day lately. It's like you ain't got nothin' to do but deal with your own problems. Maybe you ought to look around you and realize that there's things goin' on around here." The stress of the night broke my nerves, and I started shaking and crying, but I managed to keep ranting. "Maybe you got too much on your mind to realize other people got troubles of their own, but these days all you seem to do is think about your own life and ignore everybody else's."

"You near about done?" she asked. "I'm tired."

Momma came out onto the porch and stared wide-eyed at us both. "What on earth is goin' on out here? You'll wake the dead!"

"Jessie's just riled at me, is all," Gemma said. "Pretty much the same as always."

I bristled at her assertion that I was always picking fights, and I told her as much. "Ain't no normal day. Ain't no normal time with you and me, neither."

I was still crying a little, and Momma came over to hand me a fresh handkerchief she had in her apron pocket. "Gemma, Jessilyn's a little hurt inside today over the Colby girl and all. Why don't you girls talk about this again tomorrow when things seem clearer?"

Gemma gave my momma a confused glance. "What about the Colby girl?"

"She went missin'. Looks like maybe she wandered off last night or this mornin'. Took them a long while to find her."

"Is she all right?" Gemma asked.

Momma shook her head slowly. "Honey, she's pretty tore up. Has some broken bones and things. She's at the hospital over in Laurel Springs right now. Jessilyn and Luke . . . they found her at Duncan Pass, layin' underneath the bridge."

Gemma's face went pale and she dropped her purse right onto the lawn. I had wondered if she'd show concern, but I hadn't expected anything near to the look I saw on her face.

"Gemma?" I asked anxiously.

She ignored me, bent over to retrieve her purse, and said, "You let me know if you hear she's all right. I'm goin' to bed now."

Momma and I stared at one another as Gemma charged off into the house.

"You see, Momma?" I asked indignantly. "She's been like this for weeks now, all caught up in her own little world, and she can't see hide nor hair of anythin' else."

Momma didn't say anything, though I could see she was concerned just like I was. But then, there were plenty of concerns to go around.

Chapter 5

The next morning I made my way out to Daddy's makeshift office in the shed. He was sitting at his desk in the cramped space, rubbing his neck. His shoulders were slumped, and I knew just what was weighing on him the heaviest.

I approached him cautiously and set a glass of sweet tea on the desk beside him. "More money troubles, Daddy?"

"Ain't nothin' for you to worry about, baby."

I watched him closely for a minute, wondering if it would be smart to ask my important question while he was so pre-occupied. But then I thought that if he was distracted, it might be the perfect time to ask, since he wouldn't have much of his brain left for thinking about little things like me working for Miss Cleta. I decided to take the plunge. "Daddy," I began slowly, "you got a minute?"

Daddy sighed and wiped the sweat away from his eyes. "What d'you need, Jessilyn?"

"Well, it's just that . . . I talked to Miss Cleta and, well, she asked me a question, but she said I can't give her an answer till I get an answer from you."

Daddy stared at me for a few seconds. "Jessilyn, I ain't too good at thinkin' on hot days like this. You think you can say that a little clearer?"

I took one good look at the impatience spreading across his face and decided I'd better take my chance while I had it. "It's just that Miss Cleta . . . well, she's asked me to come work for her maybe two, three days a week. She says she's gettin' on up there in age, and her arthritis is actin' up, and she could use some company. So she asked me to come help her do some cleanin' and gardenin' and stuff."

"Miss Cleta asked you this?"

"Yes'r."

"And you want to do that?"

"Yes'r, I do. And I think it'd be a kind help to Miss Cleta, anyhow."

"You know I ain't too much for the idea of you workin'."

"I know, Daddy, and Miss Cleta figured as much. But I sure could use somethin' to do, and it wouldn't hurt to make some spendin' change doin' it."

"Seems you could help her out without takin' her money."

"Yes'r, and I said as much, but she won't have it any other way. And you know how Miss Cleta is when she sets her mind to somethin'." I leaned heavily against his desk and sighed. "Anyways, hard work would keep my mind off troubles. And I'd be nearby the Colbys so as to hear any news on Callie."

My hands gripped the edge of his desk so hard my knuckles paled, and Daddy reached over to peel one of them away. He tucked it inside both of his hands and sighed. "Reckon it's fine with me, Jessilyn. Long as you run it by your momma and make sure she can spare you some days. I know she's needed you to take on some of Gemma's chores along with your own now that Gemma's workin'."

"I'll ask her, Daddy." I put my free arm around him and laid my head on top of his. "You know, now that I'm workin', I can help out around here with my pay."

"Jessilyn, it's my place to make the money for this family, and I'm gonna do that. I don't want you feelin' a burden over this."

"Ain't no reason I can't help out around here. What else have I got to spend my money on that's worth somethin', anyhow?"

"That ain't the point. I got me responsibilities, and one of them is supportin' this family. And that's what I'm gonna do."

Worries were plentiful enough for us just then, so I decided to keep any arguments for another time. "Yes'r," I murmured. "Guess I'd better go talk to Momma."

Daddy squeezed my hand between his two and then let me go. "You do that, baby. And don't you worry about money. That's in the Lord's hands, and we got to trust in that."

I wasn't much sure about that, but I didn't say a word as I left him behind in the shed. I found Momma on the porch, fanning herself with a magnolia leaf.

"Sounds like a right nice way to spend a summer, Jessilyn," she said when I asked her. "I can get by just fine. Long as you can keep up with your regular chores."

So I made the trek down the road in the building morning heat, my steps instinctively slowing as I neared Miss Cleta's house. Just the sight of the Colbys' house next door got my heart racing. I put my head down and walked on, determined to keep my eyes from wandering anywhere I didn't want them to.

I found Miss Cleta fussing with some weeds in her front garden, and I immediately bent down to join her.

"Land's sake!" she muttered when she saw me. "Weeds are the doin' of Satan, the way I see it. They just pop up and bother people for no reason other than to bother them."

"Let me get them for you, Miss Cleta. Momma and Daddy agreed on me workin' for you, so I may as well start now."

She leaned back and smiled, the wrinkles beside her eyes deepening. "Well, that's happy news around these parts, and no doubt I needed some. But I'll work alongside of you while my back says it's okay. I find it ain't a bad job with you for company." She took her gardening gloves off and handed them to me. "Here. I don't want your pretty young hands gettin' all dirty."

I held my hands out to her and said, "My hands ain't pretty. Anyways, no reason why you should get your hands dirty but I shouldn't."

"Well then, I'll have to pick up a pair for you in town today. Ain't no young lady should have dirty fingernails."

We worked side by side for quite some time without a shortage of chatter before she finally stood up slowly, listing a bit to the right before she steadied herself. "I declare," she said, fanning herself with her hand. "Ain't no good to gettin' old, Miss Jessilyn. It's gettin' so I can't even bend over no more without takin' a spell."

I took the spade she carried in her hand. "I can be just as stubborn as you, Miss Cleta. I ain't bein' paid to watch you work, and since it's botherin' you to do it, I'll do it myself. Seems to me you can set and talk with me just as easy as you can pull weeds and talk with me."

Miss Cleta took a seat on a nearby bench and wiped her forehead. "Well, I'm too old to argue," she conceded with a smile.

"You ain't never too old to argue with nobody. You'll be arguin' till your dyin' day."

Miss Cleta let out a hoot and shuffled into the house to get us some lemonade. I worked in the garden for the next hour, did a little ironing with Miss Cleta bending my ear all the while, and then we settled down for some dinner. After I'd had my fill of cold ham, potato salad—and a little sweet, of course—Miss Cleta announced that she wanted me to accompany her on some errands.

"This is my goin' into town day. Lionel Stokes is due to pick me up in his taxicab soon, and I could use some extra hands if you don't mind comin' along."

"No, ma'am. A little stroll through town today would do me good. Change of scenery, and all."

Miss Cleta looked me over and waved a hand at me. "You best go on home and change into somethin' else. You've got dirt all over you, and a young lady ain't got call to go into town all smudged up."

I looked down at my clothes and nodded my head in agreement. "S'pose so. I could use a little washin'."

"Well, you go on home and wash up, and Mr. Stokes and I will pick you up in about an hour."

I hurried home, though I knew it wouldn't take me any time to get ready. Sure enough, I was finished in far less than an hour, so I sat on a porch rocker waiting for the taxi. When it arrived, I found Miss Cleta all dolled up and smelling like gardenias.

"Good day, Miss Jessilyn," Mr. Stokes said. "You look mighty fine this afternoon."

"Thank you, Mr. Stokes."

"Now, Lionel, you keep your eyes on the road and off the pretty girls," Miss Cleta said. "I don't want no accidents while I'm sittin' back here."

"I always give the ladies respect, Miss Cleta. You know that. I got my eyes in my head for sure."

"See that you do."

Mr. Stokes took a quick look over his shoulder at me. "Ain't seen much of Miss Gemma lately. She doin' poorly or somethin'?"

I cocked an eyebrow and leaned toward the front seat. "Ain't you seen her at the colored church, Mr. Stokes?"

"No, ma'am, I ain't. Seems to me she ain't been in some

weeks. My missus was just sayin' yesterday, 'Ain't seen Gemma Teague in a spell, don't it seem?' and I said I figured she was right."

I leaned back in the seat and wrapped my arms around my middle. Gemma had been claiming to go to church every Sunday morning, and now I knew she was lying to me, something I never would have expected from my Gemma.

I could tell by her sideways glances that Miss Cleta could see I was worried, but she decorously held her tongue while we were in the taxi. It was once we were out on the sidewalk that she questioned me.

"You and Gemma havin' trouble?" she asked as she studied a hat in a store window.

I pondered how much I might want to say to Miss Cleta. "Don't know yet," I replied. "Seems she's keepin' things from me. She ain't never kept things from me before."

"She's a grown woman now. Maybe she's just tryin' to figure some things out."

"If she's a grown woman now, then she shouldn't have as much to figure out, should she?"

We walked along for a while longer before she spoke again. "You think Gemma's been actin' strange lately then?"

"Yes'm."

She cleared her throat a little uncomfortably, something I didn't see Miss Cleta do very often. "She's been tellin' you she's goin' to church on Sundays?"

"Yes'm, she has. So now she's been lyin' to me, too."

"Well, I don't want to be passin' tales, but . . ."

I stopped dead and looked pleadingly at her. "Oh, Miss Cleta, if you got news on Gemma, please tell me. She's got me worried sick, and she won't tell me nothin'. Nothin' at all!"

She leaned closer to me and said, "I seen her passin' my house every Sunday mornin'. And you know she doesn't have to go past my house to get to the colored church. She goes on up the road, carrying her purse like she always does on her way to work at the Hadleys'."

"Why would she go to work on a Sunday? She don't work on weekends."

"Well now, that's what I been thinkin', and last time she went by, I called 'yoo-hoo' to her, and she never turned to look my way one bit. She seemed to be thinkin' too hard to notice me." Miss Cleta brushed a drop of sweat from her powdered forehead. "I declare, she's actin' mighty strange these days, and she done got me worried."

"I know. She's got me worried too. I told you, I'm all tied in knots."

She put a quieting hand on my back and nodded ahead of us. "Mrs. Packard's comin'," she said in a whisper. "Let her hear anythin' and it'll be all over town before you can blink twice."

True to her character, Mrs. Packard never issued us a greeting but started right in on a juicy tidbit the moment we met up with her.

"Well, Cleta, what do you think of this nasty business?" she asked in a flustered tone.

"Imogene, I ain't got a speck of an idea what you're talkin' about," Miss Cleta answered in exasperation. "As usual."

"I'm talkin' about Elmer Poe, of course. That boy's always been daft, don't you know, and now he's gone and gotten himself good and in a fix. Everyone in Calloway knew it would come to this someday."

Miss Cleta's face creased into concern the minute Mr. Poe's name came up, and she steadied herself against the side of a building. "Now, just what is everyone in this infernal town puttin' blame on Elmer Poe for?"

"For runnin' down the poor Colby girl, of course. He's always been a nuisance behind the wheel of his momma's old jalopy, and now the sheriff's gone and picked him up."

"Mr. Poe's bein' blamed?" I cried. "Mr. Poe would never have done that and just left her there. He's got one of the kindest hearts I know."

"You don't know a soul like you think you do sometimes, Jessilyn. You of all people ought to remember that."

"Well, I know Mr. Poe, and he would do no such thing."

"The girl's right and you know it, Imogene," Miss Cleta declared. "That boy's as good as they come. He don't even know how to keep a secret. Even if he hurt that girl by accident, he'd stop and care for her without pausin' to think."

Mrs. Packard seemed offended that we didn't sink our teeth into her news. "I don't need to stand here and be insulted. I just thought you'd like to hear, Cleta, what's been goin' on in this town. After all, they found his car right busted up, and it seems a clear case despite what you're thinkin'."

She skirted past us in a huff and left us to look at each other in bewilderment.

"Mr. Poe couldn't do nothin' so cold, Miss Cleta," I insisted.

She took my arm to steady herself and began walking toward the center of town. "I know that, darlin'," she said thoughtfully. "I know that as well as you do."

"Where are we goin'?" I asked as we passed by the pharmacy, where Miss Cleta had wanted to retrieve some things.

"I'm headin' over to that jailhouse and see what kind of nonsense is goin' on in this town."

I accompanied her gladly, wanting nothing more than to go to Mr. Poe's aid. He had always been so kind to me and my family, and I couldn't bear the thought of him being in jail.

"He must be frightened near to death," I murmured. "Poor Mr. Poe."

The minute we walked into the jail, Miss Cleta hollered, "Charlie Clancy! Where're you at?"

Sheriff Clancy moseyed out of the back room. "I'm comin', Miss Cleta. What's got a bee in your bonnet?"

I'd hated seeing Charlie Clancy take over when Sheriff Slater moved away, and I liked it even less now that he had Mr. Poe in his jailhouse. I didn't trust him, and I worried even more for Mr. Poe because of it.

"You got Elmer Poe in this here jail?" Miss Cleta demanded to know.

The sheriff rubbed a hand over his tired face and sighed.

"Yes'm, I do." He held up his hand when Miss Cleta began to speak again. "Now, Miss Cleta, I know just what you're gonna say, and I feel the same as you. I wouldn't have thought Elmer Poe capable of maliciousness any more'n you, but we done found his car all beat up, and he travels over the pass near every day to go look in Mr. Kearns's antique shop. There ain't no other option in light of the evidence."

"You been a lawman for some years, Charlie. You always had cases where what you seen matched up with what was true? Your own cousin was a murderous Klansman, and you didn't suspect a thing."

My stomach dropped when I heard her reference to Otis Tinker, and I swallowed hard in an attempt to push those thoughts away.

"All right now, calm down," Sheriff Clancy told Miss Cleta. "We're lookin' into things. If there's another truth to find, we'll find it."

"But now people's minds are set on it bein' Mr. Poe," I argued. "I've seen enough of this town's prejudice to know that once they make up their minds about somethin', they ain't gonna change it anytime soon. They'll make a villain out of Mr. Poe."

"Jessilyn, I know you got a fondness for Elmer, but sometimes that fondness makes people a little blind to someone's faults."

"Mr. Poe couldn't have done such a thing. I know that sure and simple."

"I want to see him," Miss Cleta demanded. "That poor

man's probably scared out of his wits, and two familiar faces would do him a world of good."

The sheriff stood there with his hands on his hips, staring at the both of us. He finally nodded slowly. "All right, Miss Cleta. You two can come on back if you like. Just don't go slippin' him no hacksaws or nothin'."

Miss Cleta smacked his arm with her pocketbook. "Get on back there with your smart tongue and take me to the boy."

It was a sad sight seeing Mr. Poe sitting in that jail cell. He had his arms wrapped around himself, his eyes red from tears. One of his feet was constantly tapping, and he was muttering things I couldn't understand. But then, Mr. Poe was usually hard to understand.

"Elmer," Miss Cleta said quietly. "You all right there, honey?"

Mr. Poe's head shot up at the sound of Miss Cleta's voice, and he jumped up and ran to us, shoving both hands through the bars.

"There, there, now." Miss Cleta gripped his hands and shushed him softly. "It'll be all right, Elmer. The good Lord's watchin' out for you."

"Ah ain't done nuthin' wrong, Miss Cleta," he said in his heavily accented way. "They's sayin' ah hurt a little girl, but ah ain't done nuthin' in muh life to hurt a little girl."

"I know that, Elmer. I know that well as I know my own name. Don't you worry none. Truth always comes out. You'll see."

"We're just wonderin' how your car got beat up and all, Mr.

Poe," Sheriff Clancy added. "Why don't you tell Miss Cleta here how your momma's automobile got so smashed up."

Mr. Poe started to get worked up again, and he looked desperately at me and then back at Miss Cleta. "Ah cain't say what happened to muh momma's automobile, Miss Cleta. Sure 'nough, ah cain't. Ah ain't even been out drivin' of late."

"Now, Mr. Poe," Sheriff Clancy said, "everybody in Calloway knows you head on over to the antique shop near every day. You sayin' you ain't been there lately? 'Cuz Mr. Kearns, he says he saw you in his shop that day the little Colby girl got hurt."

"Ah's there," Mr. Poe stammered. "Ah ain't nevuh said ah weren't there. Ah walked that day."

"That's nearly five miles, Mr. Poe," the sheriff exclaimed. "You tellin' me you walked ten miles that day?"

"Tain't but three miles the short ways. If ah walk across fields'n things, it's a shorter distance than takin' roads."

"This boy can walk six miles easier'n most in this town," Miss Cleta insisted. "He's got more stamina than you or your deputies, Charlie, I can tell you that." Miss Cleta shot a glance at Sheriff Clancy's overlapping belly. "Seems you could use a little more walkin' yourself."

"All right now, Miss Cleta," the sheriff said after clearing his throat uncomfortably. "My need for exercise ain't no evidence for court. What we need is proof that Mr. Poe weren't drivin' that day."

"Are we in America, Sheriff, or ain't we?" Miss Cleta

asked. "Seems to me what you need is proof that he did it, not that he didn't do it."

"I already got proof that he did it, Miss Cleta. I got that automobile, and that's evidence enough."

"But he said he wasn't drivin' it."

"But his word ain't enough."

The two stood there, squared off, staring each other down while Mr. Poe stood in that cell rocking back and forth.

I went over to him and placed a gentle hand on his arm. "It'll be okay, Mr. Poe. Miss Cleta and I will help you. I'll tell my daddy about it, and he'll help too."

"That little girl," Mr. Poe said to me, "she okay?"

Truth was, I hadn't heard any report since they'd taken Callie to the hospital, but I smiled wanly. "She'll be fine, Mr. Poe. Don't you worry none about that."

"She's a nice little girl."

"Yes'r. She is. And she'll be fine; don't you worry none."

The three of us left Mr. Poe after Miss Cleta gave him one more bit of assurance that he'd soon be free.

Once we were out in the front office, Miss Cleta lit into the sheriff again. "You know you got the wrong man, Charlie Clancy. Why ain't you just doin' what you know is right? You need to let that boy go."

Sheriff Clancy took off his hat and ran a hand through his mussed hair. "Miss Cleta, I got me a job to do. I gotta go on evidence, not on my gut."

"Well, you sure got enough gut to go on," she scoffed. "That ought to be plenty of evidence."

"Givin' me grief ain't gonna change nothin' for the better."

"You know, Elmer's poor daddy will be spinnin' in his grave. Judge Poe was a fine man of the law for some forty years before he passed, God rest his soul."

"I can't release a suspect just because his daddy was a respected judge back in the day."

Miss Cleta started toward the door, and I followed. But she stopped stock-still before she reached it and turned to face the sheriff. "If any harm comes to that boy because of this," she said with a shake in her voice, "it'll be on your head, Charlie Clancy."

I followed her out of the jail with a heavy heart. It certainly seemed as though the deck was stacked against Mr. Poe, and I was terrified at what they would do to him if evidence to prove him innocent was never found.

Miss Cleta and I went over to the pharmacy, where she mumbled under her breath the entire time she waited for Mr. Poppleberry to fill her order. She was as mad as a hornet.

It would have been wise, then, if Mrs. Myra Tucker had realized that Miss Cleta was mad as a hornet because she would likely have avoided saying what she said when she spotted us in the pharmacy.

The moment Mrs. Tucker called our names in her loud, nasally voice, Miss Cleta rolled her eyes and sighed. "Great balls of fire, what does that woman want now?"

"Always knew that Poe boy would come to no good," Mrs. Tucker fairly shouted to us even though she was only a few feet away. "He was always so strange, talkin' to himself and whatnot. I'm not surprised to hear of him sittin' in a jail cell."

"I do declare, Myra Tucker, if you ain't just got the mouth of the devil," Miss Cleta spat out angrily. "Anyone with a lick of sense ought to wash your mouth out with soap. Tellin' tales about that poor boy and screamin' it across the store so the whole world hears you. You ought to be ashamed of yourself!" She looked around at the handful of patrons and slapped her money down onto the counter. "You all ought to be ashamed!"

I picked up her package and followed her out the door, struggling to keep up with her spry seventy-nine-year-old footsteps.

My stomach began to whirl as it always did when trouble was at hand. There was no good to come of this. Like Mr. Poe would say, I could feel it in my bones.

Chapter 6

"Ain't this town learned enough about makin' hasty judgments?" Daddy asked no one in particular. "Ain't no one learned his lesson?"

Momma stood at the kitchen counter peeling her potatoes, a tear or two dampening her cheeks. I sat across the table from Daddy flouring dough for the potpie, but I was making a mess of it since I was thinking about a lot of things other than potpie.

"That poor man," Momma sniffed. "He's got to be scared to death!"

"He is, Momma," I said. "He's just as scared as can be. And they ain't got so much as a witness against him."

"They've got his momma's car," Daddy said. "That's all they think they need to haul that man in there, even though everyone in these parts has known him for years and knows he wouldn't never do nothin' like this. Anybody could've taken that car. He keeps the dang key sittin' inside it."

"Ain't nothin' fair around here, Daddy. This town'll turn against Mr. Poe with a snap of their fingers."

Momma put her knife down with an angry clatter. "Well, we won't," she declared. "I'm takin' that man supper every day, and just you see what'll happen if Charlie Clancy don't let me." She fished around in the potato bin for an extra and began peeling it with vengeance. "Harley, you're takin' me into town after we eat so I can take some food to Elmer Poe, you hear?"

Daddy nodded and got up from the table, slapping his leg with his hat so hard a snap echoed through the room. "I'm gonna call Charlie up and see what I can find out. Maybe I can talk some sense into him."

"Then you tell him we're comin' with supper."

We ate somberly that evening. Luke hadn't come to supper, leaving a gaping hole at our table, and Gemma still wasn't speaking to me. She sat beside me at the table, barely eating a thing. Momma and Daddy looked at her a lot, but they didn't seem to think it prudent to say anything to her.

Momma and Daddy left just after supper, and I washed while Gemma dried. When I tried telling her about Mr. Poe's dilemma, she shushed me by saying, "I don't want to talk about that."

"But don't you care nothin' about what goes on in this town no more?" I asked desperately. "I swear, Gemma, you ain't like you at all."

"I said I don't want to talk about none of it," she hollered. Then she tossed down her dish towel and ran out of the room.

I watched after her helplessly, dishwater dripping from my hands to the floor. I didn't follow her—I knew well enough she wanted to be left alone—but I couldn't help worrying.

When I was done with the dishes, I decided I'd head down to the Colbys'. Truth be told, I had no interest in going near the place for all the fear I now associated with it, but I was aching to hear news of Callie. I grabbed some leftover bread pudding and started on my walk.

When I reached the Colbys' house, I found Mae sitting on the porch swing, tears in her eyes.

"Hey there, Mae," I said softly. "You all right?"

"Just thinkin'," she said.

"I came to see how Callie's doin'. Brought you some bread puddin' too."

"That's mighty kind of you, Jessilyn." She took the bowl and set it on a table beside her. "Your momma makes a fine bread puddin'."

She scooted over to make room for me on the swing, and I sat next to her, a knot in my stomach because I hated talking to people about sad things.

"Is Callie doin' better, Mae?"

"Doc says we won't know for maybe a few days. Sent us home to rest, but I can't get no rest."

"Is Nate home?"

"He's gone into town for some things. He can't seem to sit still for more'n a few minutes."

We sat there in silence for a moment, and then I said, "Momma prays for Callie nearly once an hour. You know, she prays out loud all the time, and I can hear her prayin' for Callie and for you and Nate. And we pray for you every suppertime."

"That's mighty kind of y'all." She looked up quickly as a truck rounded the bend. "There's Nate. I guess we'll be goin' on back to the hospital in a few minutes now."

"Well, I won't keep you. Just wanted to see if there was any news. If you got some need for help, you let us know."

She got up from the swing and followed me to the porch steps. "Will do, Jessilyn. You tell your momma thanks for them prayers. And thank you for that bread puddin'."

I was on my way down the walk when Nate came walking toward the house.

"Hey there, Nate," I said, but I was taken aback by the angry look on his face.

The only acknowledgment I got was a nod in my direction and a curt "Jessilyn."

"You know what I heard in town, Mae?" he said before he even got to the porch. "They done picked up who hurt our baby girl."

Mae put her hands over her mouth in shock.

"That's right! They done arrested Elmer Poe, crazy old loon. Didn't I always say it was the dumbest thing in the world to let that crazy man behind the wheel? And now he done gone and near about killed our baby girl."

"But, Nate," I said without pausing to think, "they ain't sure it was Mr. Poe who did it."

"They got his beat-up old automobile, ain't they? That's proof enough."

Mae slumped down onto the steps, her shoulders shaking.

"But Mr. Poe wouldn't never hurt a fly," I replied gently. "He's a fine man. Even if he'd done somethin' by accident, first thing he'd do is fetch help."

"Jessilyn Lassiter, that man 'bout killed my Callie. They got enough proof they seen fit to arrest, and that's enough for me."

"They ain't got no witness, no way of knowing how that automobile got messed up."

"I think we can all figure that out just fine. They got enough to show who done it, and he'll get what's comin' to him."

"But they'll put him in prison . . . or worse."

Nate Colby pointed a shaking finger in my direction and said, "For what he done to my baby, he can burn in hell!"

Mae never uttered a word. I turned sharply and made my way home with fear nipping at my heels. I knew Nate had a good reason for how he was feeling. But I also knew that people in Calloway had a bad habit of jumping to conclusions. My memory was good enough to remember how much trouble that could cause, and worries for Mr. Poe's safety filled my every thought.

When I got home, I found Gemma sweeping the porch fast and furiously. I didn't like the looks of her, but I wasn't about to say anything. She was in no state to be reasonable, I well knew, so I kept quiet. I was never known for keeping my tongue, but I'd never been in such a position with Gemma before.

She stopped sweeping long enough to look up at me with guarded eyes. "You see the Colbys?" she asked quietly.

I nodded, not wanting to say much to her just then. "They ain't good."

She stared off into the distance for a minute and then went back to her sweeping. The methodical noise of the broom made me frustrated. "That all you got to say?"

"Ain't full of words today."

The breeze had littered the porch with azalea petals, and I slid my foot across the porch to kick away one she'd missed. "You goin' to church on Sunday?"

She stopped sweeping and looked at me. "What're you askin' that for?"

I shrugged and examined my fingernails. "Just thought they might miss you over there since you ain't been lately."

Gemma tossed the broom to the floor. "You been spyin' on me, Jessilyn Lassiter?"

"In case you didn't know it, this town has eyes. I ain't got to spy on nobody. All's I've got to do is listen. People talk."

"Well, maybe people ought to find better things to talk about."

"If you don't want them talkin' about you, maybe you ought to keep better company."

Gemma didn't say anything, but her glare was enough to burn a hole clear through me.

"'Course, maybe you ain't spendin' time with someone on Sundays. Maybe you're just spendin' some time alone somewhere." I waited, hoping she'd give me the answer I wanted to hear. But she didn't say anything, which only made me figure the worst. "Or don't Joel Hadley go to church on Sundays, neither?"

Gemma picked the broom back up so sharply, I was afraid she'd spear me with it, but she just angrily went back to sweeping. "Who I spend my Sundays with ain't none of your business."

Even though her words were harsh, her expression worried me, and I reached a hand out to touch her arm. "You got things to talk about, Gemma, you can talk to me. You can talk to me about everythin'."

She stood motionless for a moment, looking aimlessly into the distance. When she spoke, her voice came out strained. "Not everythin'." Then she leaned the broom against the porch rail, walked down the steps, and hurried away down the road.

There didn't seem to be one place I could go where worry would leave me alone.

Except Luke's.

I swept the last few petals from the porch, propped the broom against the house, and headed down the road. The evening was hot as usual, but the air wasn't so damp as I was used to and there was a good breeze to lighten my spirits. The sky was turning pink when I rounded the corner to Luke's property. He'd made a good business for himself in the last year making furniture, and when I found him, he was busy painting a kitchen table a pale shade of green.

The remaining sunlight cast a golden sheen on Luke's hair, and I stopped short to get a good, long, admiring glance at him. My infatuation with him had done nothing but grow over the last four years, and I got my looks at him whenever I could do it without his notice. When he stood to stretch his back, I shook myself out of my reverie and moved into his view.

He turned his head and smiled sleepily at me. "Hey there, Jessie. What's got you over this side of the creek?"

"Just wanted some company," I said. "Gemma and me ain't talkin'."

"That's a shame about you and Gemma."

"Ain't nothin' I can do about it. Ain't no point in worryin' about somethin' I can't change."

My words sounded very mature and calm, but they had nothing to do with my real feelings. It was just something that made me hurt inside, and I didn't much feel like talking about hurtful things.

"You hear about Mr. Poe?" I asked. "He's in the county jail, you know."

Luke stood up straight and squinted to see me against the setting sun. "What in blazes for?"

"They think he's responsible for Callie bein' hurt. They found his momma's car bashed in, and they think he hit Callie with it."

"That's a fool thing," he spat out, tossing his paintbrush down on the table. "Ain't never a day Mr. Poe would do somethin' like hurtin' a girl and leavin' her on the side of the road to die."

"I know that. Daddy knows that. Momma knows that. Miss Cleta . . . she knows it, and she already done told the sheriff he's a crazy fool, but nobody's listenin'. It's just like it was when people were hatin' on us because of Gemma years ago, Luke. People up and make decisions that don't make sense, and then they go out and hurt innocent people because of them. There ain't gonna be no hope for Mr. Poe unless they find out what really happened."

Luke ran the back of his hand over his sweaty forehead and paced the dirt path where he stood. "You say the car was bashed up?" he asked me after a couple of minutes.

"That's what they're sayin'. But Mr. Poe . . . he says he didn't do nothin' to that car. And he means it," I said adamantly. "You should've seen his face when he told me and Miss Cleta. There ain't no lyin' in that man, Luke, and you know it."

"No, there ain't no lyin' in him, Jessie, but there's lyin' in lots of other folks. You can just bet someone in this town knows what happened to Callie Colby, but they ain't sayin' nothin'. They'd rather let a poor, innocent man go to jail for doin' nothin' but mindin' his own business."

"You know that feelin' I get right in the middle of my stomach when somethin' bad's gonna happen? Well, I got it now. This ain't gonna come to no good."

Luke came over and lifted my chin with a paint-stained finger. "Don't you go losin' hope, Jessilyn," he told me seriously. "Ain't no reason to lose hope until all possibilities are used up, you hear? We got things we can do. Givin' up hope is the same as givin' up on Mr. Poe."

His voice was firm but kind all the same, and it took some of the bitter taste out of my mouth.

I smiled at him as well as I could with a heavy heart and looked down at his green-tinted hands, eager to think about anything but trouble. "Who on earth wants a green kitchen table?"

He smiled and gave the tip of my nose a tap. Then he walked back to the table. "Mrs. Polk. She's got a big new cookin' range comin' in this week that's green, and she figures she ought to have a green table to match." He bent down level with the tabletop and ran his finger over one spot in examination. "Makes me a little sick puttin' this color on a sturdy table like this, but she's the customer. Customer's always right, you know, Jessie." He stood up and winked at me. "Just don't always mean they have good taste, is all."

"I knew Mrs. Polk was gettin' a new cookin' range. She spread it all round town, and Miss Cleta told me Mrs. Polk was all full of herself. She says Mrs. Polk'd be better off gettin' a new face; that'd give her somethin' to truly be thankful for."

Luke laughed out loud, and I smiled at his amusement.

"'Course she followed it up by sayin' what an awful thing that was of her to say, and the Lord should strike her speechless for sayin' it." I bent to pick a nearby violet and twirled it between two fingers. "Then she followed *that* up by sayin' that the Lord would likely forgive her, though, since she was only near enough speakin' the truth. 'Weren't the Lord who gave her that face, after all,' she told me. 'It's a sour disposition and a greedy heart that gave her face that sorry, crinkled-up look.'"

"There ain't no more honest soul in the world than Miss Cleta," Luke said, still laughing. "Lord love a woman like that. She's got more pluck than all the women in Calloway put together."

I straightened up tall. "I got plenty of pluck myself."

"Oh, I know you got plenty of pluck, Miss Jessie. I've been on the receivin' end of it many a time."

"And you wouldn't like me as much if you hadn't been, neither," I said coyly. "You like havin' spats with me, and you know it."

"Well now, I don't know," he said, rubbing his chin in feigned thought. "Might be life would get a bit simpler if I didn't have to put up a fuss with you so much."

"No sir. You like our rows. I can see it on your face. If I were just some mouse, sayin' all 'yes sirs' and 'no sirs,' you'd be bored stiff."

"But there ain't no use arguin' about whether or not I like to argue with you, is there?" he asked with a grin. "Seems since you're near about a lady, and you ain't changed none, you ain't bound to change now. Seems you're full of pluck and sure to stay full of it."

He turned away and picked up an old rag to wipe his hands on. "Still, though . . . ," he murmured wryly. "Ain't no one said I can't put a bar of soap in that mouth of yours every now and again."

"You just try it, Luke Talley," I exclaimed tartly, "and I'll have you tarred and feathered by mornin'."

"Ain't no feathers anywhere near here, so I can figure. I reckon I got me a good chance of gettin' away with it. Heck, your daddy'd probably pay me money for it."

I reached over and picked up the green paintbrush, wielding it like a weapon, but Luke grabbed my wrist before I had the chance to catch him with it. I tripped forward into him, and for one short but glorious minute we stood there, face-to-face, his hand gently gripping my arm.

I was afraid to blink in case I'd miss anything, so I stood there wide-eyed, my heart beating a mile a minute. The fleeting brilliance of that moment passed when Luke suddenly dropped my hand like it had stung him and stumbled backward, bumping into his worktable.

Neither of us knew what to say. There was a deep silence between us, and even the crickets seemed quieter than usual. I tried swallowing, but my throat was dry, and I backed up a little bit, awkwardly fumbling for my next move.

Luke was just standing there, looking toward the ground at nothing in particular, his eyes never meeting mine.

At length, I managed to speak after twice clearing my throat. "You got paint on your trousers."

Luke seemed not to hear me for a moment; then he blinked a few times fast and bent his head down to look at his pants. "Ain't I clumsy," he mumbled uncomfortably. And then he took advantage of the opportunity to excuse himself from our strange meeting. "Better go scrub it off. I'll see you later, Jessilyn."

I watched him as he tripped over a chair and then a tree stump before managing to make it inside his house.

I knew my daddy would want me home before dark, but I still wandered home at a snail's pace, lost in a daydream.

After all, my smile lit my way home.

Chapter 7

Saturday seemed a day like any other day when I woke up. I looked out the window at the pink streaks that were starting to fill the sky and glanced over at Gemma still sleeping in her bed. She had tossed and turned until very late last night just as she had done many nights of late. I watched her there and felt the sadness of our strained friendship, hoping this day wouldn't bring more pain than I already felt.

As was common for me of late, my first thoughts were of Gemma and my second thoughts of Callie. True to his word, Luke had taken me to the hospital on Thursday night, but we hadn't had any news of Callie since. I decided to head down the road in search of some.

Old Joe Callahan was fixing Miss Cleta's roof when I passed by, and he waved a hello to me.

"Out awfully early this morning, ain't you, Miss Jessilyn?" he called.

"Same for you, Joe."

"You know Miss Cleta. She's got to have things done soon as they need doin', and she'll bother you till she gets her way."

Miss Cleta came out onto the porch, letting the screen door slam to with a clang that made old Joe jump up on that roof.

"You talkin' about me again, Joe Callahan?" she hollered.

Joe grabbed his hammer back up good and quick. "No'm, I ain't," he lied, before his words were drowned out by the sound of his hammering.

Miss Cleta, her hands squarely on her apron-covered hips, nodded at me with a smile that didn't reach her eyes. "Come on in for some banana bread, Jessilyn. Ain't nothin' else for a morning like this but some banana bread."

"I don't want to take up your time, Miss Cleta."

"It ain't takin' up my time. Just the same, I have somethin' to talk over with you."

I wandered into the house, where it wasn't much cooler than it had been outside, but the smell of the bread took my mind off the heat. Miss Cleta gave no indication of what she wanted to talk to me about for the first little while. She just rattled around in her kitchen, setting out plates and butter. I sat idly by, knowing full well any offers to help her would be rejected since Miss Cleta felt no guest should ever lift a finger and today I was a guest, not her household help. It wasn't until she was settled opposite me and halfway through her first slice of bread that she murmured a single word.

"You know, Miss Jessilyn, I think you seen a lot of unpleasantness in your short life."

I looked at her oddly and shrugged. "S'pose so, Miss Cleta. Though it seems near everyone's gone through the same sadness. People all over the place are losin' kin and whatnot. Can't see as though I'm much different from the rest."

"Well, you know God has a plan for things, don't you? Out of things that seem bad at the time, good things can come."

"Yes'm. I've seen that before."

Miss Cleta took one long sip of her tea, then a second and then a third. I could tell she was uncomfortable and unhappy though she was talking fine and pleasant, and there was a sudden tightening of my stomach as I watched her face.

"Miss Cleta," I said hesitantly, "you got some bad news to tell me, I'd like you to come on out and tell me. I ain't going to feel any better findin' bad news out from anybody else, and around these parts, I'm gonna hear about it later if I don't hear about it now."

She thought for a moment and looked like she was going to speak; then she thought twice and got up to put the teapot back on. But as she went to strike the match for the stove, she stopped and looked at me, and I could see her eyes were starting to wet.

"Miss Cleta?" I murmured nervously.

"Child, little Callie. She ain't . . ."

I pushed my chair back from the table, starting to feel suffocated. "She ain't what, Miss Cleta?"

"Honey . . ."

"You're scarin' me!"

"You know how bad she was hurt, Jessilyn."

"But she was doin' better, I thought."

"No, honey. She was just the same as ever all along. The only reason she seemed better is because she didn't seem worse. But now . . ."

"Now what?"

"She's gone, baby. Jesus took her home late last night."

I clutched my chair tightly, my thoughts whirling.

Miss Cleta came across the kitchen to console me, but she only laid a hand on my shoulder, making sure to give me room to figure things out on my own.

"Why would God take a little girl?" I asked, angry and sad at once. "She's just a little girl!"

"Honey, it's as I said before. God's got His plans, and we ain't the wiser to them. We can't understand His ways."

"Ain't no doubt we can't. 'Cause ain't none of it makes any sense." I got up and paced the room, feeling like nothing was right or familiar. I suddenly felt out of place. "Mr. Poe," I remembered suddenly. "What'll they do to Mr. Poe? They'll string him up for sure."

Miss Cleta said nothing, and I could tell by her silence that she felt the same as I did.

We stood there across from each other in Miss Cleta's kitchen, faced off over the seeming unfairness of life. I crossed my arms defiantly and shook my head.

"Honey," Miss Cleta said, "you got to believe God's got His reasons, and His reasons are always right."

"It ain't right! No'm, it ain't right!"

Miss Cleta tried to console me, but I backed away. "I've got to go," I mumbled.

"Where you goin', honey? You want Joe to give you a ride home?"

"No, ma'am. I just got to go somewhere . . . somewhere else."

Miss Cleta followed me to the door. She let me go without another word, but when I turned down the road away from my house, I heard her say, "Joe, you get on over to the Lassiters' and tell them where Jessilyn's headin'."

But I didn't want anyone to find me. I just wanted to be alone. I hurried along the road until I was out of sight and then slipped off into the woods.

I stumbled mindlessly over stumps and fallen tree branches until I reached Squalers Pond. I dropped to the ground and stared into the water, watching the reflection of the clouds, without any thought toward time. It didn't matter to me that Momma and Daddy might worry or that I'd be bitten to pieces by mosquitoes. All I knew was I was mourning the loss of life as it had been as much as I was mourning the loss of Callie.

I'd spent many moments by this pond with her, watching her toss stones into the water in search of a good splash. The memory of her laughter echoed in my head as I mindlessly fingered a rock beside me, closing my hand around it. The thought struck me that Callie would never sit by this pond with me again, and I squeezed the rock hard, hoping the pain from its jagged edges would cut the pain in my heart. But it didn't numb it one bit.

I was oblivious to anything else around me until a long shadow fell over me. I looked back to see Luke standing behind me.

"Jessilyn," he said, "your momma and daddy are mighty worried about you. You all right?"

I hadn't cried a tear that whole time by the pond, but now I could feel them behind my eyes, determined to come out. It was all I could do to say two simple words in a broken whisper: "Callie's gone."

Luke gently pulled me to him and my sobs came in short gasps. "I know, Jessie. And I'm sure sorry," he murmured. "I'm sure sorry."

I let myself cry for a couple minutes more before pushing away from him. I looked into his face desperately. "They got Mr. Poe for hittin' her, Luke. They'll kill him now."

Luke's jaw tightened, and I could see in his eyes he knew I was right. "Did you hear any news? Anyone done anythin' to Mr. Poe?"

"No, but they will. You know it."

He took me by the arm, his touch kind and gentle despite his angry posture, and we traveled the short distance home without saying a word. When we rounded the corner to home, I saw Daddy leaning on a fence post mopping his face with a handkerchief. The minute he saw us, he straightened up tall and approached us with rapid steps.

"Baby, are you okay?" he asked after one look at my face. "We been lookin' everywhere for you."

I ran to him, and though he was hot and sweaty, I let him take me in his arms. "We have to help Mr. Poe, Daddy. He ain't got no one else."

"Think we might have some trouble brewin' in town," Luke said. "Mr. Poe ain't likely to get a fair trial now."

Daddy let me go and gave me a soft push toward the house. "Jessilyn, you run on in and tell your momma you're back. She's been sittin' by the phone hopin' for someone to call about you."

I wandered off, but I slowed my pace to hear what they might be saying with me gone.

"Ain't no good to come from things like this," Luke told my daddy. "Mr. Poe ain't got a bad bone in his body, and this town's bound to treat him no better'n an animal now."

I stopped at the porch steps to glance behind me, and I saw Daddy shake his head wearily. "I'll go fetch my rifle."

Daddy mounted the steps past me, but I turned again to look at Luke. He had pulled his pistol from his waistband and was checking to make sure it was loaded. A chill went down my spine as I watched him there, weapon in hand. I pictured him being threatened by other men with guns, angry men wanting nothing more than to exact vengeance, and my heart began to beat fast and hard so that I could feel it in my throat. I stood there for a minute before I found my feet and ran down the steps toward him.

"Luke," I called out. "Luke!"

He quickly replaced his pistol and looked at me with worry in his eyes. "What's wrong, Jessie? You all right?"

"I'm okay," I stammered breathlessly. "It's just . . . I wanted to say . . . I want you to be careful, is all."

He smiled halfway. "I'm always careful, Jessilyn. Your daddy and I are just goin' into town to check on Mr. Poe. We ain't really expectin' a fight or nothin'. We're just bein' prepared."

"Luke," I said with a shake of my head, "I ain't no baby no more. Lyin' to me don't make no sense. I know people, and I know what they can do when they're blind angry. Ain't no use tryin' to convince me that there ain't gonna be no trouble. I know better."

Luke pushed his hat back on his head and looked into my eyes. "I reckon you're right at that, Miss Jessilyn," he said, his voice soft but certain. "You ain't no baby no more, sure enough."

"'Bout time you realized that."

"Well then . . . ," he wondered aloud. "What should I say? I'm used to sayin' things to make you feel better."

"You can't make me feel better all the time, Luke. Sometimes things are just bad any way you slice it. All you need to say is you'll be careful—and mean it."

"All right then," he said quietly. "I'll be careful, Jessie. So long as you don't go followin' behind us when we leave."

"Huh?"

"Don't tell me 'huh.' I know you, Jessilyn Lassiter. The

minute we're outta sight, you're gonna get it into your head to follow behind us."

"I wasn't goin' to."

"Uh-huh," he murmured. "Just the same, you listen to what I'm tellin' you. I can see in your face you're thinkin' different than you're sayin'."

"Don't you go tellin' me what I'm thinkin'. I got me a mind of my own, and ain't nobody gonna tell me what I'm usin' it for. I said I ain't thinkin' of followin' behind, and I ain't."

He raised both palms in front of himself. "Hey there, don't get so feisty," he said, giving me a cockeyed grin. "I'm just sayin' . . ."

"Maybe you shouldn't just say. Maybe you should let me make up my own mind, instead of tellin' me what it is."

"Every time I turn around, I find you two spattin' about somethin'," Daddy said as he made his way down the steps. "Jessilyn, your momma's already fixin' some supper for the Colbys, and she's wantin' you to fix up a cobbler if you're feelin' up to it."

Just hearing the Colbys mentioned brought my senses back a bit, and I swallowed my frustration at Luke and nodded at Daddy. "Yes'r. I reckon puttin' my hands to work would help me feel better." I leaned up and planted a kiss on Daddy's cheek. "You'll be careful, Daddy, won't you? I'm worried there's trouble comin'."

"Baby, don't you worry none. We'll be fine."

I nodded without conviction and walked toward the house. Halfway up the porch steps, I stopped to look at Luke.

He was walking to the truck in that familiar loping gait of his, but the minute I turned around, he turned too, walking slowly backward as he peered at the porch. I gave him a sad, halfhearted wave, and he smiled, tipped his hat at me, and disappeared into the truck.

I wasn't much of a praying girl, but I said a quick one for Daddy and Luke as I stood there in the heat of summer, worrying for the two men I loved most.

Chapter 8

Momma was sniffling about every fifteen seconds, and though I could understand why she was crying, I wished she weren't. It only made me think about Callie Colby even more, and what I wanted just then was to forget. But my momma cried when she found a dead bird, so asking her to stop crying about such a horrible thing as Mae and Nate Colby's losing their baby girl was out of the question. I just tried to think of something else as I coated blueberries with flour in Momma's big green mixing bowl. The slam of the screen door announced someone's entrance, and Momma and I looked up to find Gemma coming around the corner.

She took one look at the odd scene of the two of us, elbow-deep in flour and cooking grease, our faces stained with tears, and dropped her purse in a panic. "What's goin' on?"

Momma couldn't talk, she was too upset, so Gemma looked at me. "Jessie, you tell me what's wrong."

I swallowed hard twice to push down the lump in my throat and simply said, "Callie Colby died."

Gemma's face paled two shades, and I saw her grip the doorframe so that her knuckles paled too. Her knees seemed so unsteady, I jumped up in case she needed help to stay standing.

"Gemma," I said, "you okay? You need to sit down?"

She didn't say a word, and even Momma seemed shocked at her reaction to the news. There wasn't a single body in Calloway who wouldn't feel a solid stroke of sadness on hearing such a thing, but Gemma hadn't ever been around the Colbys as much as I had, and I never expected to see her so torn up over the loss of their daughter.

Gemma closed her eyes tight for a few seconds, used the wall to steady herself, and then stumbled down the hall and up the stairs. Momma and I exchanged a glance before I wordlessly followed Gemma upstairs. I found her on her bed, sobbing into her pillow, and I could tell by the sound that she was trying her best not to let anyone hear.

"Gemma," I murmured, touching her shoulder lightly, "is there somethin' I can do for you?"

She said nothing, and for the next several moments I sat there and let her cry, tears slipping from my own eyes all the while. I had just risen to leave when she sat up suddenly and looked at me with desperation. "What's goin' to happen to Mr. Poe?" she asked, her voice rising in pitch.

I got a chill at the reminder of what Luke and Daddy were walking into, and I rubbed my arms to fight it off. "Don't know. Daddy and Luke went off into town to see if there was any trouble brewin'."

"There will be trouble. You know it!"

"I reckon," I said sadly. "Sheriff Clancy's got him safe at the jailhouse, though, and even if he is a hardheaded boor, he's bound to do his duty by him."

Gemma sat there on her bed, slowly shaking her head back and forth. Then she hopped up and started to take off her work clothes.

"What're you doin'?" I asked.

"Goin' out."

"Goin' out where?"

She just kept getting dressed, the tears still coursing down her cheeks.

"Gemma Teague, you tell me where you're goin'," I demanded.

She still held her tongue, and I went around to look square into her eyes, where I could usually find what she was thinking. "Are you goin' into town?" I asked with surprise.

Still she didn't reply.

"Why would you want to go into town?"

"Because Mr. Poe's in trouble," she moaned. "He needs help."

"And how are you gonna help him? What are you gonna do that can help?"

"It ain't a matter for figurin' on, Jessie. I just gotta go, and I'm goin'."

"There'll be trouble there. Daddy and Luke took their guns with them and everythin'."

She slipped her feet into her shoes and walked past me. "Ain't no matter. I'm goin'. There's gotta be some way I can help."

"Just what d'you think a colored girl's gonna be able to do in settlin' down the people in Calloway?" I asked, determined that the only way I could stop her was by being painfully honest.

She slowed her steps and stared at me. I stood by waiting for her to slap me silly. Instead, she just blinked twice, bent over to grab my shoes, and tossed them at my feet. I looked down at the shoes and then back up at her.

"You're right," she said. "They won't listen to a colored girl. Guess you're comin' too."

And then she marched out the bedroom door without waiting for me to follow because she knew I would. There was never a time when one of us was about to step into trouble that the other one didn't follow to keep watch. Most of the time it was the other way around, but today it would be me following Gemma into trouble, and I let out a long sigh as I slipped my shoes on and chased after her.

I grabbed Gemma on the stairs and whispered, "There ain't no way to get by Momma. She's waitin' on me to make that cobbler. She'll be hollerin' for me in minutes."

Gemma just continued downstairs, stopping outside the kitchen.

Momma looked sadly over at us and said, "Gemma, you all right, honey?"

"I need some air, is all. You mind if Jessilyn comes for a walk with me?"

Momma tipped her head sideways and gave Gemma an understanding but sad smile. "Sure enough, honey. I'll finish up the cobbler."

Gemma nodded and turned slowly away from the door, but when we were out of Momma's sight, she hauled me outside like a cat with dynamite on its tail.

"You lied to Momma," I hissed when we were on the lawn.

Gemma ignored me.

"Gemma Teague!" I exclaimed. "I ain't got any idea what's put the burr under your saddle, but you just lied to my momma and you've got me involved, and I want to know what's goin' on."

She kept going down the road, but I could tell by her expression that she would tell me soon enough. I kept quiet and waited, but it wasn't until a mile in that she started to speak, though she never slowed her steps or looked in my direction.

"Mr. Poe didn't kill Callie Colby," she said.

"I know that. He couldn't have."

"But you only know that 'cause you know Mr. Poe. I know that 'cause I was there when Callie got hurt."

Her hand still clutched my arm tightly so I couldn't stop in my tracks like I wanted to, but my feet wouldn't work right, and I stumbled along after her in shock.

Finally I managed to pull her to a stop and grabbed her face in both my hands. "Tell me what happened," I pleaded. "I want to help you."

Gemma's eyes were glassy and shimmering with tears, and the pain in her face made my heart hurt, but I stared at her, willing her to tell me what I knew she didn't want to have to put into words.

"I thought we hit a deer," she whispered absently. "I told him to slow down. I told him to get out and see. But he'd had too much to drink, and he wouldn't stop. He just wouldn't stop!" Her voice reached a crescendo, and then she dropped to her knees on the side of the road and let her face fall into her hands.

I knelt down beside her with a stomach full of knots. "Gemma, please. Please tell me who was drivin'."

"Joel Hadley," she said at last.

"Joel Hadley!"

"He'd been drinkin' at their party, but I let him drive me home anyways. His car broke down near Mr. Poe's house, and he said we'd take Mr. Poe's car instead. I told him no, but he said we had no other way but to walk and he wasn't walkin' all that way." Her words came in streams like they'd been caught up in her for so long that she couldn't keep them in any longer.

"I told you not to trust him," I said softly. "He ain't no good."

She shook her head sadly. "He seemed to like me, Jessie.

He really did. He was always actin' sweet on me, and it . . . it made me feel good to have him pay me attention."

"Gemma, you ain't got to have a no-good like Joel Hadley around to get attention. You're worth more'n that."

"I ain't been thinkin' straight, is all. Ever since he started payin' mind to me, I been thinkin' all wrong."

I took her face in my hands again and swiped her tears away with my thumbs, but they kept coming so fast I couldn't keep up. "Gemma," I whispered, "calm down and tell me what happened that night."

She looked away from my face and stared into the distance like that night was playing itself out behind me. "He'd been drinkin', I could tell, and I knew I'd best not go with him, but he was actin' a gentleman. He even offered me the front seat, and I thought maybe he'd had a change of heart, so I decided to go with him. He was just fine when we started out. Then he stopped on the road near Mr. Poe's house and he started . . . he tried to . . ."

I grabbed her hand tight enough to squeeze the blood out of it. "Did he hurt you? . . . Gemma!" I exclaimed when she didn't speak up. "Answer me! Did he do anythin' to you?"

She shook her head slowly and looked into my eyes. "I got away before he could, and he chased after me and said he was sorry. He said he was sorry and he'd just get me home . . . but we couldn't because the car wouldn't start back up, and he got out all mad and cursin', and I started walkin' down the road."

"Then what?"

"Then he saw we were near Mr. Poe's house, and he said we'd just borrow Mr. Poe's momma's car, and I said no. I said it was same as stealin'. But he said I was bein' uptight, and I didn't want him to think I was some dumb girl, worryin' about everythin'."

"But he'd been drinkin'. He wasn't fit to be drivin' no more."

"I know. I know I should've tried to stop him or at least walked on home, but I was all mixed up." She was pacing now, wringing her hands so tightly I thought she'd peel the skin right off. "I'm no fool of a girl, Jessie," she told me in a near sob, as though I needed to be told some such thing.

"I know you ain't, Gemma," I said as consolingly as I could. I reached out to touch her shoulder but she wouldn't be moved to stop her pacing. I stepped back a bit and waited for her to sort out her thoughts.

"He kept makin' me out to be a worrywart and all, tellin' me I was scared of every little thing, and he said he'd thought I was the sort of girl that wouldn't go gettin' silly over nothin'." She turned her eyes to me with an expression full of panic. "You were right, Jessie. You warned me not to trust him, but I wanted him to like me. I don't know why. I just wanted him to like me, and I thought he did."

"I don't care none about bein' right just now," I told her as softly as I could though my mood was strung high as a kite. "I just want you to be okay." I reached for her again and this time she stopped and let me take her by the shoulders. "You ain't been okay for a while now, Gemma Teague, and I just want you back, is all. I want my Gemma back."

"I ain't the old Gemma no more," she cried in short gasps. "If I hadn't been so worried about not makin' Joel think me foolish, I'd have kept him from drivin' that car. Or at least I would've made him stop to see what he'd hit." She said that last word with a broken voice that mirrored her heart, and I knew she blamed herself for Callie's death as though she'd done the killing herself.

"Gemma, you can't take this on yourself. It was Joel Hadley killed that girl, not you."

"But I could've stopped him from gettin' in that car. And maybe if I hadn't been there, he wouldn't have been so feisty and he might've paid more attention to where he was goin'. He was cursin' me when he hit her, tellin' me I'd led him down the path and then put up a fuss over nothin'. It was because of me he wasn't payin' much attention."

"Don't you go makin' excuses for that Hadley boy. That's the problem with him altogether. Ain't no one ever let him take the blame for nothin', and now he just goes around doin' things he should be blamed for but knowin' he won't."

Gemma couldn't stop her tears for anything, no matter what I said, and my heart ached for her. I was losing my Gemma, all body and soul of her, and I wanted to fix it all but didn't know how. Callie Colby was dead and Mr. Poe was in jail awaiting a biased trial, and there was no way to push back time.

"Are you sure, Gemma, that Joel hit her? Are you sure?"

"There ain't no way around it, Jessilyn. We had the car; we hit somethin' right up along the bridge. . . . There ain't no way around it. And all this time I knew what happened and let Mr. Poe go to jail instead of sayin' the truth." She crumpled to her knees again, weeping till I thought she'd have no tears left.

"There ain't no sense in wallowin' in nothin'," I told her with firmness. "What's done is done, and ain't no way to do anythin' but move on and keep more wrongs from happenin'."

"But we can't do nothin'. Nothin'! When I told Joel about Callie and what must've happened, he said his bank holds your daddy's mortgage, and he threatened to take the farm away. Why do you think I ain't come clean before today?"

"He threatened you? He threatened my daddy?"

"And you know he'll do it too. Ain't no one in this town's goin' to take my word against his. He'll just tell them I'm lyin' and then take your daddy's farm away." Gemma stopped wailing but her breathing came in staccato hiccups and tears still rolled liberally down her face to wet her dress. "Poor Mr. Poe," she murmured. "I don't know what to do, Jessie. I can't think straight no more."

"You ain't got to think straight. I'll do the thinkin' for us." But despite my words, I didn't know what to do any more than Gemma did. I craned my neck to look upward as though the clear blue sky would open up and give me an answer that would make everything right.

There was no revelation from the heavens, but there was

a determination that built in me all of a sudden. No matter what Joel Hadley had threatened, there had to be some way to outweigh him, and I was determined we'd find it.

I marched over to Gemma and took her stoutly by the shoulders. "Mr. Poe needs our help, and we're gonna give it to him, so you best stop your bawlin' and get up on your two feet, Gemma Teague. We got work to do."

Chapter 9

Though Gemma never stopped her quiet crying the whole way into town, she did manage to make the trip, and when we came in sight of the jail, my heart sank to find that my fears had been justified. About a dozen men stood outside of the jail talking all at once so that their words sounded like nothing but a buzzing beehive. Right up on the front steps stood my daddy, gun in hand. Behind him, Luke leaned against the doorway in a nonchalant fashion that I well knew, one that implied ease but was tensed up for battle underneath. He held his pistol in one hand, his arms crossed, his hat pulled down so that no one could see much of his eyes but he could still see theirs.

Daddy was talking too, amid that buzzing hive of revenge seekers, but there wasn't much anyone could do to hear one voice at a time, and I figured there wasn't a man among them that heard a word anyone but himself was saying. Finally Daddy turned to Luke and gave him a sharp nod. Luke returned the nod and pointed his gun into the air, firing one earsplitting shot.

I had seen it coming, so my heart only sped up a bit, but poor Gemma jumped so high I thought she'd hurt herself coming down. The rest of the people in town stopped dead, even the angry men who'd come for Mr. Poe.

Luke tugged at the brim of his hat. "Seems we're all talkin' at once here," he drawled. "So now, why don't everyone just turn their attention to Mr. Lassiter and we can try and sort things out?" The whole time he talked, he waved his gun around like it was an extension of his hand, and I figured it was his way of showing people he'd use that gun if he had to and be quite comfortable with it.

Eager to hear all, I grabbed Gemma's hand and pulled her closer to the jail, though well out of sight of my daddy and Luke. There was no doubt if either saw us they'd send us packing right off.

Daddy cleared his throat and said, "Well then, now that we got some order here, why don't everybody just calm down and speak one at a time?"

"We want Elmer Poe," Delmar Custis called out, one of his grubby hands holding a rope up high. "Seems to me you got a pretty good idea what we come for."

"But see, that ain't exactly a rightly excuse, Delmar," Daddy told him in reply. "This here's a law-abidin' town, and our laws say a body's got a right to be considered innocent until proven otherwise. So now, why don't you boys head on home and wait for the trial to be over and done. I'm sure you'll see some sense by then."

"Ain't no trial necessary," Walker Mason shouted back. "We got all the evidence we need. Ain't nobody in this town got any doubts who done killed that girl."

This started all the men talking loud again, and Gemma and I used the distraction to get closer to the jailhouse. We hid behind a willow tree to the right of the stairway and tipped our heads sideways to hear better. Two squirrels scurried past us and up the tree as though fleeing the crowd. The men started to mount the steps, and I felt the hair on my arms stand up.

Daddy raised his gun to point it straight at Delmar Custis since he was at the head of the pack, and I wondered desperately where Sheriff Clancy and his deputies were. It seemed for all the world that Luke and Daddy were the only two people guarding Mr. Poe.

"You best back on down," Daddy shouted over the din. "What you boys are plannin' would be a big mistake, and I don't aim on lettin' you make it. Y'all just get on home to your families and let the law take its course."

There was no change in the men at that point. They seemed carried away by blind rage, and I realized for the first time that Nate Colby was at the center of the group. He hadn't said a word, but he was standing there with them, his fists clenched by his sides, a look of pure hate on his face. It was then that he pushed his way past the rest of the men and mounted two steps to stand square in front of my daddy's gun.

"You got no right to keep me from doin' what any daddy's got a right to do." Nate put one finger on the barrel of the gun and pushed it sideways a little. "What would you do if someone killed your baby girl, Harley? You tell me that. What would you do?"

Daddy's face wrinkled up in pain at the thought, but he shook his head slowly and said, "I know what I'd feel like doin', Nate. But God help me if I ever got close to doin' what I'd feel. Ain't no healin' from actin' out of hate and rage. Now why don't you head on home to Mae. I'm sure she's needin' you right about now."

"Not so much as my baby needed me," he cried out in anguish. "Not so much as she needed me when that man in there ran her down in cold blood."

Daddy lowered his gun a bit and leaned forward to put a strong hand on Nate Colby's shoulder. "Listen here, Nate. I don't rightly know what's goin' on inside you, but I can tell you this. We ain't certain sure Elmer Poe had anythin' to do with what happened to your girl. Truth of it is, he says he had nothin' to do with that automobile on that night. Now, we got to take time to find out the truth, hear?"

Nate had one hand on his hip and used the other to tip his hat back so he could look into my daddy's eyes without obstruction. "My little girl's dead, Harley. You hear what I'm tellin' you? My girl ain't got no life left in her, and you want me to worry about waitin' for facts and figures? We got all the truth we need to have, and I want that man to pay for what he done."

Up close, I could see the chilling looks on the men's faces, and my heart began to pound faster and harder. There was murder in the eyes of most. I knew because I'd seen that look before in my life. I was afraid for my daddy. I was afraid for Luke. And I was afraid for Mr. Poe. To say nothing about Gemma's broken spirit. I was just plain afraid for everything.

Two of them men started to advance toward Daddy, and Luke cocked his pistol with a very blatant movement. I leaned forward and readied myself to pounce at any man I could get my hands on if help was needed, but my sharp movement sent the leaves of a nearby bush to rustling, making Luke look quickly toward our hiding place.

Our eyes met, and Luke narrowed his at me so that he left no doubt about his feelings. He was mad as a hornet at me for coming into such a dangerous situation, and I knew I would be in for a good lecture by both him and Daddy. And Momma would no doubt put her own two cents in. But I couldn't think about that now, and I returned Luke's hard gaze with one of my own. The way I figured it, I was a grown woman, and I didn't need Luke Talley telling me what I could and could not do. I stiffened my shoulders rebelliously and stood up straight, revealing myself to all of them.

"Nate," I said with a bit of a shake in my voice, "Mae's awful broke up, so I hear. If you want, I'll go back with you to help her."

Nate's look of malice softened a bit at my words, but his

jaw still held tight in determination. "I ain't goin' home right now, Jessilyn."

"Momma's makin' some good food for you, and we can stop by on the way to get it. I know you don't feel like eatin', but it'll do you good."

"You go on home and get it yourself. Mae's sure to like your company. Maybe you can get her to eat somethin'."

"I'd be happy for you to come with me, Nate."

He didn't take his eyes from my daddy's, but he said to me, "I got other things to do right now. You go on without me."

I left Gemma cowering beside the steps and ducked beneath the railing, climbing up to stand behind Daddy. "I can't go on without you, Nate, 'cause it seems to me you're threatenin' my daddy. Just the same as you would have wanted to protect your baby girl, so I want to protect my daddy."

"Your daddy's a grown man," Daddy growled at me. "And I told you to stay behind, Jessilyn."

"Yes'r, but somethin' came up to change things."

"What somethin'?"

"I can't tell you, sir."

Daddy knew better than to take his eyes off the man in front of him, but I could imagine the look he would have given me just then if he could have. "Jessilyn, you best tell me what's goin' on."

"I can't tell you, Daddy. You just have to trust me."

I felt a hand on the back of my shirt as Luke pulled me closer to him. "You best get out of here," he whispered in my ear, "before you get hurt."

"I ain't leavin' you alone."

"Jessie, I don't want you gettin' hurt."

I didn't reply. I just kept my eyes on Nate, almost wishing him away. He didn't make a move toward Daddy. In fact, his face seemed to soften a bit, but he still held his position firmly.

"You do anythin' here, Nate," Daddy said quietly, "and your Mae loses you and her girl all in one fell swoop. You'll go to prison for murder and leave her all alone."

"Ain't murder if it's justice."

"Law says you ain't got the right to carry out your own way of justice. Law says you'll go to prison. And you just might take these men along with you."

Nate blinked a bit faster as though fighting back emotion.

"You turn away, Nate," Daddy continued, "and I figure they'll do the same."

"He ain't got control of everythin' around here," Mr. Custis said. "Not a one of us wants that crazy lunatic roamin' these streets to run down our own families. Gettin' rid of Poe gets rid of danger to all of our families, the way I see it."

"Stand down, Delmar," Nate Colby growled. "This ain't your battle to fight."

"Way I see it, it is," Mr. Custis said, pushing past Nate. He stuck a finger in Daddy's chest and poked him twice, hard. "I don't see no badge pinned to your shirt, Harley Lassiter," he snarled, poking him with each word he spoke. "You best get on out of my way until you get sworn in official-like."

Daddy could stand a lot but he didn't like getting poked;

that I well knew. Momma once told me that Daddy had had only one fight in all his life. Daddy made his excuses by saying that the boy had been asking for it for a long time, but when I asked him what had finally made him angry enough to fight, Daddy said, without even looking up from his newspaper, "The boy poked me."

I remembered that story now and backed up closer to Luke, afraid of what my daddy was going to do. I saw the muscles in his neck tighten and his free hand clench into a fist. Then he reached up, grabbed Mr. Custis by the front of the neck and squeezed, just enough to take away a bit of his air.

"You listen here, Delmar Custis," he said through clenched teeth. "I'm a generally peaceful man by rights, but you're forcin' me to get nasty. Now you just calm yourself down and get off this property before somebody gets hurt. You hear?"

Mr. Custis squirmed uncomfortably, his head stuck in an awkward upward turn. His eyes were wide and his lips moved as though trying to speak but unable to.

Just then, I heard a rifle cock, and I looked up to see Joe Dailey point his rifle straight toward my daddy. Terror filled my mind, and I reached a hand back and grabbed Luke to steady myself. I felt his hand on my shoulder in a tight grip, but his other hand held the pistol off in front of me, pointing at Joe Dailey.

"You best stand off, Luke," Mr. Dailey said. "Lest you want me to shoot Mr. Lassiter here. And you best let Delmar go, Harley, 'cause we aim to have what we came for." He moved a foot closer so that the gun was only inches from Daddy's chest. "Now let him go."

Daddy let Mr. Custis go but he still held his gun in front of him at the ready. Nobody budged for those few seconds that seemed to me like hours. We all stood without flinching, afraid that any sudden movement would set one of those guns off.

A couple more men took advantage of the moment to move quickly forward, and I again readied myself to pounce, but a shot sounded in the air that brought us all to attention. Fear crawled through my veins and made my hair stand on end, and I desperately scanned my daddy from head to toe to make sure he was all right. He stood there without a wound, his eyes as wide as everyone else's, and I looked frantically around to see who had fired that shot and if anyone had received it. That was when I caught sight of Sheriff Clancy standing on the bottom step, his arm raised, pointing his pistol into the back of Joe Dailey's head.

No one said much of anything, and no one moved either, but Sheriff Clancy kept his gun steady. "Don't think I won't use it, Joe Dailey," he said to the man at the other end of the barrel. "I ain't got as much of a conscience about such things as some do."

Joe's face melted into dismay, and he let the gun drop slowly to his side.

"All the way down, Joe. I want that rifle on the ground."

Joe dropped the gun and raised his hands slowly up next to his ears in a show of surrender.

"All right, then, boys," the sheriff shouted. "Move on out before I got to lock you all up."

"Lock us up in there with Poe," one of the men muttered. "We can take care of him good and simple that way."

"I'd send you over to Spokeet County, is what I'd do. I'm sure Sheriff Hobbes would welcome the sight of you. He gets lonely over there since they ain't got but a handful of people livin' there these days. Heck, he'd put a welcome mat on his front door."

"That man in there," Mr. Custis said, pointing toward the jailhouse. "That man's responsible for killin' a little girl, and you're gonna protect him?"

"That man in there," Sheriff Clancy replied, "is *accused* of killin' a girl. He ain't convicted. You boys ain't got any right or responsibility to judge him lest you're on a jury, and I can tell you right now, ain't a one of you that will be on his jury after today. Now you all best scatter before somebody gets hurt."

Not one man budged, as though each was waiting for another to move first. The looks of murderous determination had faded only on the faces of Nate and Mr. Dailey, and Mr. Dailey's had faded only because of the gun at the back of his skull. Sheriff Clancy usually had a fair amount of respect from everybody in town, but on this day, his skills at convincing the men to listen were waning.

"We'd better see Elmer Poe hang for this, is all we're sayin'," Clem Spangler argued. "That man don't hang, you can be sure he ain't gonna be safe in this town till his dyin' day."

From below me, I heard a sob, and I looked down to see Gemma jump from behind the bush for the first time since all the trouble had started. "Leave him alone!" she cried out. "Ain't one of you here knows what you're talkin' about."

"Gemma!" I was desperate to keep her from going on, knowing full well that prejudice lived on enough in Calloway to cause Gemma all sorts of trouble if anyone found out she was part of what had happened.

Gemma tried to say more, but I leaped over the railing in an unladylike way that would have given Momma a faint and grabbed Gemma by the shoulders, whispering, "Ain't nothin' gonna be helped by you sayin' somethin' right now, Gemma. You just wait, hear?"

"I gotta tell, Jessie," she whispered back frantically.

"Not yet. Not here. Not without proof."

"For pete's sake, Jessie," Luke leaned over to whisper. "You brought Gemma in on this, too?"

"I ain't brought her in on anythin'," I hissed. "She's the reason we're here."

"Gemma," Daddy said softly, "everythin's gonna be all right, honey. You just wait over there, and once this is settled, Luke and I will take you and Jessilyn home."

"That's right. This ain't got nothin' to do with you, Gemma Teague," Mr. Custis said. "You best keep out of it altogether."

"But he didn't do it."

"Then a judge and jury will see to it he's let go," the sheriff said. "We'll just let things work out the way they should."

I squeezed Gemma's arm hard and she turned away from the crowd and said nothing more.

Sheriff Clancy nudged a couple of the men with the barrel of his gun and said, "That's enough of this now, boys. Everyone move on out before somebody gets hurt."

Daddy didn't lower his gun until the crowd was good and scattered. "Where in blazes have you been, Charlie?" he muttered. "You always leave your prisoners unattended while a mob's out to get 'em?"

"Simmer down. There weren't no mob when I left. I just ran over to the pharmacy for a minute."

"A minute? We were holdin' them off for a good ten, Charlie."

"What'd you run to the pharmacy for?" Luke asked with a sneer. "Run out of chaw?"

Sheriff Clancy stared at him hard and held up a paper sack. "Matter of fact, I did."

Daddy sighed and stepped aside as Sheriff Clancy climbed the steps to go into the jail. "Luke, you watch out for the girls while I have a word with the sheriff."

Luke nodded his reply, but the second the door shut behind them, he vaulted over that railing the same as I had and landed in front of me, his face red with anger. "What the sam hill were you thinkin' of doin', Jessie? You tryin' to get someone killed?"

"It weren't her fault," Gemma told him, but I shushed her with one palm in the air.

"Just who do you think you are, Luke Talley?" I demanded.

"You think you got the right to tell me what to do and what not to do?"

"Matter of fact, I do."

"Then you'd better think twice, 'cause lest you're my daddy or you got a badge, you ain't got no right tellin' me what to do."

"There ain't no use arguin' over nothin'," Gemma said with a pleading tone. "This ain't Jessie's fault. She come on my account."

"Gemma tells you to jump off Goggins Bridge, you gonna do it, Jessie?"

Luke's fatherly words made me fume. "Come the day my daddy runs out of lectures to give me, I'll call on you, but till then, you can leave off tellin' me things I can hear at home. I swear, you think you can boss me over everythin'."

"You come on into town when you knew how dangerous things would be, and you think I'm not gonna be upset that you put you and Gemma in a bad spot?"

This time it was Gemma who got tied up in knots, and she stamped a foot. "It weren't her fault, I told you!"

I put an arm out to keep her back. "Stay out of this, Gemma."

"Now, listen here," Gemma said, her senses regained for the first time since she'd told me all. "I got enough on my mind without hearin' you two argue over nothin'. I'm a grown woman, and I've got a right to do as I please, and you ain't got no say over it. Jessie's here because I wanted to come and she wouldn't let me come alone, and that's all there is to it." She brushed past us, charged up the steps, and headed toward the jailhouse door.

"Where you goin'?" I asked.

"To see Mr. Poe."

"Gemma," I said, reaching through the rail to touch her hand, "it's gonna be okay."

She studied my face for a minute before nodding, her weary eyes piercing my heart.

We watched her enter the building, and then I sank down into the dirt, my knees suddenly feeling like jelly. I sat there for a few moments just waiting for Luke to start in on me again. But I wasn't there long before the sound of a ruckus reached my ears, and I jerked my head around toward the jailhouse, where Gemma was being escorted out by Sheriff Clancy. Daddy was beside the sheriff, talking animatedly. I hopped up, and Luke and I walked quickly toward them, my stride outdone by Luke's, two to one.

"What's goin' on?" Luke asked all three of them at once.

"He won't let me see Mr. Poe," Gemma answered.

"I got enough trouble round here right now, Gemma," Sheriff Clancy said. "I need to lock down the place till I get some more help. I ain't got but two deputies today, and the one inside ain't worth a hoot. The other one's on a call. I got some help comin' in from Spokeet County that'll be here tomorrow. You come on back then."

"We're here now, Charlie," Daddy said. "Luke and me can help you keep watch while Gemma goes in for a few minutes. You can see the girl's got a real itch to see the man."

"Harley, I got ways of doin' things, and I got to follow my own rules. If I let you in now and then somethin' happens to Elmer, I'll have heck to pay."

Daddy dropped his chin to his chest in resignation; then he reached out and put a hand on Gemma's back. "Looks like we'll have to come back tomorrow, Gemma," he said, his voice filled with compassion. "I'll drive you in whenever you like, all right?"

I knew Gemma appreciated Daddy's promise, but I also knew that it didn't satisfy her much. The poor thing was pure and simple dying to see Mr. Poe. I figured she wanted to see with her own eyes that he was alive and well. She just walked down the steps like she was walking to her own death. I scurried over to her and took her arm, helping her to a bench under an oak tree and settling her there until Daddy and Luke were done talking to Sheriff Clancy. When they were through, the two men walked to where we sat and eyed us both.

"Everyone okay over here?" Daddy asked. His arms were folded tightly against his chest, and I could tell by his body language that he was angry. I waited for him to lecture us, but he obviously decided against it. "Guess we'd better head on home," he said without waiting for us to answer his previous question. "I gotta get some wood to fix the shed before we go. Luke, you want to come over and give me a hand loadin' up?"

Luke bobbed his head in agreement, though I could see he was reluctant to leave the two of us alone. Apparently Daddy was too, because he pointed a stern finger at us and said, "Don't you two go wanderin' off or nothin'. I expect to find you here when we come back in about fifteen minutes."

We didn't say anything, but he took our silence as an answer that we would and strode off with Luke in tow. Gemma watched them as they walked down the sidewalk, and the second they turned the corner out of sight, she was off the bench like a shot.

"Where in God's green earth are you goin'?" I called after her.

She said nothing, and with a long sigh, I heaved myself off the bench and followed after her, fairly well knowing what she was planning without her telling me. I followed her to the back of the jailhouse and down the hill that dipped to the basement floor, where the cells were. I caught sight of the metal bars across the windows and had a fearful feeling that they might not be good enough to protect a man from an angry crowd like I'd seen that day. I bent over low to keep from being seen by anyone while we peered into the windows looking for Mr. Poe's cell.

He was sitting on his cot, his knees tucked up under his chin, arms wrapped around his legs. I had a fleeting thought that he was good and limber for a man in his late sixties, but I doubted his ability to ever defend himself against any capable man.

Gemma sat on the ground and peered into the long, narrow window, tapping against one of the bars.

Mr. Poe looked up quickly, fear in his eyes, but the fear melted when he recognized us.

Gemma lay down on her stomach and put her face to the bars. "You okay in there, Mr. Poe?" she asked, her words slow and deliberate to keep from sounding upset.

Mr. Poe jumped up from his cot and moved to the window as fast as his legs would carry him. "That you, Miss Gemma Teague?"

"Yes'r, Mr. Poe. And Jessilyn too."

"Hey there, Miss Jessie," he said with a nod in my direction.

By now, I was lying on my stomach next to Gemma, tears building in my eyes to once again see that man, sweet as honey, sitting behind bars.

"Cain't look at muh Injun pennies," he said in his usual mumbled speech. "Cain't look at muh bottle tops or muh skippin' stones or muh butterflies."

"Sheriff won't let you keep any of your collections here, Mr. Poe?" I asked. "Did you ask him if you could?"

"He says ah cain't." He began to pull at his earlobe nervously. "Them's all by their lonesome, all muh things. Sure 'nough, they's alone."

Mr. Poe had always been "special," according to Momma, and I'd always known him to talk a little funny and be hard to rouse once focused on something, but he was smart as a whip in his own way. Just now, though, his senses seemed dulled, and he was far more anxious and distracted than I'd ever seen him before. I was worried for his mind as well as his body.

"I think I'll have my daddy talk with Sheriff Clancy, Mr. Poe," I told him. "Maybe he can convince the sheriff to let you have a collection or two to look at."

Mr. Poe's face broke into a smile full of such hope that I was terribly afraid of what he would feel like if Daddy didn't manage to talk the sheriff into it. I hoped I wouldn't regret making the offer.

"Sure'd be nice, Miss Jessie," he said, the *s* sound whistling through the empty space where his two front teeth had been. "Indeedy, it'd be nice. I ain't got nuthin' in here to c'llect."

We left him with smiles that were much lighter than our hearts, and I put a hand on Gemma's shoulder as we went. It was as though I could feel the weight resting there, and I wished I could carry some of it for her. But sometimes, there just isn't much a person can do no matter how much they wish they could. Daddy had told me before that sometimes the Lord lets us feel the weight of the world so we figure out how to let Him carry it for us. I reckoned then that this was Gemma's turn, but I hoped good and hard that she'd figure it out fast.

Chapter 10

I woke up the next day to find Gemma's bed empty. She'd been up at the crack of dawn for the past two mornings, and I hadn't seen her much at all. I decided to make sure I spent time with her that day, so I pinned my hair up quickly, put on one of my light dresses, and ran downstairs to the breakfast table.

"You seen Gemma this morning, Momma?" I asked as I buttered a biscuit with quick strokes.

"She ran off for church about fifteen minutes ago now, I guess. Suppose she wanted to make Sunday school this morning. Didn't eat any breakfast, but I saw her fill her pockets with a plum and two biscuits. Seems that girl's not eatin' her fill these days," she murmured, staring out the window at nothing. "Girl's got me worried."

I didn't tell her I felt the same. Momma seemed preoccupied, absentmindedly tapping a finger on the counter while she gazed outside, so I didn't say anything to her in reply. I just stuffed my biscuit down and grabbed another plum to put in my own pocket. Even though it was hot already at this early hour, I knew where Gemma had gone with her pockets full, and I was determined to join her.

"Maybe I'll catch up and walk her to church, Momma. She could use some company now, I think."

"That's a nice idea, Jessilyn. Maybe she'll confide in you. Daddy and I will pick you up at the colored church."

"Oh no, that's okay," I replied almost too quickly, knowing full well church was not where Gemma was heading with that food in her pockets. "I'll walk. I can cut through the woods and make it on time."

"You'll get your dress all in tatters."

"I'll be careful. And anyways, if Gemma decides to talk about somethin' important, won't it be strange if you and Daddy come ridin' up in the middle of it?" I could feel my right eyelid twitch a bit under the strain of stretching the truth to my momma, but I tried to console myself that it was for Gemma's sake. "It ain't a long walk, Momma. I'll be fine."

Momma bit her lower lip for a moment in consideration before relenting. "All right, honey. We'll see you at the church."

I grabbed another biscuit and scurried out the door before she could reconsider. The sun was already beating down something fierce, but I made my way along the road, humming a bit to make the time go faster. I was sweating from top to toe by the time I reached town. I figured it didn't matter too much since I didn't plan on seeing anyone but Mr. Poe and Gemma. When I came near the jail, Sheriff Clancy was on the stoop peering at the sun and smoking a cigarette. He flicked some ash over the side rail, and I breathed a deep sigh of relief to see it land on ground that was no longer cluttered with angry men. The sheriff must have made his threats worthwhile enough to keep them away for the time being, but I wasn't so sure it would last.

Sneaking around a big oak tree, I paused as Sheriff Clancy dropped his gaze to squash his cigarette under his shoe. Then, when he turned to go inside, I rushed around the corner of the building to the back, where Mr. Poe's window was.

I wasn't surprised to see Gemma there, lying on her stomach with no thought for the dust she was collecting on her skirt front. She had her chin resting on her folded arms, a cockeyed smile on her face.

"There you are, Mr. Poe," she was saying. "That works, sure enough."

Once I crept up behind her, I saw for myself what she was talking about. Mr. Poe had a long, narrow wooden box that he was carefully maneuvering through the small spaces between the bars in his window, his tongue stuck out in concentration.

"Sure 'nough, it done fit, Miss Gemma," he said in his lazy drawl. Then he got an awkward, childlike expression on his face and looked behind him nervously. "Don't know 'bout what the sheriff would think, though. Might say ah cain't have it."

"But that's what I brought the box for, Mr. Poe. It's our special secret. Don't the sheriff or nobody got to know."

"Ah don't know, Miss Gemma," he said, scuffing one shoe noisily on the cement floor. "Don't know if ah should be keepin' secrets."

"It's not so much a secret, Mr. Poe," I said softly, sneaking up to join Gemma at the window. "It's just friends sharin' a memory, is all. You know how you showed me your secret berry-pickin' spot when I was little? It's like that. Don't hurt nobody. It's just a special bit of happiness that friends share."

Gemma peered at me over her shoulder and gave me a soft, grateful smile. I smiled back and lowered myself onto my stomach beside her.

But Mr. Poe still looked conflicted, and I saw him wince and blink hard twice, trying to make up his mind.

I didn't know what was in the box, but I could guess. "Got some special things in there, Mr. Poe?"

"Yes'm. Got me some mighty good coins in there and five good stones." He nodded and repeated, "Yep. Five good ones. Miss Gemma, she know how tuh find good smooth stones. Five good ones too."

"Gemma's always been good at pickin' stones," I said, though I'd never seen her pick up a stone to do anything more than chase a raccoon away. I moved a little closer to the window and whispered, "Seems she's gone to a right bit of trouble to bring you some little happiness. Maybe you best keep this little old secret so's she won't be feelin' sad and hurt. You think maybe so?"

Mr. Poe's brow wrinkled up even more, and after he finished blinking several times fast, he said, "Reckon yer right, Miss Jessie. Reckon muh momma always told me tuh show proper thanks when friends treat a body kindly." He looked expectantly at me. "You reckon muh momma would think so now?"

"I think she would, Mr. Poe. Ain't no harm in this here little secret. None at all that I can see."

Mr. Poe thought for a moment and then smiled at Gemma. "Mighty nice of you, Miss Gemma. Mighty nice."

"No trouble at all, Mr. Poe," she said, relief written all over her sleep-deprived face. "Now, that box should fit nice under your cot, I think. If you just slide it under and all the way into the corner, I think it'll stay our secret."

"Seems you could use some refreshment, Mr. Poe," I told him. "Want some of this here plum?"

"Mighty kind of you, Miss Jessie, but Miss Gemma here, she done already bring me biscuits and a plum." He rubbed his thin stomach. "Don't think ah could take another bite jest yet. And you be sure tuh thank yer momma fer the good suppers she's bringin'. Sure makes a body feel cared fer."

"Sure enough, Mr. Poe. You sure you don't need anythin', then?"

"Miss Jessilyn, I got muh Bible and muh prayers, so ah got me all ah need."

The smile he gave me was worn and not at all like the bright, innocent smiles I'd always seen on his face. For the first time in his many years on this earth, Mr. Poe was learning what it was like to have the world come against him, and I was sad to see his carefree face so changed.

For all that I hated some of how the world had treated me, just then I would have wished Mr. Poe's grief were mine.

❧

Luke watched me impatiently over the chessboard, his chin resting on the edge of the table. "A man can only stare at them squares on the board for so long, Jessie, before it all just starts to mix together. I'm gettin' cross-eyed."

I sighed and rolled my eyes. "Luke, I ain't never buggin' you to hurry on your turns."

"That's because I don't take twenty minutes to do it."

"If I'm so tiresome, then I don't know why you even bother playin' with me."

"Ain't no one else around here who likes chess."

"Well, I'm flattered I'm only good as a last choice. Maybe if you teach Duke, he'll play better'n me."

Our basset hound picked his head up and gave me a mournful look before dropping his head back down under the table.

"Guess he don't want to play chess with you," I told Luke,

my mouth turned up in a wry smile. "Maybe you're not so good a chess partner as you think."

"I never claimed to be a good chess partner," he said, leaning back in his chair to catch the slight breeze that had kicked up. "I only claimed to be able to finish makin' up my ever-lovin' mind in less than an hour."

I glared at him for a minute, but he just kept his face pointed upward into that breeze. I went back to staring at the board even though I wasn't thinking a bit about chess. I was thinking about Gemma and Mr. Poe and trying to figure out any way I could do something but sit around waiting for things to get better. Luke's porch rocker creaked as he began to stir back and forth.

"I'm tryin' to think over here," I said.

"Well, I'm trying not to fall asleep over here."

"You play the game like you're sleepwalkin' anyhow. What's the difference?"

Through the open windows I could hear Daddy sigh all the way from his chair in the den. "Can't we never have a quiet Sunday afternoon without you two arguin' about somethin'?" he muttered. "I swear you spat like a married couple."

The very mention of me and Luke in the same sentence with the word *married* made my heart flutter, but I just fingered one of my knights and tapped my foot a little to ease my nerves.

Momma was sweeping the porch, and she stopped and peered through the window screen. "You makin' a point about married people, Harley Lassiter?" she asked sharply. "You sayin' we argue all the time?"

"Now, Sadie, don't let's start. I didn't mean nothin' by it."

"Why shouldn't I start somethin'? That's the way married couples are, ain't it?" She propped her broom against the wall and made her way inside. "S'pose we best be like all them other quarrelin' married folks."

Daddy's sigh was louder and longer this time, and I fought off a smile as best I could. I peered at Luke to share my amusement with him, but he was staring hard at his hands resting on the table, his cheeks red as beets.

Now, I'd seen Luke Talley happy, sad, angry, irritated—any which way you could think, I'd seen him. But I'd never once seen him as uncomfortable as I saw him now. His toe tapped so much my king wobbled from the vibration and he squinted hard at the board like he was losing his sight.

But I was enough of a woman to guess at what was going on inside his head. I hadn't missed that it was Daddy's mention of marriage that had set those cheeks on fire. There'd been a glimmer of hope of late that I'd finally started to get his attention after four long years, and I wasn't made up of the stuff that would keep me from making him suffer . . . just a little.

"You feelin' sick or somethin'?" I asked after a minute, one corner of my mouth twitching in an attempt to keep from smiling.

He jerked like I'd pinched him. "What're you talkin' about?"

"I said, are you sick or somethin'? You got red cheeks like you been sunburnt."

He squinted at me. "Well, maybe I'm sunburnt."

"You sayin' you done got sunburnt sittin' on this here covered porch for forty-five minutes? 'Cause you weren't sunburnt when you got here."

"Jessie, you tryin' to be ornery or somethin'?" he asked, his tone harsh.

My mouth finally slipped up into a half smile, but I narrowed my eyes to compensate. "I'm just bein' concerned for you, is all."

"Well, seems to me you worry too much."

For the next twenty minutes Luke hardly even looked at me, and once he started to squirm like there were ants in his pants, I felt a twinge of shame for making him so nervous. I purposefully put my queen in danger as my way of apology, but Luke missed the chance twice. It was like playing chess with a statue, and as the game went on in uncomfortable silence, I started to get annoyed at his failure.

"What in tarnation," I finally cried. "You got sense in your head or not?"

"What are you talkin' about?" he asked, his brow wrinkled like an old hound dog.

"I just gave you the game, and you ain't even got the sense to see it."

"Well, what'd you give me the game for? I ain't no charity case."

"I was just tryin' to be nice, is all."

153

Under his long, dark lashes, Luke gave me that "evil eye" that Daddy was always saying Momma gave him when he got ornery. "Fine!" he snapped. "If you don't want to play, you don't have to cheat. You can just say so."

"Fine! I say so. I quit! You can play chess with someone else from now on if you're goin' to sit there and daydream the whole time." My words came out with conviction, but I didn't mean them. The way I saw things, if he was daydreaming about me, he could play me in a bad game of chess anytime he wanted. But I was just stubborn enough to want the last word.

Luke kept giving me that evil eye, but I met it head-on. I wasn't one to back down from a challenge any time, but when Luke's eyes were staring me down, I never had any interest in looking away. Even when they were full of anger, those blue eyes were two of my favorite things to look at.

The whine of the screen door broke the spell, and we looked up to find Momma peering out at us.

"Thought we'd make some good ice cream," she said lightly as though she hadn't caught the two of us in an angry glare. "You up to crankin', Luke?"

Luke smiled for the first time in a half hour. "Yes'm. Some ice cream sounds mighty nice about now."

"It's hot enough, there's no doubt," I said. "I best track down Gemma and see if she wants some."

"Gemma's out on a walk, baby. She said she'd be back later on. Seemed she needed some thinkin' time to herself." Momma's face creased a bit in worry, and I understood how she was feeling. Even though I knew Momma didn't really know just how much thinking Gemma had to do these days, I knew she had a good idea that Gemma was having a good and hard time. I figured that on her way back to the kitchen, Momma would be whispering a heartfelt prayer for our Gemma, and I hoped it worked. Gemma needed all the help she could get.

Momma came back outside, and while I watched Luke get to work, I had to try hard not to sit and worry. I wondered where Gemma was and why she was out on this hot day taking a walk. Gemma hated hot days, and as long as I'd known her, she'd never liked taking walks on them.

After a while I glanced over at Luke. His face was all red and he raised one hand to wipe his forehead with the back of his wrist. I put aside my worry and went over to see if I could help.

"Here, I'll do some."

"It's all right," he said pleasantly. "I'm doin' fine."

"But you're all hot and sweaty. I can take a turn."

"Gonna be hot and sweaty on a day like this any which way, Jessie. I was hot and sweaty playin' that there game of chess."

"Well, ain't no reason for you to keep doin' it when I can help. You go on and get yourself some sweet tea, and I'll crank some." I reached out and put my hands against his, meaning to take over his job, but he pushed my hands away with a sharp quickness that startled me.

"Luke, it's our ice cream. If I want to crank it, I'm gonna crank it."

"Don't need no help," he said, his ears turning a color that matched his face. His voice took on an agitation I didn't expect when he finished, "If a man says he don't need no help, Jessilyn, he don't need no help."

I watched him, my stomach in knots because Luke's voice held a sternness that I wasn't accustomed to hearing from him. Momma was coming out the door when Luke spoke, and even she stopped short at the sound of his voice.

"I was just tryin' to be nice," I said softly. For once, I didn't feel like arguing back, and I went to the door to take the glasses of sweet tea Momma was carrying.

"You doin' okay there, Luke?" Momma asked carefully. "I got Harley busy fixin' the screen on the back door, but he says he'll be finished in a quick minute, so he can give the crank a turn for you when he's done."

"He don't have to worry," Luke said in a tone that was much kinder than the one he'd given me. "I've got it taken care of."

Momma gave me an odd look before she disappeared into the house, but I glanced away. I didn't want to answer the question her eyes asked. The way I figured it, I was only guessing at things, and I didn't want to say anything to anyone unless I knew for sure. Just for now, whatever was happening between Luke and me could be something special, and I wanted to keep it to ourselves.

Luke wiped his forehead with his wrist again, and I noted that his ears were still that funny pink color.

"Ain't no woman can figure a man, Jessilyn," my momma had told me once not long ago. "I guess they're God's way of remindin' us ladies that we can't know everythin'."

The way I saw it just then, I wasn't even close to knowing everything.

But I was starting to learn.

Chapter 11

I could hear Daddy's angry voice all the way upstairs, which worried me since my daddy only yelled when he got good and mad. I could tell as I made my way down the steps that he was yelling at no one in particular. He was just ranting and raving, and when I reached the hallway and peered cautiously into the kitchen, I could see my momma sitting in a chair at the table, her gaze focused on nothing in particular.

"Ain't no reason I got to crawl on my hands and knees to no man, Sadie. Will you just look at me?" Daddy asked, holding out his calloused and worn hands. "Here I am, forty-three years old, and I got to be bound to a man like Coble Hadley."

"You ain't bein' bound to him," Momma said softly. "You're bound by no man, Harley Lassiter, and there ain't no reason to lose hope yet. This drought may look bad, but we'll be able to pay our mortgage somehow."

"I'm as bound by him as any man. The man can take away my farm, I don't pay him on time. Ain't no mornin' I don't get up hopin' I can manage to find the money I need every month."

"Ain't never been a time the Lord's let us fall into hard times we can't handle. Ain't never gonna be a time."

Daddy rested his hands on the kitchen table and looked Momma square in the eye. "I'll tell you somethin', Sadie Louise," he said with a face so earnest it made my stomach tie up into a big, painful knot. "Ain't never been a time my faith's been tested like it is now. Some days, I don't know where God is. Sure don't feel like He's right here."

I didn't know much about faith, but I knew that whatever it was, my daddy had it, and it had always given me peace. To see and hear him in this way, doubting what he'd always held so strongly to, turned my world upside down.

Momma reached out and grabbed Daddy's hands so tightly, her own hands shook. "Ain't nothin' in this world that'll ruin us besides losin' our faith, Harley. There ain't nothin'! You hear? We can lose everythin' and still make it by, but if you start losin' that solid faith that makes you who you are, we may as well drop dead here and now. 'Cause there ain't no livin' like that."

Daddy's head drooped and then slowly, wearily descended onto Momma's hands. I watched guiltily as Momma put her head down onto his, and when I realized they were both crying softly, I ran off, feeling like a traitorous sneak. I couldn't remember ever seeing my daddy cry.

We were in more trouble than I'd realized, that summer on the Lassiter farm, and I was filled with rage toward the Hadleys. After all, they were the reason my daddy was feeling so distraught. They were the reason my Gemma was suffering. And they were the reason Mr. Poe was sitting, disillusioned and heartbroken, in a dirty jail cell. Anger started to creep into my heart like the ivy that choked the trees in the cemetery, and I started to head instinctively toward the meadow, desperate to see Luke.

But it struck me that Luke would be at the factory this Monday morning, and I made my way down the road at a much slower pace, thinking too much for my own good and wondering where I would go now. I was angry and sullen, and I wanted to take my anger out on something, anything.

It was unfortunate that Joel Hadley's car came down the road at that moment.

It was unfortunate because I could feel the heat creep up the back of my neck, and I knew that I was about to say a lot of things I would later regret. I may have grown up some bit in the last years, but I was still not so smart about taking stock of things before I said them.

"You seen Gemma?" he asked me as he pulled his car to the side of the road without any sort of greeting. "Ain't seen her for work today."

"I don't need to talk to nobody about Gemma. Gemma can do her own talkin'."

"Seems to me you can do plenty of talkin'. I ain't never known you to shut up."

"I *said* I ain't gonna do no talkin' about Gemma. You want to ask her somethin', you ask her yourself."

"Well, that's gonna be kind of hard seein' as how she ain't around." He opened the door of his fancy car and stood up to lean on it all cool and casual, and I was certain he'd gotten that pose from the cigarette ad hanging in Parker Hayes's tobacco shop. "Now, here's what I want you to do," he said like he was talking to a three-year-old. "You go on home like a good little girl, and you find Gemma, and you tell her we're waitin' for her to get on down to work." He blew out a long stream of smoke. "You think you can do that all by yourself?"

"There'll be snowballs in hades before I do anythin' you tell me, Joel Hadley," I spat back.

"Funny you should mention hell, seein' as how you'll fit in right nice there."

I had a sore spot about hell because I was afraid I'd end up there since I'd never really believed in God and the Scriptures like my momma, daddy, and Gemma did. I didn't want to end up in the burning hellfire Pastor had preached about, and I didn't take kindly to hearing a man like Joel predicting I'd spend eternity there.

I stared at him for a good thirty seconds and then eased up alongside his car, running my hand along the back of it. "This sure is a pretty car," I said slowly. "It's a good thing you didn't kill Callie Colby with this one. Would've been a shame to mess up a treasure like this."

The minute I said it, my heart started to flutter like it had wings. Only it didn't feel anything like it did when I was with Luke.

Joel Hadley pulled his cigarette away in mid-drag and clapped eyes on me that were filled with a mixture of fear and hatred. I watched him toss the rest of his cigarette onto the ground with one fierce motion and strut toward me like a prowling lion. "What did you say?" he asked in just above a whisper.

I didn't say anything in reply, and all I could wonder was why, if I was to lose my ability to speak, I had to wait until after I'd let Joel Hadley know that I knew what horrible thing he'd done. I was sure Gemma was going to kill me.

If Joel didn't finish the job for her first.

He came to a stop only when his toes touched mine, and though I was gripped by a sudden fear, I forced myself to meet his enraged gaze.

"You accusin' me of somethin', girl?"

The very nearness of him infuriated me. I didn't like to be put upon by anyone, especially not arrogant men with big heads and nasty reputations, and my anger overtook my fear in one fell swoop.

"Dang right I'm accusin' you," I said hoarsely. "I'm accusin' you of plenty. And I'm tellin' you right now, Joel Hadley, if the both of us are gonna end up in hell, I'll take comfort knowin' you'll make it there first, hangin' from the end of a rope."

The image of him swinging from his neck made him sick

inside. I could see it in his eyes that were only inches away from my own. But he grabbed my arm in a grip that was stronger than I'd ever imagined and returned my stare, looking angry enough to kill. Despite the possibility that he might be inclined to do just that, I hadn't the sense to shut up.

"You may think you've got one on me and Gemma, but evil deeds are always found out, and someday you're gonna pay for killin' that little girl." I dug a finger into his chest because I knew it was just the kind of thing that infuriated my daddy, and I wanted nothing more than to push every button in Joel Hadley's body. "You best look over your shoulder every minute of every day, because one day, when you least expect it, they're gonna come lookin' for you. One day you'll hear loud voices, and you'll look behind you and see a crowd of men comin' toward you. Angry men. Carryin' ropes and guns and lookin' for blood to pay for Callie's that was spilled all over the road that night. They'll be comin' for you. And they won't be listenin' to pretty excuses and angry denials. All they'll be comin' for is to break your skinny little neck."

All of the rage I'd felt over the past week had come pouring out in that one reckless speech, and despite the fact that I knew I could face desperate consequences for it, I felt a giant weight lifted from my shoulders. Just then, I didn't care what happened to me, so long as Joel Hadley paid for what he'd done.

"I ought to kill you," he whispered loudly, the break in his voice betraying his fear. He put a hand up to my neck. "I ought to squeeze the life right out of you."

Joel's sweaty hand flooded my mind with memories of that horrifying day four years ago when I'd felt Walt Blevins's hand on my neck because he hated me and my family for taking in Gemma. I knew what it was like to have someone squeezing the life out of me, and I never wanted to feel like that again. Walt Blevins had tried to kill me because I'd accused him of being the bigoted coward that he was, and here I was being threatened again for accusing another coward.

In my head, I could hear my mother saying, "Jessilyn Lassiter, one day that blunt tongue of yours is gonna break your momma's heart." I knew what she'd meant when she'd said it. She was afraid I'd pay a terrible price for confronting people to their faces, but the way I saw it, an evil man ought to be told that's what he is. I figured maybe God had given me just the sort of words to do it.

I stared right at Joel even though my heart pounded into my throat. "Then you'll swing for two killin's," I managed to say without my voice shaking.

Joel hesitated and then pulled his nervous hand back, his entire face and body betraying the fear my accusations had raised in him. He turned away from me, and I used the chance to bend over slightly, hoping a good strong breath would make my knees stop shaking. When he turned around, he was tugging at the open collar of his shirt, sweat beading on his forehead. I stood up straight to face him and watched as he methodically raised his hand and pointed at me.

"You think you're gonna go around town makin' wrong

accusations against me, Jessilyn Lassiter, you got another think comin'."

"I ain't makin' *wrong* accusations."

"You think you're all smart and know more'n everybody else. *But you ain't*," he said, using that pointing finger of his to jab in my direction with each word. "And I'm tellin' you, if you start spreadin' rumors, I'll make good and sure you pay."

"You threatenin' me again?"

He took a few steps closer and it was all I could do to keep from taking a few steps back. But I stood my ground as he moved within five feet of me and put his hands firmly onto his hips.

"Seems to me your daddy's got some accounts to settle," he said.

The mention of my daddy made my blood run cold. "You leave my daddy out of this," I demanded. "This is between you and me."

"No you don't, girl. You don't get to make all the rules." He raised that active finger of his again and jabbed it in the air toward me. "Now you listen here. I got me more power than you think I got, and I'm tellin' you right now, you best think twice if you want your daddy keepin' that farm of his."

"I said you leave my daddy out of this." My mouth was dry, every muscle in my body tensed, and I narrowed my eyes at him.

Joel ignored me with a shrug and made his way back to his car with a forced swagger. "Ain't me who's bringin' him into it; it's you and all your crazy talk." He climbed back into that car of his and flashed me a Cheshire cat grin. "You have a good day now, you hear?"

I watched him drive off, my eyes watering from the dust he kicked up in my direction, and I knew from my fingers to my toes that bad things were right around the corner. One more time I'd gone and opened my mouth when I should have kept it sewn up, and now I'd stepped in it something good.

I let my weak knees buckle now that Joel couldn't see and leaned against a nearby aspen. Sliding down onto my backside, I tucked my knees up against my chest and stared at the silvery leaves above my head. A steady breeze had picked up, shaking those leaves into a whispery chorus, almost as though they were talking to me. They'd be telling me I was stupid, I figured, and whispering warnings of the bad things that were in store for my family. Because there was no doubt that I'd brought ruin to us all with my loose lips.

Even the trees knew it was true.

Chapter 12

I was only four years old when Gemma and her parents came to live on our farm, but from that first day, I liked her better than any child I'd ever known. Mostly I'd stayed away from other kids. They were noisy and irritating and didn't want to play the same things I wanted to. The way I saw it, I was better off doing things on my own.

But with Gemma, it was different. Even though she was two years older than me, she'd made me comfortable right from the start. She had a fiery nature like me, though she wasn't as eager to tell people what she thought as I was. She'd tell *me*, though, in no uncertain terms. If she didn't like what I was doing, she'd tell me so and give me a good shove to finish off with.

Times hadn't changed much, I was thinking as I watched Gemma's face that evening after I'd confronted Joel Hadley. It was just as much a tangled mess of fury and despair as she could muster when we were children, except there was a level to it that we'd never reached before. I'd told her about my run-in with Joel, and as we stood there in the shade of Daddy's gazebo, I braced myself for the shove I figured was coming my way.

"Jessilyn Lassiter," she growled, her face scrunched up beyond recognition, "I swear I ain't never goin' to tell you nothin' again in my whole life. You realize what you done got us into?" She took two steps toward me, her hands balled into tight fists, and repeated, "Do you?"

"Gemma, I didn't mean to—"

"'Gemma, I didn't meant to,'" she mocked. "Same as what you say every time you go shootin' your mouth off without thinkin'. For a girl who don't mean to all the time, you sure do manage to cause a lot of trouble."

I didn't bother saying anything else at that moment. I just stood there biting my lip, waiting for her to lay into me some more. I was feeling like I'd eaten my worthy share of crow, and I stood by passively waiting for my just desserts to follow. But the minute she gave me her next angry words, I stopped being so humble.

"You think you're all grown-up," she seethed. "All grown-up. And you can't even keep your mouth shut about important things. You ain't nothin' but a baby, Jessilyn. Never will be."

Now she'd done it. Now she'd gone and plucked my nerves, and I wasn't feeling so much like taking what she dished out anymore.

"Don't you go callin' me things, Gemma Teague," I shot

back, my body stiff with rage. "Don't you dare go callin' me a baby, tellin' me I ain't actin' grown-up. How grown-up is it for a girl of nineteen to go wooin' a man who ain't got no more interest in marryin' a poor colored girl than he's got in doin' an honest day's work?"

I backed up a step since Gemma's face twisted into a look I'd never seen before. One that seemed to speak of violent things.

"Ain't no time I ever said nothin' about that boy marryin' me," she said in a whisper laced with poison. "Ain't no time. He ain't nothin' but my boss."

"You kept company with him much as you could. What's that tell you? Does that say you wanted him to be nothin' but your boss?"

"What I want is none of your business."

I recoiled at the tone in her voice, and for the first time that summer I felt the full effect of Gemma's strangeness. It was starting to eat right into my soul, and all my anger melted into fear that I was witnessing the beginning of the end of Gemma and Jessilyn. "Once was a time you wanted all your business to be my business," I murmured. "Lord knows, ain't never been no time I didn't want my business to be yours."

Gemma put her head down and stared at her feet. "Guess times can change."

I could've sworn my heart dropped from my chest to my feet when I heard those words come from my best friend's mouth. I'd never thought to see the day she'd push me out of her life.

"You want me done with you, Gemma?" I asked, my voice cracking in dismay. "You sayin' that?"

Gemma just stood there staring at her shoes, keeping me in suspense all the while. Then she lifted her head without looking me in the eye and said, "I'm sayin' I can't be friends with someone I can't trust."

"Gemma . . ."

"I trusted you!" she cried, finally meeting my gaze. "Now I'm gonna lose my job, and your daddy's gonna lose his farm, and all because you can't keep your mouth shut." She crossed her arms and shook her head. "Uh-uh!" she muttered. "Uh-uh! Ain't no way I can trust you never again."

Then she turned away from me and walked back through the field, the weeds slapping her legs as she went. I watched her go, my heart breaking with each step she took. There was no strength left in my legs, but I willed myself to turn away. I couldn't watch her go without feeling sick to my stomach, and the only thing I could think of was to find someone who still cared for me, who'd tell me that everything would be all right. I thought of Momma and Daddy, but they'd gone into town.

I grabbed my swirling stomach and staggered toward the only other place I could think to go.

Luke's.

But I didn't make it there before I crossed paths with Buddy Pernell. He was busy patching the roof to his daddy's shed, but he stopped cold, his hammer ready to strike a nail, and smiled down at me.

"Hey there, Jessie," he said kindly, almost too kindly. "You're a sight for sore eyes."

Rumor had it Buddy had been crushing on me since the summer I'd turned thirteen, and I'd spent a good bit of time avoiding him because of it. Back in that summer Buddy had been a wild boy, and he'd nearly drowned me in the swimming hole on my birthday. But his daddy had taken a firm hand with him from that time, and even I had to admit he'd grown up just fine. I figured he had a guilty conscience over nearly killing me, which any boy with some sense would, but the way he catered to me was something silly to my mind.

Momma had always insisted I let him be nice to me. "He's just tryin' to clear a guilty conscience, Jessilyn," she'd said to me all those years ago when Buddy had started fussing over me. "When a body sincerely wants to make amends, you ought to let him. It's just Buddy's way, is all."

"Hey there, Buddy," I said with as much a smile as I could muster.

Buddy climbed down his ladder and hopped past the last two rungs. "You got that sad look about you, Jessie," he said, dropping his hammer and wiping his hands on his pants. "You got problems?"

"Just things, is all. Nothin' for you to worry about."

"Well now, it seems a body's got to talk about things when they're worryin' her mind. Sure enough, I know that feelin'. If you got things to say, you can say 'em to me."

There was no doubt I had things to say, but I wanted to say them to Luke Talley, not Buddy Pernell. But his face was as sincere as it could be, and I was dying to talk to someone. I stared at Buddy for a minute, wondering at the wisdom of telling him about me and Gemma.

"Got some fresh-made lemonade inside," he told me, nodding toward the house. "Why don't you set yourself on down and have somethin' to cool yourself off with. Then, if you feel like talkin', you can talk. All right?"

I hesitated a second and then nodded. I couldn't deny that a tall glass of lemonade sounded like heaven to my parched mouth, so I made my way to the Pernells' shaded porch and sat in a squeaky rocker.

The two of us sat there sipping our lemonade for the next ten minutes. I didn't say a word, but Buddy said enough for both of us, talking about all the chores that needed done around their house and how he was looking forward to fall, when he wouldn't have to be doing so much hard work in the heat.

Then after I'd finished my last sip of lemonade, he set his glass down on the worn floorboards and asked, "You and Gemma in a fight?"

I lowered my glass slowly and eyed Buddy, wondering when he'd become a gypsy fortune-teller. "What's that you're sayin'?" I asked hesitantly.

He leaned back in his chair and folded his arms behind his head. "Seems to me anytime you're real sour is when you and Gemma are havin' a dustup." He returned my look of surprise with a wink. "See there, Jessie? I know you better'n you think I do."

The breeze had picked up, and I tipped my face to catch it, thinking over my options about what to tell Buddy, if I was even going to tell him anything at all. He watched me debate with myself before I finally relented.

"It's just, she's my best friend," I said with a sigh. "You know how I mean. It's no good when things ain't right between us."

"She do somethin' to rile you up?"

I shook my head slowly with a grimace full of shame. "It's Gemma who's mad at me, not the other way around. She's all fired up."

"She'll get over it soon enough, the way I see it."

"Not this time."

"Jessie, ain't no time you two had a spat longer'n a few days. It'll be good as new soon, you can mark my word."

"Things are different this time," I murmured, tucking one knee up under my chin. "Ain't nothin' usual about this fight."

"Ain't like you to do nothin' to rile her up that bad," he told me, a reassuring smile on his face. "Maybe you're worried over nothin'. You shouldn't feel so bad."

I knew he was trying to be nice, and under better circumstances maybe I would have had more appreciation for his tone. But just then, with all the worries stirring my stomach up into a twister, I didn't take too kindly to his argument that things weren't so bad as I thought.

"Were you there?" I asked him sharply. "'Cause from my

way of seein' things, if you weren't there, you ain't got no way of sayin' how I should feel."

Buddy sat up a little straighter when I spoke, and he donned an expression of discomfort that made me feel bad for speaking so harshly. But only a little.

"I didn't mean nothin' by it, Jessie," he said, his voice rising a bit higher in his eagerness to reassure me of his good intentions. "I was just tryin' to help."

"Ain't nothin' you can do to help," I told him in a softer tone. "Ain't nothin' anybody can do." I said that with enough conviction to let Buddy know I didn't want him to say anything more about it, but I didn't mean every bit of it. Luke would help in some way; I was sure of that. I didn't know what he would do, but suddenly, sitting on Buddy Pernell's porch drinking lemonade was no longer a good idea to me, and I couldn't stand the wait that it would take me to get to Luke's. I hopped up quickly, handed my empty, condensation-covered glass to Buddy without looking at him, and said, "Gotta go. Thanks for the lemonade."

"Hold on, Jessie," he called after me, but I was at the bottom of the steps by this time and didn't stop to listen.

"Gotta go," I repeated, adding, "See you at church" in hopes of making some amends for returning his kindness with my short temper.

"I didn't mean anythin' bad, Jessie," he hollered.

I stopped at the street and turned to look over my shoulder. "I know," I replied sincerely. "It's okay. I've just got somewhere to go."

Buddy followed me down the steps and paused at the bottom, wringing his hat in his hand nervously. "Well, I was gonna ask you somethin' before you go."

My feet were itching to get to Luke, but I figured I owed Buddy for being so kind to me even when I stuck my claws out, so I cocked my head to the side and pretended more interest than I felt.

He paused for a few seconds, and I stood there impatiently, wishing more than anything that he'd just up and spit it out. Finally he did, and I immediately took my wish back.

"I was just wonderin' if I could take you to the Independence Day dance this year."

My heart popped into my throat, and I was suddenly covered in hot prickles even though I felt shivery. I stared awkwardly at him, my mouth hanging open in disbelief. No boy had ever asked me anything like that before, and I had no idea how to respond. This was something about growing up that my momma hadn't covered. But then, we'd never needed to cover it before since I hadn't been interested in any boy except Luke since the day I turned thirteen.

So I did the only thing I knew how to do. I walked away.

"I gotta go," I told him again, and without answering him, I left him behind as quickly as I could without looking like a coward.

I could hear him call after me, but I ignored him. When I was well out of his sight, I slowed my pace a bit, beads of sweat dripping down my neck. I felt like a horse's behind for leaving him high and dry like that, and my mind began to swirl with insecure thoughts that turned into anger as I walked.

How dare Buddy Pernell ask me something like that while I was wound up about me and Gemma. I was in no state to be put on the spot, and he should have known better than to ask me like that, out of the blue. The way I saw it, he was just another selfish boy who thought he was so great that I'd feel pleased as punch to be courted by him and that his attentions would make all my worries go away.

All those thoughts made me feel better for being a coward . . . at least a little.

The sky was just starting to hint at sunset, and I took a deep breath of the summer air as I hurried down the road. There wasn't one single person I could tell about me and Gemma, but being with Luke usually took my mind off things, and my spirits lifted with just the anticipation of see-ing him.

That was how I ended up with at least a little smile on my face when I broke through the tree line at the front of his property. I could hear all sorts of clattering going on in Luke's house, and I wondered what sort of fixing up he was doing now.

I walked up his front steps and peered into the window. "If you're doin' spring cleanin'," I said loudly enough to be heard over his noise, "you're runnin' late."

Luke jumped a little when my voice startled him, and he tossed aside an old field-working boot with ferocity. The boot knocked over a cup full of water, and I quickly backed away from the window so none of the scattering droplets landed on me. I was so surprised by his angry display that my eyes must have been wide as saucers, but Luke didn't seem to notice.

He just pointed at me and said, "Don't you go sneakin' up on me, Jessilyn. Ain't I told you that before?"

I'd had enough of people trouble, and I bristled at his tone. "I ain't sneakin'. If you hadn't been makin' all that ruckus, you'd have heard me comin'."

Luke glared at me a few seconds and then turned away, shaking his head so hard that his short blond hair fluffed up into a peak.

I pulled away from the window and warily made my way inside, peeking around the doorway first. "You lookin' for somethin'?"

He didn't answer me at first. Instead, he rubbed the back of his neck, a sign of stress I'd seen in him just the day before.

I didn't much like being ignored and particularly not after the day I'd had. "Ain't you gonna answer me?" I asked him determinedly. "I said, are you lookin' for somethin'?"

"I'm just missin' a tool I need. It ain't nothin' to concern you," he muttered, kicking a dirty sock across the wooden floor.

"Maybe I can help," I managed to squeak out. Since when had anything to do with Luke not concerned me? "That's all I was thinkin'."

Luke rubbed the space between his eyes and sighed,

letting his shoulders drop into a defeated pose. "Jessilyn, I ain't in need of your help." He stopped himself short, hearing the sharpness in his own words. "It just ain't somethin' you need to be worryin' about, is all."

His words were said with restraint and laced with enough honey that they should have made me feel a bit better. But they meant little to me. His whole body told me that what he really wanted to say to me would have cut me like a knife.

More than anything, I felt like crying, and that made me even madder because I hated crying. All in the space of one afternoon, two of the most important people in my life had taken to despising me. At least with Gemma I knew why, but I had no way of knowing why Luke seemed to want me out of his sight as much as he did right then.

I could see that asking him was of no use, and after a minute or so of watching him avoid looking at me, I just turned around and walked away from a man for the second time that day.

Chapter 13

There was a storm in the air on Tuesday morning just as much as there was a storm in my heart, and with my chores behind me, I wearily put my walking shoes on to the tune of Momma humming while she sewed.

"I'm headin' into town to get some things for Miss Cleta. You need anythin'?" I asked, peeking into her tiny sewing space.

She stuck her needle into a cushion and looked at me with consoling eyes. "You all right, baby?"

I shrugged and fingered a piece of green muslin that lay spread out on a wooden chair. "Just feelin' cooped up, is all."

"Feels like rain today. Worries me you'll get caught in a cloudburst."

"Ain't like I've never been caught in one before."

She put down her half-sewn dress and stood to pull me close. "Gemma won't stay mad long, Jessie. Whatever it is you two are dustin' up about, it'll work out."

My shoulders sagged with worry but not only from remembering my troubles with Gemma. I was still stinging from Luke's rebuke the night before too. I just melted into her arms for a minute and let her comfort me as only a momma could. Then I smiled wanly and said, "I'll be all right, Momma. Sure you don't need nothin'?"

"No, baby, I was just in town last night. You have a nice walk and be careful. Duck into a store if it starts to come down on you."

"Yes'm." I made my way downstairs and packed up a few things for Mr. Poe, grabbed one of Daddy's fine ripe tomatoes from the pantry, sprinkled some salt on it, and set out on my way. Tasting the cool juice from the tomato did nothing to ease the intense heat of the still-early morning, but I kept on the road into town, determined to check up on Mr. Poe.

The sheriff was standing on the front steps when I reached the jail. He was smoking a cigar, and he tipped his hat at me when he saw me coming.

"Got a hot day for such a long walk, Miss Jessilyn. But then, we ain't got nothin' but hot days no more." He cast a glance up into the sky, squinting against the sun as it popped out from its cover of clouds. "Those storm clouds are teasin' us today. Sure could use some rain."

"It'll rain," I told him confidently. "I can smell it in the air." I climbed the steps and stood in front of him, well off to the side to avoid the suffocating stench of his smoke. "I'm here to see Mr. Poe. Seems to me there ain't no law against me seein' a prisoner in your jail."

"Well, I suppose I could work somethin' out there," he said with a slow drawl. "Providin' you behave yourself, that is."

I bristled at his response and stood up straight, my five feet seven inches matching up to his short frame. "What kind of trouble are you talkin' about, Sheriff? I ain't never been in no trouble with the law."

"You ain't never been so determined to see a man go free, neither. I don't want you goin' and takin' liberties with my prisoner. I know you and Gemma have been sneakin' him things. I already done took away a box of one of his crazy collections." He took off his hat and wiped his forehead with the back of his hand. "Doggonit, you know I can't have you interferin' in police business."

"Maybe if the police wasn't so bound to make a poor innocent man miserable, I wouldn't go interferin'. And anyway, all we did was bring him some treats. Seems a man unjustly accused can't hurt so much from gettin' treats."

He replaced his hat, took two puffs on his cigar, and looked at me through narrowed eyes. "Ain't no reason you girls had to do it in secret. I'll let the man have some treats. Just depends on what the treats are."

"You wouldn't even let us see him."

"That was when there was trouble stirred up. The boys around here have eased off a bit. Seems they're willin' to wait for trial and let the law take care of things. Wish you'd do the same. I got rules in my jail, Jessilyn."

I reached into one of my dress pockets and held out a handful of stones. "Brought these for Mr. Poe's collection. And I brought him some of Momma's dried figs." I pulled a bag out of my other pocket and revealed it to him. "You got rules about these things, too?"

"Can't let him have the stones. Could be a weapon."

I rolled my eyes to the heavens and sighed. I never enjoyed dealing with people that didn't use the sense God gave them. "When's the last time you saw Elmer Poe hurt a body with a rock? He ain't no David with a sling. He just wants 'em to look at when he's sittin' all cooped up in that dingy old cell."

The sheriff puffed another circle of smoke in my direction, and I waved it off angrily, sick of the smoke and senseless words that kept coming from that man's mouth.

"Listen here," he said, his patience waning. "You can let him have those figs, but that's it. Now, if you want to come in here, fine. But I'm tellin' you, those rocks stay outside. You hear?"

I looked at the thick, stubby finger he pointed at me and bit back the sharp words that sat on the tip of my tongue. Finally, after taking a minute to compose myself, I dropped the stones onto the jailhouse steps, letting their clatter interrupt the silence between us. I held up the bag of figs to show it was all I had with me. "Now can I go in?"

He finally stubbed the ugly old cigar out on the metal railing and flung out a hand in an exaggerated gesture to usher me inside. I was disliking him more and more by the minute.

"My daddy says ain't no way Mr. Poe done this," I told the sheriff as I followed him back to where they were holding Mr. Poe. "Ain't just me and Gemma that thinks it. Ain't just Daddy, neither. There's plenty of folks that know he ain't capable."

"Ain't what folks think that I run my town on," he said sharply.

"Sure about that?" I asked, opening my mouth that one step too far like I usually did. "It's an election year, ain't it?"

He whirled around on me with a quickness I didn't know a bulky man like him could possess and glared at me with a look I'd never seen in his eyes before. "Talk like that'll get you in trouble, little lady. You best bite your tongue before I send you out of here good and quick."

He startled me enough that I took a long step back, but my gaze never left his. "I done known you a long time, Sheriff. For the life of me I can't figure why you're treatin' Mr. Poe so bad. He ain't never been nothin' but good to you."

"I'm done talkin' with you, Jessilyn," he told me. "You want to see Elmer Poe, then you go on back and do it. I ain't gonna argue with you no more."

I stared at him for a few seconds longer, then stormed past him into the short, stuffy hall that led to Mr. Poe's cell.

"You got ten minutes," Sheriff Clancy called before he slammed the door behind me.

I reached Mr. Poe's cell and tapped on one of the bars to

get his attention without startling him. He was all curled up in the corner of his cot, staring at the narrow patch of cloudy sky that was visible through his window.

"Hey there, Mr. Poe," I said softly as he turned to look at me.

He sat up to greet me, but his movements were slow and labored, his face creased far more than I remembered it. "Hey there, Miss Jessilyn. Didn' hear ya comin'."

"I thought you'd like some company."

"Sure 'nough." A dim smile crossed his face but never reached his eyes. "A body needs comp'ny tuh get by."

A knot formed in my throat as I looked at his face that was so saddened by betrayal and confusion. He shuffled over to me, wrapping his hands around the bars for support, and just stood there with his head dipped down, his eyes focused on the tips of his worn shoes. I'd never seen Mr. Poe with shoes that didn't shine like the moon, and it struck me that all I'd known this man to be seemed to be slipping away from him.

I pulled the small sack from my pocket and held it between the bars. "Brought you some of my momma's dried figs. I know you like them."

"That's right kind of ya," he said, taking them with a shaky hand. "Right kind. Tell yer momma Ah said so."

"Yes'r. I'll do that."

I watched him as he made about the business of getting into the bag of figs, but his motions were slow and uncoordinated. The paper sack crinkled loudly as he tried to unfold the top and reach inside. It must have taken him a solid minute before he even managed to open the top, but once inside, his hand wouldn't grasp one.

"Cain't find 'em," he muttered.

"Here, I'll help you, Mr. Poe." I gently took the bag from him and reached in to pull out two sugary figs. "They get stuck together sometimes, is all. Maybe we can rip the sack some so you can see them." I tore the bag halfway down the side and rolled the top down to form a paper bowl. "There you go. Now you can get at them good and easy."

I leaned against the bars and watched as Mr. Poe shuffled back to his cot, slumped over his knees, and fumbled with the figs. Even eating seemed a chore to him, but at length he managed to swallow one.

"Mighty good," he murmured, his head continuing to nod slightly as though he had no ability to control it. "You tell yer momma ain't nuthin' tasted better tuh me than these here figs."

"I'll do that, Mr. Poe." For another minute I watched him without saying a word. He was just sitting there, staring at the other fig in his shaky fingers. Finally I leaned in closer, sticking my head as far through the bars as I could manage, and quietly said, "Mr. Poe. They bein' good to you in here?"

He didn't seem to hear and I raised my voice a little. "You hear, Mr. Poe? I was askin' if they's treatin' you good in this here jail."

He lifted his nodding head. "They's just doin' what they has to. S'what the sheriff says."

"But they ain't bein' rough with you or nothin'?"

For the first time he perked up a bit. "Oh no, Miss Jessilyn. They ain't hurt me. No, ma'am. They's just gotta keep me here, is all."

"You sure you're feelin' all right? Maybe they should have the doc come take a look at you."

"Ain't nuthin' wrong with me. Old Mr. Poe, he ain't never sick." He gave me a wobbly smile. "Ah take after muh daddy, s'what muh momma always said."

"And your daddy weren't never sick, is that it, Mr. Poe?"

"Nope. He weren't never sick. Me neither."

"So you're doin' all right in here, then?"

He nodded and slowly took a bite out of the fig in his hand. "Just wish ah could have muh things to look at. Ain't got much to do with muh days." He reached under his pillow and pulled out a worn, leather-bound book. "Got me a Bible here, though, and I figure that's 'bout all a man needs tuh get by. I got the Lord by muh side. Ain't nuthin' better'n that."

"That's fine," I said, though I was still fuming at Sheriff Clancy for leaving this poor old man in a dirty cell, alone and with nothing to occupy his time. "S'pose it's nice to have somethin' to read, then."

"I got me the Lord's words," he said, tapping a finger on the cover of the Bible. "Got me all ah need when ah got me the Lord's words."

"Yes'r," I murmured, even though I didn't think a worn Bible was enough to keep Mr. Poe from losing his health and happiness.

Sheriff Clancy opened the hall door, sending an echoing squeak bouncing off the cinder block walls. "Time's up, Jessilyn. You need to be on your way."

I gave him a venomous glare and then I turned my attention back to Mr. Poe. "I got to go now, Mr. Poe. But I'll be back to visit as much as I can, you hear?"

"Yes'm, ah hear ya. Tell yer momma a kind thank-you for the figs. They's mighty good."

I smiled at him and nodded, but he seemed to be looking through me rather than at me, and I backed away sadly.

"That man ain't fit," I told the sheriff before I even got through the door.

"Ain't nothin' done wrong to that man," he said, and I could tell how annoyed he was with me by the sigh built into his words. "We've got him three square meals a day, plenty of water, and he's got a Bible to read. I even let him see the paper every mornin'."

"Well, that's right kind of you, Sheriff. Seein' as how he's been a loyal citizen of this here county for his whole life, it's good to know you don't let him starve or go without knowin' the important news of the day."

The sarcasm in my voice was evident in a way that would have made my momma blush in three different shades, but I didn't care just then. I was good and mad for seeing what was being done to my old friend for no good reason.

"Seems you could do better by him by findin' out who really killed Callie Colby so Mr. Poe don't have to sit and rot back there in that old cell while the real killer goes free."

"See here, Jessilyn Lassiter," he warned. "You ain't got no call to tell me how to do my job. Your daddy were here, he'd give you a tongue-lashin' for your wild talk."

"If I gotta be the only one who'll stand up for Mr. Poe, then I'll do it, even if my daddy gives me a tongue-lashin'. That man's near about dyin' slow back there, and you ain't givin' no respect to what kind of good man he is. He's used to takin' long walks in the sunshine and talkin' to people in town, and here you've got him all cooped up in that dim light, starin' at nothin' and talkin' to no one."

"What d'you expect me to do for him? Bring in entertainment? I got enough work to do here, tryin' to find out all I can about this case."

"Then if you're workin' so hard, why ain't you found out who's really guilty? Seems you shouldn't have so much trouble figurin' it out since he lives in your own town."

Sheriff Clancy had popped in some chaw and I watched with irritation as he readjusted the lump at the side of his mouth. "Jessilyn," he said, his eyes narrowed thoughtfully, "you know somethin' I should know about this here case, you best be tellin' me if you want your Mr. Poe to get back to his walks in the sunshine and all."

I struggled not to gulp audibly when he said that, and though there was a burning desire in my soul to tell the sheriff all about Joel Hadley, Gemma's angry face flashed across my memory, and I caught my tongue. I didn't know what to do. I wanted more than anything to see Mr. Poe walk out of the jail free and Joel Hadley dragged in to take his place. But

I couldn't imagine what would happen if my daddy lost his farm because of it. Losing the farm would mean bad things for all of us. Not to mention that Gemma would hate me forever for breaking my promise. I felt trapped.

"I ain't sayin' I know nothin'," I told him. "I'm just sayin' you ought to find him if you're a good sheriff."

"You said somethin' about him livin' in my town. How would you know that?"

"I don't know nothin'," I lied quickly. "I'm just figurin' no one but a local would travel that road that time of night. It ain't a road that leads much of anywhere, so out-of-towners wouldn't be usin' it."

The sheriff stared at me for a minute before leaning down to spit in a tin cup, and I cringed at the sight of it.

"So, you don't know nothin'?" he asked again, his eyes betraying his suspicion. "Well, I suppose you'd tell me if you did, seein' as how it'd be sure to help out your friend Mr. Poe."

"You keep callin' him my friend."

"Well, ain't he?"

"Was a time he was your friend too, Sheriff. Was a time you'd see fit to treat a friend of yours better'n this."

My tone was much softer this time and more pleading in nature.

Sheriff Clancy looked down at his feet and let his shoulders droop in resignation. "Miss Jessilyn, I got me a heap of troubles right now, and I'd sure like to help Elmer Poe get back to his own home and out of trouble. But I got me a job to do, and I got to do it. That's it in a nutshell." He pulled his hat tighter onto his head. "You best get on, now. Looks like rain, and you got to walk back home."

I could see he was done talking, and that meant I needed to be done trying to convince him he was wrong. I'd said all I could, and he hadn't budged. I returned his gaze for a moment before I turned and left him behind. I didn't like losing fights. There was a part of me that felt I should always be able to figure out a way to make things right. But I had found out in the past, and I was finding out again, that the world is full of things no amount of trying can fix.

Chapter 14

Daddy's head was hanging low when he came in from the fields the next evening, and I could see weariness written all over his face.

"You got any smiles for a tired man, Jessilyn?" he asked me when he caught the sad look on my face.

I wanted so much to tell him my worries, but I could see he had enough of his own, so I smiled as best I could. "It's too hot for a full day's work, Daddy."

"Too much work to be done. The heat can't matter on days like this."

"I'll get out there and work some tomorrow. I ain't got to go to Miss Cleta's if you need help."

"Baby, no," he said sharply.

Daddy didn't think women should do labor like that, and though I knew he was unlikely to change his mind,

I persisted. "It ain't no trouble. I'm young yet, and you know I got me more energy than a plow horse."

He sighed. "Jessilyn Lassiter, there ain't never a day I put my girls to work in heat like this, and there ain't never gonna be a day. If a man can't find a way to provide for his own family without seein' his girls near about faintin' in the fields, then what good is he?"

Daddy's vehemence was something I'd seen only rarely, and I knew enough to hold my tongue. He sighed again and clomped through the house without even taking the time to remove his boots outside like he usually did.

I went on inside to help with supper and found Momma absentmindedly slicing green tomatoes. It was clear by the muddy footprints on her clean floor and by Momma's strained expression that Daddy had already passed through here, leaving the wake of his worries behind him.

"Daddy ain't happy," I murmured, testing the waters to see if Momma was willing to talk about it.

"Tryin' times, honey," she said lightly, her voice quavering. "That's all. We've made it through them before."

I tied an apron around my waist, grabbed a long knife, and set to work with the carrots. "He says he won't let me help."

"You ought to know he won't."

"But these are different times. I ain't a child no more, and he ain't never been close to losin' the farm before."

"Not that you know, Jessilyn," she interrupted. "Times were once when we didn't know how we'd keep things runnin'. Ain't that long ago that money was scarce all over this country. It was God's hand and your daddy's smarts that kept us afloat while others were sinkin', and it'll be the same this time."

"Did you tell Daddy so?"

"I tell your daddy so every day, baby. He just ain't feelin' it in his bones right now." She dipped tomato slices in batter and tossed them into a hot skillet. "Jessilyn, you got enough worries of your own." She wiped her hands on her apron and gently brushed a few stray hairs out of my face. "I can see it in your eyes. Don't you go tryin' to carry ours too. We've always worked things out, and we'll do the same now."

"But, Momma, that ain't easy for me to accept now that I'm old enough to help. I want to do somethin'."

"You already are." She took my face in both of her hands and drew closer to me. "Baby, just seein' your face every mornin' gives your daddy and me all the strength we need. We look at you and we see how good you're growin' up. It makes us right pleased to see how fine you've become, and we're feelin' blessed just as much as we did when times were more secure. Only thing that would make things better . . ."

Her voice trailed off, but I knew what she'd considered saying. She was burdened because I didn't know Jesus, and I knew it preyed on her heart like a curse. But I couldn't say something was for me when it wasn't, so I just smiled at her lightly. "Momma, I want to make you happy. . . ."

"I know, baby. I know." She gave my cheek one soft pat

and padded across the floor to tend the tomatoes. "The Lord will bring it to your heart when the time is right."

I didn't know why I couldn't feel like Momma did when it came to faith, but I just couldn't, and the last thing I knew how to do was to be something I wasn't. I looked at my momma, standing there at the range on her bare feet, her shoulders heavy with worry but her heart light with peace, and I wished I could know what she knew. There was no peace in any part of my body or mind just then, and I would have given anything to know what that felt like.

⚘

The last time I'd seen Luke, I'd been left feeling sore. He hadn't been by our place since, and when I'd asked Daddy about it, he'd just said Luke must have something on his mind.

"But what is it he's got on his mind, Daddy?" I asked. "Maybe we could help."

"Reckon I don't know, but there's times a man's just got to work things out for himself, baby. This is one of those times for Luke. He'll work it out. You ain't got to worry about him."

But I didn't believe him, one of the few times when I found it too easy to doubt my daddy. There had been times enough when I'd seen Luke angry at other people, but there had never been a day I'd known him to be downright angry with me. No doubt I could frustrate the life out of him, but his true

196

temper had never touched me once before that evening, and now it lay on my heart like a bruise.

I watched Daddy head out to his hard day's work, finished drying the breakfast dishes, and started upstairs to get myself fixed up for work at Miss Cleta's. I didn't see hide nor hair of Gemma that morning, and the loss of her was paining me something fierce while I made my way to Miss Cleta's.

"Got somethin' on your mind," Miss Cleta said with an exaggerated nod when I climbed her steps. She hopped up out of her rocker and opened her screen door. "You need an éclair."

I didn't think an éclair would solve anything, but I followed her inside and ate it nonetheless. Working for Miss Cleta, it was a good thing I was skinny by nature. By midmorning, she sent me over to Mae's house with a platter of cookies.

"She probably won't eat them, bless her heart," she told me. "But I keep tryin'. That girl's so thin these days, I swear that baby inside her won't have nothin' to live on."

She was right about Mae, I found with sad certainty when I arrived. Mae was sitting on a chair in front of a window, her weary face staring into the glass without seeing. I knocked on the door and braced myself to talk to her, but she didn't move a muscle.

"Mae," I called softly through the screen. "It's Jessilyn Lassiter."

She still seemed unaware of my presence, so I opened the door and poked my head around the doorway to look at her. "It's Jessilyn, Mae. Can I come in?"

The movement of my head roused her attention and she looked slowly in my direction.

"Oh, Jessilyn," she drawled lazily. "I didn't hear you comin'."

"Wish you'd tell my momma that. She always tells me I clomp my feet too much," I said, hoping some humor might lighten the air a bit. "But then, I always tell her I can't help it because my feet are so big."

Mae smiled, but it was the smile of someone who was trying to show something she didn't feel. Her skin was pale, her eyes drawn, and her normally plump figure had grown thin and bony. She started to stand, but I was afraid she would topple over from sheer exhaustion.

"No need to get up, Mae," I said hastily. "I can find a seat myself." In truth, I had to look hard for a good place to sit down, her house was in such disarray. It was unlike Mae in its untidiness. She'd always run a tight ship with her cleaning and cooking, and I'd never seen her things out of order.

I cleared off a chair so I could sit and then walked the platter over to her. "Some cookies from Miss Cleta." When she hesitated, I shook the platter lightly to get her attention. "They're good," I reassured her.

"Miss Cleta always makes good things," she murmured, taking one, though I figured she was mostly taking it to keep from arguing with me about it. "She's always brought us good things."

I sat down and laid the platter on the floor, the only place

I could find for it. "She's right kind that way," I said, nibbling on a cookie. "Right kind."

It must have been five minutes before another word was said, and the silence was more deafening to me than any noise could have been. Mae never took a single bite of that cookie; she just stared at an undefined spot in front of her with eyes that didn't seem to be seeing.

Finally I spoke up just to break the quiet. "I sure do like Miss Cleta's brownies. You ever tried one, Mae?"

When she said nothing in reply, I continued nervously. "She's got some mighty fine tarts too. I like tarts. But then, I like near about anything that's sweet. I got me an over-developed sweet tooth, so my momma likes to say." I was rambling, and I knew it, but the way I figured it, someone had to talk, and words weren't likely to come from the ghostly figure sitting stock-still across from me. "As a matter of fact, Miss Cleta's bakin' a coconut cake right now for me to take home to my family. I told her not to, but she insisted. I think it's her way of showin' kindness to people."

I moved my head from side to side trying to catch Mae's gaze, but it seemed an impossibility to do so.

"So . . . Miss Cleta says she's makin' a plate of ginger-snaps too, since my daddy loves them so much and he's been workin' so hard. I said a coconut cake would go over just fine, but she said, 'A hardworkin' man needs somethin' to lift his spirits at the end of the day, and your momma's got enough to do without slavin' in the kitchen on a hot day.' And I said, 'But, Miss Cleta, ain't you slavin' in the kitchen on a hot day?' And she said, 'To me it ain't slavin'. To me it's a happy way to pass my time. I ain't got all the things to do your momma has.' So now she's over there whippin' up a cake and some cookies. Bet that oven's got the whole house heated up right toasty."

My long rant did nothing to change Mae's shattered expression. "You like gingersnaps?" I asked helplessly. "I figure they're best on a cold day with some hot cider, but my daddy, he likes them any which way."

Mae stirred a bit, and I leaned forward in my seat to catch her attention. "You like gingersnaps, Mae?" I asked again.

A slight smile broke the blankness of her face, and she slowly aimed her eyes at me. They were so glassy, I couldn't tell what was behind them, but I figured it out quickly enough when she said softly, "My Callie loved gingersnaps."

My throat went dry, and the bite of cookie in my mouth felt like sand when I tried to swallow. I knew gingersnaps were Callie's favorite. Hadn't I seen my daddy sitting on the front porch sharing a plate with her more than once? Why did I have to open my mouth like that?

I was never so sure of my social graces, and I was even less sure now. Before I could say any more, a tear trickled down Mae's cheek and landed on her untouched cookie.

"She'd sit there with one of Miss Cleta's cookies, right there in that chair where you're sittin'," she said with a break in her voice. "And she'd smile like a Cheshire cat. Made a mess of crumbs on her good dress, but Miss Cleta, she'd just laugh at the sight, so I didn't never make much fuss over it."

She was talking to me, but then again she wasn't, and I looked around the room uncomfortably, panicking inside, trying to think of some way to step out of the mess I'd stepped into.

"You know, Miss Cleta would like to see you, I'm sure. You want to come back with me to see her?" I asked.

But Mae was unaware of my words; she just kept rambling on. "Callie loved near about all sweets. But then, she liked near about everything. She was such a happy girl. . . ."

Her voice quavered, and she dropped off into a swell of tears. I jumped up, nearly upsetting the tray of cookies at my feet, and rushed to her side.

"Mae, I'm sorry," I told her, my own voice breaking with emotion. "I didn't mean to upset you."

She was inconsolable, her shoulders heaving. I ran out of the house to fetch Miss Cleta, but I ran square into Nate Colby before I reached the sidewalk.

"What're you screechin' around here for, Jessilyn?" he asked. "You got fire under your feet?"

I looked up into a face worn with creases just like Mae's and shook my head. "It's Mae."

"What about Mae?" he asked, his tone more serious now. "She sick or somethin'?"

"She's all upset," I said though my throat was choked with unspent tears. "I done said somethin' that reminded her of Callie and she got all upset."

He turned quickly to head up the steps. "Ain't people got enough to do in their lives that they ain't got to go sayin' things to upset grievin' folks?" he muttered as he left me behind. Over the sound of Mae's wails that had begun to float out through the window screens, he said, "Maybe you best not come around right now, Jessilyn. Mae's got enough troubles."

The door slammed behind him and he left me there on the sidewalk with a lump in my throat that wouldn't budge. It was all I could do to trudge back to Miss Cleta's house without losing every bit of composure I had left.

"Oh, baby, it ain't your fault," Miss Cleta said once I'd managed to tell her about my tragic visit with Mae. She untied the apron at her waist and wiped my tears with it. "Our Mae's been cryin' nearly all the time since the sad event. I should've warned you."

"I shouldn't have said nothin'," I nearly wailed. "I'm always sayin' things that ain't right."

"Now, don't you go puttin' blame on your small shoulders, Jessilyn. Ain't nobody can talk to Mae without her thinkin' about her baby girl. Ain't nothin' but time that's goin' to remedy that." She gave me a plate covered in tinfoil. "You go on and take this cake home with you and tell your daddy he'll get some fine gingersnaps tomorrow. I ain't had time to make them yet."

"But I ain't even done no work for you today."

"Honey, you had a right bad time of it, and I feel responsible since I sent you over there. You just go on and take the day off and take your pay with you."

"I can't take no pay for work I ain't done," I argued.

"Every job gives paid days off every now and again," she rallied back. "At least any job that's worth workin'. Now I'm the boss, and I say you get a paid day off, and that's all there is to it, you hear?"

I looked at her face and knew I'd never win this argument. "Yes'm," I said with a slight nod. "Sure is good of you."

"Ain't nothin'. Now you head on home and get some rest and stop thinkin' so much about troubles. A girl your age shouldn't be carryin' around so many. You read a good book or somethin'. And make sure it's a book about people who ain't got no troubles."

"Yes'm."

I walked down the porch steps and left her behind, and though I knew she meant every consoling word she had said to me, I still felt like a child and a failure. I didn't know how to help Mae or anyone like her and I wondered if I ever would.

As I walked home, the cake icing was melting in the heat, dripping down the side of the plate to stick on my fingers, and I was grateful for it because the stickiness was a distraction from my anxious thoughts. All I wanted from life then was a way out. I felt helpless and hopeless, surrounded by events I couldn't handle or control, and I felt alone in the midst of it.

Daddy was resting on the front steps when I came up the walk, and he tossed me one of his worn but loving smiles. "Miss Cleta sendin' goodies home again?" he asked eagerly.

"Coconut cake." I slumped down on the step beside him and set the cake on the porch behind me, ignoring the melting icing. I licked my fingers and shook my head. "She's always makin' somethin'."

He peeked under the tinfoil, dipped a finger in a puddle of icing, and said, "And God bless her for it. This'll be a fine endin' to what's sure to be a fine supper by your momma."

I smiled and laid my head on his shoulder. "You takin' a dinner break?"

"Already had my dinner break. I was just sittin' out here thinkin' about you."

"Me?" I asked, raising my head to look at him. "What for?"

"Just wonderin' what's on that mind of yours these days. Seems we ain't done much talkin' of late."

"What'd you want to talk about?" I asked, though I was afraid of his answer.

"Oh . . ." He leaned back and peered at the sky for a moment. "Guess I was just thinkin' about my baby girl and how she used to be full of smiles and how now she seems all troubled and lonely."

I looked away from him and swallowed hard. "I ain't troubled and lonely, Daddy," I lied badly.

"Baby, you think I'm a stupid man?"

"No, sir!"

"Then how come you think I'll fall for talk like that when I can see trouble written all over your face?"

I had no answer for that, so I just looked off into the

distance at the tops of the trees as they swayed in the breeze. We had never gotten the rain I'd been so sure we'd get just days earlier; the weather had been cloudy and threatening without giving us any measure of relief. Today was no different, and the unrelenting wind seemed to tease us all by tossing the dry dirt up into clouds that would never produce the rain we needed.

"You want to tell me about it, baby?"

I sat there for a while longer and then shook my head slowly. "Can't" was all I said.

"Since when is there somethin' you can't tell me?" he asked. "Sure you don't just mean you won't?"

I whipped my head around to look him square in the eye. "No, Daddy. That ain't what I mean. I mean just what I say. I can't. I wish I could, but I can't."

His face twisted up in worry, and he furrowed his brow when he met my gaze. "Jessilyn, I'm your daddy. I can't just set by and not know what's troublin' my baby girl. Now, you done this once before when that Blevins boy was botherin' you, and I thought we agreed you wouldn't do it again."

"Daddy, I got reasons that I can't tell you. I don't want to do it. I want to tell you, but you got to understand, I can't."

There was no doubt my daddy was miserable at the idea of not prying more, but I knew he could see the sincerity in my words.

"You can trust me, Daddy," I told him. "I ain't in no trouble myself. It's just somethin' I got to hold on to right now, but it ain't me who's in trouble."

"Then who is it?" he tried one last time. "Is it Gemma?"

I sat there, tight-lipped, and knew my silence would tip him off. "Can't say nothin', Daddy," I repeated.

He scratched the bridge of his nose, though I figured it didn't really itch, and I could see him thinking things through for a minute. Then he looked at me and said, "Well now, baby, I figure I got to respect your feelin's." He put his arm around me and gave my shoulders a good squeeze, and though we sat on that porch for another fifteen minutes in silence, I knew better than to believe that was the end of the conversation. My daddy had enough clues to go on, and he wasn't the stupid man he'd accused me of thinking he was. There may have been a lot of doubts in my mind just then, but there was one thing I had no doubts about at all. My daddy would pick and prod until he found out my troubles all on his own.

When it came to his girls, my daddy would stop at nothing to make things right.

Chapter 15

By the time I turned seventeen, there were some things I'd figured out I couldn't change. Like the way I was too young for Luke to fall in love with yet, or how Gemma would always think she was the boss of me, or how those freckles ran across my nose like footprints. But there were some things I could change, the way I figured it, and I woke up that Saturday morning on Independence Day, determined there was one thing I could do something about. I rolled off the bed and stepped on the sheet that had puddled beside me on the floor since nobody wanted anything unnecessary touching their body in heat like this.

Gemma was already gone, and I knew she'd be heading into town to check on Mr. Poe just like she did most early mornings. It flashed across my mind that I wished she had asked me to go to town with her like she would have when she liked me better, but I knew she just couldn't be happy with me right now. The thought broke my heart, so I pushed it out of my mind and hurried about the room getting dressed.

I went into the bathroom to splash some water on my face and found my hair had popped up into uneven waves from the humidity, but I'd long ago given up on it. I ran my comb through it quickly and avoided looking at my suntouched face too long. I didn't much care for my pert little freckled nose or my green cat eyes. They were nothing like the women I'd seen in magazines and motion pictures, so I avoided looking at them altogether.

Once I'd finished readying myself, I ran downstairs, grabbed a piece of corn bread, and scurried out the door.

By the time I reached the edge of Luke's property, I'd started questioning my decision to come, but there was no way I was turning back. Even if I had to drag him out of bed, I was going to find out why he'd been staying away from our house. I hadn't seen him since he'd yelled at me in his house, and I was done wondering. Come hell or high water, he was going to tell me what was wrong.

His back door was hanging open, and I could hear water splashing around the other side of the house. When I stepped around the corner, I saw him there in the sun, his suspenders hanging to his sides, his top half covered only by a white undershirt that didn't have any sleeves. He was standing in front of a table with a big steel tub full of water on it, washing up.

The second he saw me, his blue eyes flashed with surprise and embarrassment. "Jessilyn!" he hollered, yanking his suspenders up like they would keep me from seeing his undershirt. "What're you doin' around here this time of the mornin'?"

"I want to talk to you," I said with no uncertainty. "Right now."

"I ain't even dressed."

"You got pants on, ain't you?"

"I ain't got no shirt on."

"Don't go makin' excuses to me. I've seen you in only your swimmin' bottoms before. You ain't no more naked than that right now. You're just tryin' to avoid me like you've been avoidin' me all week."

He turned his head away from me and went back to scrubbing his hands. "I'm busy, anyhow."

"Not busy enough." I crossed over to where he stood, ignoring the droplets of water that splashed onto my cropped pants. "You ain't never gonna be busy enough to avoid hearin' what I've got to say to you."

He didn't look up from the water, but he stopped scrubbing and splashing, and I took that as a sign he was ready to listen.

"I came over here that night to talk to you," I began. "You know that? I was in trouble, and you told me you wanted to help when I was in trouble, so I came on over to talk to you and all I got was more trouble."

He let out a long, worn-out sigh but never lifted his eyes

from the bucket. He just leaned his elbows on it like he needed support. "I didn't mean to give you no trouble, Jessie. Honest, I didn't."

"Then why'd you yell at me like that? You were mean as a hornet."

"I was havin' a bad time of it, is all."

"I told you I'd help."

"I didn't want no help, Jessie," he said, finally meeting my gaze. "Sometimes a man's just got to care for things himself."

"You sound like my daddy now."

"That so bad?"

"No, but you ain't my daddy. My daddy's my daddy. But you . . ."

He pushed his arms up straight so his hands rested on the water tub, his arms tensed so that every muscle showed through, and gave me a look that made my knees weak. "But I'm what?" he asked slowly.

My heart was pounding, my mouth was dry, and I wasn't sure I'd be able to answer his question much less take a breath. "Well . . . ," I finally managed to murmur, "you're . . . you're Luke."

"What's that supposed to mean?"

"It means you ain't my daddy. I don't expect you to treat me the same way he does."

Luke let go of the tub and stood up straight, grabbed a nearby towel, and wiped his hands. "And how do you expect me to treat you, Jessilyn?"

"What do you mean, how do I expect you to treat me?

I expect you to treat me like a friend. Like someone you can trust. That's what I mean. You been stayin' away from us, and I figure there's somethin' botherin' you, but if you can't trust me enough to tell me what it is, then what kind of friendship do we got?"

"Seems to me you're all balled up in knots these days too, but you ain't told me nothin' about it, neither."

My eyes wandered awkwardly around the yard like I thought I'd find a good rebuttal hiding behind a tree, but I knew he'd pegged me good. "That's . . . different," I answered feebly.

He dropped the towel on the ground and took a step toward me. "How's that different?"

"I . . . I don't know," I mumbled. "It just is."

He stepped directly in front of me, blocking the early morning sun so he looked like a dark shadow. "Ain't nothin' I don't want to help you with, Jessilyn. Even if I was actin' mean as a hornet the other day."

"You sure?"

"I was upset when you found me then; that's all."

"Then why are you stayin' away from us?"

His eyes flitted around the yard at anything but my face, and I took the chance to study his expression for anything that would give away his thoughts. "I ain't been stayin' away from you," he said slowly. "I've just been . . . busy."

"Busy with what?"

"Just busy, is all. I wasn't meanin' to be rude or nothin'."

I didn't like or accept his excuse, and I told him as much.

"Seems to me you oughtn't be too busy for friends if you want to keep them."

He studied my face for a minute and then said, "Sure enough, I ain't interested in losin' them."

"Well then," I murmured, "I guess we'll be seein' you for supper most nights again."

A smile touched one corner of his mouth. "Reckon you will."

I instinctively took a step toward him, but I immediately regretted it because it broke the spell that had settled between us. He suddenly jerked away to retrieve the towel he'd tossed to the ground, leaving me to stand awkwardly alone. But I wasn't willing to let the moment pass so quickly.

I reached into my bag of womanly tricks and came out with a handful of jealousy. "I saw Buddy Pernell the other day. He sure was sweet to me. Asked after me and all."

"Buddy Pernell. What's he up to these days? Nearly drown any more girls lately?"

"You know good and well Buddy's done some fine growin' up these past years. He's turned into a real gentleman."

"That so?" Luke murmured those words and went back to that water tub to dunk his whole head in. Soaking his head didn't seem like much of a romantic gesture, and I could see his attention turning away from me quick as a wink, so the second his head came back up, I said the first thing that came to mind.

"I'm goin' to the Independence Day dance with him tonight."

Now, I knew I hadn't done anything but turn tail and run when Buddy asked me to that dance. My first thoughts when I let those words out were how I hoped Buddy hadn't gotten himself another date and how quick I'd have to hunt him down and take him up on his offer. But it was the best weapon I had, and I used it.

Luke bobbed his head to check for water in his ear and then furrowed his brow at me, his wet hair standing up in peaks. "You say you're goin' to the dance with him?"

"That's right."

"Your daddy know about this?"

"What difference does that make? Buddy Pernell's respectable. Ain't no reason my daddy would say I can't go to the dance with him."

"Maybe so, but maybe he don't like you goin' places with boys nohow."

I put my hands on my hips just like Gemma does when she gets sassy and squared up to him like an angry bull. "I ain't no little girl, Luke Talley, no matter how hard you try to convince yourself of that. I'm full grown, and I can go to a dance with a boy if I want to."

"That's right; he's a boy. He ain't no man." Then he cocked his head to the side and added, "And you sure as sunshine ain't no woman."

Those words were a slap in my face, and my cheeks felt hot like they really had caught a good backhand. "You're just jealous," I shot back.

"Jealous?" he cried out vehemently. "Me?"

"That's right. Because I found someone else to spend time with, that's why."

"Buddy Pernell!" he grunted. "I ain't never been jealous of Buddy Pernell a day in my life."

"I didn't say you was jealous of Buddy Pernell," I said, stepping closer to him just to make sure he heard me good and clear. "I said you was jealous of me spendin' time with someone else."

"That's plain stupid."

"Maybe so. But you're the one who's jealous. Not me."

"You know what, Jessie? You go ahead and go on a million dates with Buddy Pernell, and you see how much I care. I can guarantee you I won't spend more'n two seconds thinkin' about it."

His words were knife sharp, but they cut me in a whole different way than they were meant to. I could see by those pink ears of his that I'd gotten under his skin just like I'd planned, and I calmed down with uncharacteristic ease.

"That's just fine with me." I let a mischievous sort of smile crawl onto my face as I backed away from him with small steps. "See you at the dance."

And then I walked away. I'd had the last word and was proud of it. There wasn't any part of me that didn't know with absolute certainty that I'd seen jealousy on Luke Talley's face, and I was filled with more hope from one giant insult than I'd ever been by a thousand tiny pleasantries. There was meaning behind that insult, sure enough.

I walked away from him with the swagger of a confident woman until I rounded the corner out of sight.

And then I hightailed it over to Buddy Pernell's.

I may have been full of all sorts of vinegar when I'd called Luke jealous, but now that I was getting ready for the Independence Day dance with Buddy Pernell, my hands shook like wind-tossed leaves.

"What'll I say to him?" I asked Momma as she finished pinning my hair up for me. "We ain't goin' to have nothin' to talk about."

"Sure you will, baby." Momma looked at my reflection in the mirror and smiled around the bobby pin in her mouth. "You two have known each other for years."

"But we ain't never gone on a date before. I ain't never gone on a date with *nobody* before."

"Everybody's got to have their first date sometime. Don't you worry none." She pulled the bobby pin from her mouth and winked at me in the mirror. "Everythin's goin' to be all right."

But Daddy wasn't feeling things were all right. I could see it on his face as he stood in the doorway of their bedroom, watching Momma fix my hair.

"I hope Buddy's daddy taught him how to treat a lady," he murmured.

"Oh, Buddy Pernell's been taught fine manners, Harley,"

Momma scolded. "He's grown up to be right finer than he was when he was a troublemakin' boy. His momma and daddy saw to that."

Daddy was already dressed in his best clothes, and he watched me uncertainly. "Don't you go leavin' the party with him, Jessilyn," he cautioned. "Ain't no good that goes on outside in the dark at those dances."

"Yes, sir."

"And don't you go dancin' too close."

"Harley," Momma said. "She ain't a little girl no more."

"Don't mean I can't give her no rules at all."

"She'll be fine. Just don't go gettin' her all riled up over nothin'."

He threw his arms out to his sides in exasperation. "It ain't nothin' I'm talkin' about, Sadie. I'm just givin' the girl some fine things to think about. Ain't a girl that can be too careful about growin' boys." He pointed in my direction. "And you make sure you don't get any funny-tastin' punch."

"Harley!" Momma cried again. "Buddy Pernell ain't like that."

"I'm only sayin'. Ain't no tellin' what boys will do when they get the drink in them." Then he rolled his eyes and sighed. "Think of that, will you? Think of our baby with some boy who's sneakin' beers and smokin' and whatnot."

"Harley, we seen plenty of Calloway boys take the drink, but Buddy Pernell ain't one of them. You've gotten yourself so worked up you're seein' Buddy Pernell as a smokin', drinkin' hooligan. Heavens, his momma's a temperance woman."

"Don't mean nothin' if a boy's got a mind of his own."

I sat on the bench and watched the reflections of my momma and daddy as they argued, but I didn't say a thing. I knew all too well what Buddy Pernell was like on the drink. I'd had to fight him off at the dance four years ago on this very day, and the memory of it only made me more nervous now. But I'd never told my momma and daddy about that time with Buddy, and I certainly wasn't going to do it now that I was getting ready to walk out with him.

By this time my stomach was in one tight knot, and I stood up with a jolt when a knock on the door sounded downstairs. "He's here," I yelped. "We ready, then?"

"I s'pose," Daddy sighed. "Guess ain't no one around here but me who'll listen to reason."

Buddy looked as fine as I'd ever seen him, but he could've been a movie star and he'd still never give me butterflies like I got when I was with Luke. I said hello with as much sincerity as I could around my shaky voice, and it was a good thing I managed since all my daddy could do was give him a grunting "Evenin', boy."

Momma flashed Daddy a glare of warning and told Buddy he looked as handsome as his daddy, which, knowing Buddy's daddy, I didn't think was much of a compliment, myself. I just did my best to put on a smile and let Momma keep the conversation up while we walked down the road to the Sutters' barn.

There was once a time when every Independence Day dance was held in Otis Tinker's barn, but that stopped happening when I was thirteen, ever since Mr. Tinker was hanged behind the courthouse for killing two men. It wasn't lost on me, either, that it had been that last dance at the Tinkers' barn when the boy walking beside me had taken drunken liberties with me. It all seemed a lifetime ago that Mr. Tinker protectively pulled Buddy away from me, but I could still remember it with ease. Just like I could remember how different he'd looked the day he saved me from Walt Blevins's violent hands by putting a bullet through his heart. That day, he didn't look like the man I'd known all my life, and he didn't look like a hero who had come to the rescue of his good friend's little girl. All Mr. Tinker looked like was a man poisoned by hatred, one who would gladly kill a man for betraying his devoted stand against racial equality.

It still seemed it would take two lifetimes to spoil Mr. Tinker's dreams because Gemma still wasn't walking to the dance with us. Tonight, just like every other year, she was at a separate dance for colored folks. And just like every other year, we would be sitting across the lake from each other later that night, watching the same fireworks from different sides.

But then, Gemma and I were separated by more than a lake these days.

I could hear the music before we arrived at the barn, and I reached over to give Daddy's guitar a pat. "You plan on playin' tonight, Daddy?"

"S'pose I will," he replied, lifting it up to test the strings. "The old girl's probably out of tune, I ain't played her in so long."

"Ain't no reason for you not to," Momma told him. "I'm always sayin' you ought to play us some songs in the evenin's."

"Got some tired fingers in the evenin's," he said somberly.

We got silent, and I could feel the heavy weight of money troubles sliding back over us, threatening to choke out the levity I'd hoped this evening would bring. Buddy reached out to take my arm and lead me inside, breaking the spell enough to take me by surprise and make my daddy raise an eyebrow. Momma put her elbow into Daddy's ribs to keep him from saying anything, and then she gave me a soft shove in the back so I'd move rather than stand still in one spot out of nervousness.

The barn was already filled with thick smoke—a mixture of cigarettes, pipes, and cigars—and I strained my eyes to scan the room, searching for familiar faces. One familiar face in particular.

Buddy did the usual polite thing and went to fetch something to drink, and that was when I spotted Luke sitting in a chair propped up on the two back legs, his feet resting against a support post. He was dressed up all fit and handsome, and those butterflies started to stir in my stomach. Momma and Daddy were immediately caught up in talking, so I left my spot and wandered over to Luke, making sure to straighten my skirt before I did.

"Evenin', Luke," I said in my best woman's voice.

He'd been staring off into nothing, and the sound of my

voice startled him so his feet slipped off the post and the chair legs crashed to the floor with a bang. He glanced at me in embarrassment, stopping to take a second look that thrilled me to the bone.

"Jessilyn," he said in a one-word greeting, standing up to tower over me.

"Didn't mean to startle you," I said.

"You didn't." But his cheeks were flushed and I could see he was uncomfortable. He took one more look at me and then his eyes moved back to the same nothing he'd been staring at when we came in. "You look right nice tonight, Jessie."

"Momma fixed my hair" was all I could manage to reply without letting my nerves show.

Luke tapped his foot in time to the music and said, "Thought you were comin' with Buddy Pernell."

"I did. He's gettin' some drinks."

Luke leaned against the post he'd had his feet up on. "Seems to me a man shouldn't leave his date right off they get to a dance."

"He's just makin' sure I ain't thirsty. Ain't nothin' wrong about that."

Buddy came up and interrupted us, handing me a glass full of punch. "Hey there, Luke."

"Pernell" was all Luke said, his eyes narrowed in Buddy's direction.

"Don't Jessie look fine tonight?" Buddy asked, beaming at me in a way that made me feel wretched to the core for using him to make Luke jealous. "I swear, you're the prettiest of the bunch, Jessie."

Luke crossed his arms and sighed so loudly I could hear it over the thumping bass. I caught his eye and flashed him the same sort of warning my momma flashed at Daddy, but I didn't feel anywhere near as irritated as I looked. He could cross his arms and sigh all he wanted because I knew just where those reactions were coming from.

I just hoped Buddy didn't notice.

Luke rolled his eyes in response to my look, and I had to tip my head down to try to hide the smile I couldn't hold back.

"You feel like dancin', Jessie?" Buddy boomed, his voice twice as loud as the music behind us.

In truth, I didn't, but my momma hadn't raised a girl to come to a dance with one boy and spend her time with another, so I nodded and smiled. "That'd be nice, Buddy. Luke, would you hold my punch for me?" I asked, knowing just how little he wanted to be left by himself as my official drink holder.

He took my glass with a glare that should have given me cold shivers rather than melt my heart like it did, and I just kept on smiling at him. Buddy was already making his way out to the dance floor, his hand held out in expectation of mine joining it. I took another look back at Luke. "You can have it if you want. I can just get another one."

"Oh, I'll have some, all right," he whispered loudly, taking my arm to keep me from leaving. "Ain't no tellin' what's in this here drink. He probably put alcohol in it to loosen you up."

"Luke Talley!" I said with more shock than I really felt. "You ain't got call to talk like that to a lady." I shook my head and told him, "You sound just like my daddy, anyhow, thinkin' a fine boy like Buddy Pernell would do somethin' so cheap."

"You're too trustin', Jessie; that's your problem."

By now Buddy was in the middle of the dance floor alone, still holding his hand out. I smiled at him to let him know I was coming and then removed Luke's hand from my arm. "I'm bein' rude all because you're worryin' over nothin'. You can test all my drinks tonight if you want to. There ain't nothin' to hide, anyhow."

I could feel Luke's eyes burrowing holes in Buddy's back during the next two dances, and I felt a little sneaky for enjoying it so much when Buddy was being nothing but a gentleman.

By the time we took a break, Luke was still standing there with my drink in his hand, looking none too happy.

"My punch make you drunk yet?" I whispered when we reached him.

"You think it's so funny," he whispered back. "But you'd be thankin' me if I'd found somethin' in it."

I was sure Buddy was wondering what we were talking about, but he didn't say anything. He just helped me into a nearby chair and offered to get some food. "Get you somethin' too, Luke?" he asked.

"I already got myself a couple helpin's while you two were dancin' so close out there."

Buddy nodded, seemingly unaware of Luke's snide remark, and left us. Luke sat next to me and I narrowed my eyes at him.

"What's wrong with you?" I demanded, though I knew very well what was wrong. "You're bein' downright rude."

"And you ain't? Hangin' all over Buddy Pernell like he was a coatrack."

"I was not!"

He looked past me and shook his head slowly. "Whatever you say, Jessie."

"If I'd been inappropriate, my daddy would've been on me in two shakes," I told him. "You're just overreacting."

"Ain't got no reason to overreact. I'm tellin' like I see, is all."

"Then you ain't seein' right." I crossed my arms and sat back in my chair, making sure to smile when Buddy headed back to us with a couple of plates. "Food looks right nice, Buddy. It was nice of you."

"Ain't nothin' to wait on a pretty girl like you, Jessie."

Luke rolled his eyes again and started tapping his foot so hard he made the table shake. I gave his leg a good kick under the table. He shot me a harsh look, but at least he stopped the table from wobbling.

While we ate, Buddy was as attentive as could be, and the whole time we sat at our table, Luke pouted like a four-year-old. I made a memory of it to tell my momma how Luke acted. The way I figured it, if he could act like a child, he couldn't be all that old for a seventeen-year-old like me.

I watched with a smile as my daddy made his way into the band and started playing his guitar with a skill that I had missed seeing. There was a time when Daddy would bring that guitar out nearly every evening, and I'd sit outside on the porch with Gemma, listening to the music float through the window screens. But Gemma and I didn't sit on the porch together these days. And Daddy didn't play his guitar in the evenings, either.

Buddy winked at me and scooted his chair back, but before he could ask me to dance, Luke stood above me.

"Like to dance, Jessie?" he asked, his jaw tense.

My eyes shot up to meet his, and I'm sure my face must have been written all over with the shock I felt. I stumbled to say something but my tongue quit on me.

Luke glanced at Buddy and said, "You mind?"

"Jessie's free to dance with anyone she wants," Buddy said somewhat regretfully. "She ain't got to dance every dance with me."

Luke turned his attention back on me and held out a hand. "Well?"

"I s'pose." I eyed Buddy for a second. "You sure that's all right?"

Buddy shrugged, taking his turn to pout. "Like I said, Jessie, ain't any girl that's got to dance all the dances with one man. You go on and have fun."

"Well . . . ," I murmured, trying to figure out how to make

my legs work again so I could stand up. "I guess if Buddy don't mind . . ."

"Buddy don't mind," Luke reassured me with impatience. "Like he said."

I managed to stand, and I took Luke's hand with a trepidation I'd never felt before when I was with him. The short walk to the dance floor seemed like a beautiful eternity; despite the fact that he was acting like a spoiled child, I reveled in every step I took beside him, his hand around mine. The song was slow, and even though Luke was careful to hold on to me respectfully, I was still close enough to him to break out in goose bumps that I hoped he didn't notice.

It wasn't often I found myself in Luke Talley's arms. More often than not when I did, it was because I was crying like a child, letting his shirt soak up my tears. But I'd never found myself in his arms like a woman before, floating across the floor without words. It was like we'd danced right out of one of my daydreams.

I peeked up at him, but he was looking over my head. "Luke?"

"Hmm?"

"You ain't got to dance with me just to be polite." I studied his face carefully, wondering what truths I'd find there.

"I ain't."

"You sure?"

"Jessilyn, it ain't that big of a deal. It's just a dance."

My eyes lowered involuntarily to his chest. It was a big deal to me.

"Besides, the longer you dance with me," he said, "the less time I have to worry about Buddy Pernell pawin' at you."

My eyes popped back up at him. "He ain't pawin' at me."

"You hear that boy? He's all 'Jessie's this' and 'Jessie's that.' 'She's just the prettiest girl in the county.'"

"So what? There somethin' wrong with him sayin' nice things to me? The way I figure it, a girl's got a right to hear nice things about herself once in a while. Lord knows you ain't goin' to do it."

"Who says I ain't never said nice things about you?" he countered, his blue eyes icy. "I say nice things about you all the time."

"Since when? You ain't never told me I was the prettiest girl in Calloway."

"It don't hold I got to give you the same compliments Buddy Pernell gives you. I can come up with my own nice things to say, can't I?"

I wrinkled my nose at him. "You're just makin' excuses. If you don't think I'm pretty, you ain't got to say a word. It don't bother me any."

"Jessie, I ain't never said I don't think you're pretty." He caught the tip of my shoe under his own and stopped to readjust himself. There was no doubt I had him worked up into a nervous lather.

"Not sayin' I am is near about the same as sayin' I ain't."

"Fine then, you're pretty."

They were the words I'd wanted to hear for four years, but

I wasn't going to take them when he was saying them just to shut me up. "Whatever you say," I muttered. "It don't mean much when you yell it."

We had slowed our steps out of time with the music, and he nearly stopped when he put one hand under my chin and tipped it up. "I don't make a habit of sayin' things I don't mean, Jessilyn," he said in a voice so quiet it barely cleared the music. "If I say you're the prettiest girl I've ever seen, I mean you're the prettiest girl I've ever seen."

There weren't any words on my mind for a few moments, and I stared at him in silence before managing to murmur, "You never said I was the prettiest girl you've ever seen."

"Well then, that's what I meant to say."

I studied his eyes for the sincerity he claimed, and to my delight, I found it there. For about half a minute, we shared a look that told me a thousand things that added up to one—Luke Talley had a spirit that was connected to mine, and no time or place or difference in years could change that. I watched him wordlessly until a screeching guitar chord sounded throughout the barn, snapping our attention away from each other.

I turned to find Daddy's watchful eyes on us, and I knew exactly why he'd lost his way on the instrument he knew so well. He exchanged a look with me and then with my momma, and I knew there would be a discussion between them in bed that night. Daddy would say that I was growing up too fast and who did Luke Talley think he was dancing so close with his baby girl? And Momma would tell him I wasn't his baby girl anymore, and times were coming when Daddy would have to realize that.

But just then, I wasn't so much worried about that conversation as I was happy to have known, for at least a few moments, that my hope wasn't completely unjustified. I turned my eyes back to Luke's, but he'd seen Daddy's face too, and he was more scared of him than I was.

Our moment was over, and Luke walked me back to where Buddy waited with an unhappy face and another plate of ham biscuits.

Luke was nervous for the rest of the night. He watched my daddy as though he were waiting for Daddy to pull a pistol out of his pocket and shoot him dead right there in the Sutters' barn.

For my part, I fairly drifted through the evening, barely hearing a word of the pleasant chatter Buddy kept up for the next two hours. He was a fine boy, I was sure, and he thought the world of me, but I was no good at this courting thing, and I felt out of place every time I tried to interact with him. It was enough for me to just let him talk and keep my mind focused on my dance with Luke. That way I was comfortable. But every time I had to dance with Buddy, I only wanted to be dancing with Luke, and I felt clumsy and out of sorts, stepping on his toes so much I was sure he'd be buying new church shoes come Monday.

When it was time for the fireworks, we all walked to the lake together. On our way, Daddy made sure to wedge himself in between me and Buddy, and Luke made sure to keep himself far away from me while Daddy was around. At the lake, Momma made good and sure to pull Daddy down beside her, leaving Buddy to sit next to me. Luke plopped down onto the grass behind us all.

I peered across the lake to where all the colored folk sat, and after a minute I spotted Gemma sitting alone, her back against a big oak. Every year that I'd known Gemma, I'd hated not being able to share the fireworks, but she always refused to cause a stir by sitting with us, and she wouldn't let me come sit with her, either. Gemma could be stubborn that way sometimes.

But the real problem was that this year she wouldn't have sat with me even if the world had suddenly gone color-blind. Sitting there with Buddy Pernell beside me and Luke behind me, I wondered at what a long way we'd come since the day Luke saved me from Buddy in the swimming hole.

And I marveled at what a long way we still had to go.

Chapter 16

God must have been trying to teach us a lesson, so Miss Cleta had told me most mornings I'd gone to work for her that summer. Miss Cleta saw a lesson in every hard time, and those hot, dry summer mornings were no exception.

"The good Lord's got a reason for everythin'," she told me as I wiped my feet on her front mat the Monday after my first date.

I hadn't slept much that night, and it didn't help to be attacked by clouds of heat when I stepped outside that morning. It felt like getting hit in the face with a wet mop, and I was pouring sweat by the time I got to Miss Cleta's.

"Don't see as how heat like this can have a reason, Miss Cleta," I murmured with a heavy tongue. I tripped as I moved inside the house and gave her a little grimace. "My legs ain't workin' this morning. Too hot for a body to work right."

"Oh, there's a reason for this heat, Miss Jessie," she assured me, ignoring my ungraceful entrance into her house. "If there's one thing I know, it's there's a good reason for everythin'. It's knowin' that truth that gets me through this crazy life."

I decided not to argue. "Yes'm," I muttered. "Anyways, I'd rather spend a hot mornin' over here than at home doin' nothin'."

"You know what they say about idle hands," she told me, clearly in agreement with my statement. "Though what we'll be doin' this mornin', I don't know. There's to be no outdoor work, that's for certain. I don't want you keelin' over with the heatstroke."

"Yes'm. You got any dustin' needs done or anythin'?"

"Just did the house last night when I couldn't sleep."

"I couldn't sleep, neither." I ran a finger over her mantelpiece while she wasn't looking. Her eyesight wasn't as good as it once was, and I sometimes went back over her work to fix it up a bit. "Well, you got some dishes need washin' or some floor cleanin' to do?"

Miss Cleta shook her head, and I wondered fleetingly if she was wasting her money on paying me to help her. It seemed she got her work done just fine without me.

"I'll tell you what," Miss Cleta said with a sudden look of certainty. "We'll be ladies of leisure today. What do you think of that? I had Mr. Stokes bring me in some of those silly ladies' magazines, though heaven knows why since they're filled with nothin' but nonsense. We can put our feet up, have some lemonade, and read some things that don't mean much of anythin'."

"I could use a little bit of nothin', Miss Cleta. But don't you go payin' me for doin' nonsense."

"Now don't you go tellin' me how to pay my employees, Jessilyn Lassiter."

"I wouldn't feel right gettin' paid for no work. You know that. You already gave me a paid day off last week."

"Well then, I'll give you some work. This afternoon we'll fix up somethin' nice for Mae and Nate's supper and you can run it on over. You know, she ain't been up to doin' much, especially with the baby so near to comin', and Nate . . ." She trailed off, seeming to think twice about telling me her true thoughts about Nate Colby. "Well, she could use some good food in her condition, is all, and I'm sure he'd be happy with some nourishment too."

My heart skipped a beat at the mention of Mae's name. I hadn't seen her since I'd made her cry, and Nate had warned me not to come by, after all. But Nate was a man so eaten up by heartache and revenge he hadn't even shown up for Callie's funeral. I figured most of what he said these days didn't stand to much reason.

I knew Mae needed help, but I felt unqualified to help her, and knowing what I knew about how Callie had died, it was hard to even look Mae straight in the eye.

"You sure she wants company?" I asked, removing a dead rose from a vase of flowers Miss Cleta had sitting on her kitchen table. "Maybe she needs some quiet."

"You don't have to stay long. And don't you worry none about Mae gettin' upset. You can just take the food on over, get her settled with it, and come on back here."

Truth be told, I wanted nothing of it. I'd had enough confrontation already, and I didn't want to have to find some way to be good to Mae without letting my fear and guilty conscience show through. But I knew Miss Cleta would take that food over herself if I didn't, and as spry as she was, carting all that food over to Mae's still wasn't something she needed to be doing.

True to her nature, Miss Cleta noted my anxiety, and she put a small, bony hand to my cheek. "You got problems weighin' on you, Jessilyn Lassiter," she said sweetly, her head cocked to one side. "Ain't still about your daddy's farm, is it?"

Not wanting her to dig too deeply, I forced myself to smile back and said, "S'pose so, Miss Cleta. With this dry, hot weather, there's always a worry hangin' over our farm."

"Well then, I guess we'd best get your mind off of things." She poured two tall glasses of lemonade, dropped some berries into them, and nodded her head toward the living room. "We'll use the good sofa today."

I followed her in and retrieved the magazines from the shelf she directed me to. I felt almost sinful sitting on Miss Cleta's treasured sofa, but I settled in over a piece of short fiction. Every now and again Miss Cleta would let out a hoot and show me some silly picture or outlandish dress pattern.

It was a day for enjoying good company, and we certainly

took advantage of it, eating food and chatting like girlfriends at a slumber party. But when the clock struck four, my nerves started to fray. I knew I'd be expected to tend to Mae soon.

Miss Cleta stretched and yawned. "Reckon we got some cookin' and bakin' to do. Ain't nothin' like kitchen work to clear a woman's mind." She hurried to the icebox and poked her head inside. "Question is, what do we fix without heatin' the house up more than it already is?"

An hour later I walked slowly to Mae's house with a tray of ham biscuits, a bowl of pickled beets tottering danger-ously on top. Over one arm I carried a shopping bag filled with corn bread and fried okra, and Miss Cleta had topped me off by sticking a pastry box filled with chocolate-covered strawberries under one arm. I was breathless from the effort of balancing everything with precise skill, and breathless-ness was no way to help my frayed nerves.

I had no words to say to Mae when she opened that door. There were dark circles under her once-brilliant blue eyes, and the house behind her showed increased signs of neglect.

"Jessilyn," she murmured, forcing a soulless smile. "Miss Cleta got you to work again?"

"Yes'm."

Mae opened the door wider in a gesture that urged me to come in. "Best not call me *ma'am*, Jessilyn. You'll be makin' me feel old. You ain't no little girl no more, you know."

I smiled at her, but my lips were shaky when I did it, and I bit my lower one to avoid letting her see it. "I best set this down before I drop it all," I said to give me something to do. I set about putting the containers on her crowded kitchen table. Flies circled the food immediately, and I swatted them away with a wave of my hand. "Darn flies are a sight this summer. Can't keep 'em off with a stick."

Mae put the cold foods in the icebox and then leaned back against it heavily. "Ain't noticed the flies much," she murmured, her gaze set on nothing in particular. "Ain't noticed much of nothin' these days."

I said nothing and began to clear the table that had become a gathering place for old newspapers, dirty tin cups, and stale bread crusts. In the streaming afternoon sun, glistening particles of dust floated through the air, telling unspoken stories of Mae's grief.

"I best get some of this cleaned up," I told her. "You just rest, and I'll pick up a bit, okay?"

She nodded lamely and flashed me a wry smile. "Ain't had much energy lately."

"You got yourself a baby comin'. Ain't much you should be doin' in this heat but restin'," I said as much to soothe her, but I knew the reason for the messy house had nothing to do with Mae's pregnancy. I threw some crumbs into the trash bin and smiled at Mae. "Can I get you somethin' to drink?"

She just shook her head and continued to rest against the icebox.

I scooped up an armload of newspapers, stumbling over a pair of dirty work boots on my way to drop the papers at the front door. "I'll take these papers home and get rid of them for you."

I could tell by her silence that she wasn't hearing me, and when I returned to the kitchen, I found her in the same position she'd been when I'd left her thirty seconds earlier, still with an unnerving blank stare. I stepped in front of her gaze, hoping to get her attention, but she was still as a statue, barely blinking.

"Why don't you let me help you sit down?" I asked. "I'll clear off that comfy chair in the den so you can take a load off, okay?" I hurriedly attacked the crowded overstuffed chair, pulling the pile of unknown items into my arms in one fell swoop. A few things slipped from my grasp and tumbled to the floor, and I glanced down to avoid stepping on them.

Mae's silence only made my shaky hands worse, and I made more of a mess than I'd begun with just trying to help. I went to Mae and put my arm about her waist to usher her over to the chair. "You look all thin these days. Best put some meat on your bones."

Mae said nothing and wouldn't move a muscle. I could feel her breath coming in short spurts, and I realized that her blouse was soaked with sweat.

I looked at her pale, clammy skin and murmured, "Mae? You all right?"

Without speaking, she clutched the edge of the icebox, her fingers turning white with the pressure.

"Mae?" I asked anxiously, my voice rising in fear. "What's wrong?"

The whole of her weight was on me now, and I struggled to keep her from falling to the floor. Slowly I buckled my knees and managed to lower her gently, letting her head down last. She turned onto her side and tucked her knees up, her breathing now coming in loud gasps, and it wasn't until I felt the wet floor beneath my feet that it occurred to me what was wrong.

"The baby's comin'," I exclaimed, mostly to myself. "Dear Lord, it's comin'." I wiped sweat from my own forehead, then leaned close to her face and said, "Mae, you just rest here while I go get Miss Cleta, okay? She can come set with you while I get Doc to come help, you hear?"

I was out the door in a flash, tripping over the stack of old newspapers on my way. Despite the fact that pain shot up through my foot, I didn't slow my pace for a second. Poor Miss Cleta was startled out of her rocker when I rushed into the house, letting the screen door slam behind me.

"What on earth?" she hollered when she caught sight of me. "You're enough to make an old woman catch her death."

"It's Mae's baby, Miss Cleta! She done broke her water all over the kitchen floor."

"I'll go to her," she assured, pushing me through the door as she spoke. "You put wings on those feet of yours, Miss Jessilyn, and go fetch the doc quick as lightnin'."

I ran down Miss Cleta's porch steps and square into Luke.

"Where're you goin' in such an all-fired hurry, Jessie?" he asked me, that edgy tone still coloring his voice. He pulled me to a stop with a firm grip on my arms. "Watch where you're goin'!"

If my mind hadn't been heavy with the weight of worry over Mae and her baby, I would have turned all my frustration and hurt feelings out on Luke and the harsh way he'd often taken with me of late. But as things were, all I could do was shove his hands away from my arms and breathlessly tell him to get out of my way.

"I've got to get Doc," I insisted loudly. "Let me go!"

My mention of the doctor pulled him out of his insensitive mood, and his face changed from frustration to fear.

"Who's sick?" he asked quickly. "Miss Cleta?"

"Mae!" I called as I ran past him. "She's havin' the baby."

I looked over my shoulder when I heard the screen door slam.

"Luke, the good Lord sent you here," Miss Cleta told him in relief. "You've got longer legs'n Jessilyn. Run on off to get the doc. Mae ain't got much time."

Miss Cleta carried a tapestry bag that hung by two wooden rungs over her arm. She was moving at a pace I didn't think she had in her, and before I could say anything else, Luke ran past me so fast he stirred up a breeze.

"Let the boy get help," she told me. "I'll need you here."

"But what'll we do if he doesn't get Doc here in time?"

"I delivered enough babies back in my day, Miss Jessie. It's poor Mae I'm worried over. She's in a bad state in her mind right now, and I'm worried she might not have much strength for what's ahead."

My blood chilled with her words, but I appreciated that she was treating me with enough respect to tell me the frightening truth. Behind Miss Cleta, I entered Mae's house with trepidation.

We found Mae right where I'd left her, but she was far worse than she'd been moments earlier. Her hair was matted with sweat, strings of it sticking to her crimson face. Her breathing came in quick, short gasps. But what frightened me most was the vacant expression on her face. Despite her obvious pain, Mae Colby looked into space, her eyes still focused on something that didn't exist.

I flashed Miss Cleta a desperate look, but she couldn't console me in any way. She only shook her head slowly, her mouth clenched.

"We've got to get that baby out," she murmured. "This poor girl ain't got the will to live."

Suddenly I felt my whole body tense up with complete devastation. Nate Colby had lost his daughter, and I'd seen firsthand what sort of fiery hell his mind had been thrown into since then. I couldn't imagine what he'd do if he lost his wife and possibly his new baby all in one hot summer.

I dropped to my knees and mopped Mae's forehead with the bottom of my dress. "It'll be all right, Mae," I said, my words coming out in barely more than a whisper. "It'll be okay. You'll see. Hang on, and we'll help you through just fine. Me and Miss Cleta . . . we'll be here for you. Just hang on."

But while I spoke, I saw nothing in those eyes but surrender, and I felt as though my life were draining away with hers.

Miss Cleta knelt at Mae's feet, and I heard her exclaim in dismay. "Ain't much longer now," she said, rummaging through her worn-out bag.

"What should I do?" I asked anxiously.

"Just stay where you're at, Jessilyn. You're doin' a fine job. Just try and help her through the pain."

I turned my attention back to Mae, and though her eyes remained lifeless, I could feel her hand tighten on mine, giving me some hope that there was enough strength left in her to help her bring another life into the world.

A picture of Callie flashed through my mind, and I felt tears prick at my eyelashes. We'd already lost one young life in Calloway, and I wanted more than anything at that moment to see her little brother or sister bless our town with the life we'd lost at the hands of Joel Hadley.

Mae's face never changed, but I could tell when the pain was at its worst because she'd grip my hand hard and her breath would catch in her throat.

"Breathe for me, Mae," I begged. "You need some air. Keep breathin'."

"This baby's comin'," Miss Cleta determined. "It's comin' fast." Then I heard her exhale sharply. "It's comin' out backwards," she told me, and in her voice I could hear the same fear I felt inside me. "We're gonna need Doc. Dear Jesus, bring that man to me quick."

Her plea to Jesus brought to mind all the prayers I'd heard my momma send up to Him over the years, and I recited every word I could remember while I leaned over

Mae. Momma's prayers were nothing fancy, and they weren't rhymes or Scripture verses. They were just words, conversations. But I said things as I thought my momma would say them now.

I wished she were there to do it for me.

I was leaning so close to Mae that I could feel her breath on my cheek, and I was startled by a sudden moan that escaped through her parched lips. I backed up quickly, my heart racing so fast I almost couldn't feel it. Her face was still painted with the same ghostly expression. Sounds of emotion coming from a face devoid of it was such a contradiction, it stirred up fear in my heart of a kind I'd never known.

"Miss Cleta?" I asked, so many questions combined into one name.

She knew what I was saying just by calling out to her, but there was no easy answer to give. "I don't know, honey. Just keep holdin' on to her."

Miss Cleta's grunts of exertion told me the baby wasn't having an easy time coming, and I prayed harder and harder, begging God to listen, begging Him to send help.

But none came. It was just me and Miss Cleta and a woman who looked to be dying slowly before my eyes. Mae was pale and clammy, and when I saw the puddle of blood at her feet, I knew we'd lost her as good as if her heart had stopped beating already. I just knew in my bones that we'd be laying Mae down beside her daughter before the week was out.

"She ain't comin' round," I cried to Miss Cleta. "I can't hear her breathin' barely at all."

"I got her," Miss Cleta called out, her voice shaking with exertion and fear. "I got the baby girl out. You stay with Mae, now," she said firmly. "That girl needs you."

But she didn't need me. Not anymore. I took one look at the baby and glanced back to her mother to find that Mae had held on only long enough to bring her baby into the world. Those eyes that had held such a vacant stare through her agony had at least relaxed into a sort of complacency, and I reached up slowly, my hand shaking so much I could barely control its movement, to close her weary eyes.

"It's all right, Mae," I whispered, my tears flowing freely. "You rest now. We'll watch out for your baby. Don't you worry none."

My words came out in sobs, but over them I could hear the baby utter her first cries, and I found my sobs combined with laughter out of relief that we hadn't lost them both. But my laughter dissolved back into body-wrenching sobs in a few seconds, and I laid my body across Mae's, full of heartache and anger.

The screen door slammed, and I looked up to see Dr. Mabley and Luke rushing into the room.

Dr. Mabley took one look at the scene before him and sighed, his shoulders dropping in helplessness. "Is she gone?" he asked me.

"Yes'r."

"Then the Lord bless her soul," he murmured before taking the baby from Miss Cleta's arms. She followed him into the living room, leaving me and Luke alone with what I once knew as Mae Colby.

"She died," I said to Luke, unable to look him in the eye. "I prayed to God and everythin', but He took her anyway."

Luke came over to me and pulled me away. And though I clung to Mae, reluctant to leave her alone, he managed to move me away. He grabbed an apron and laid it over her face before reaching out to me. I fell into his arms and let my tears come out in painful moans.

He lifted me up into his arms and carried me outside, past the new baby and away from the death. I was shaking from head to toe. Luke set me down on the Colbys' front porch and pushed my hair back from my forehead.

"Stop breathin' so hard, Jessie," he ordered. "You'll faint dead away." His face was creased with a hardened expression, his jawbone poking out. "We ain't got need for the doc to have to start tendin' to you."

He talked harshly, but he watched me with worried eyes. I was starting to feel dizzy. Mae's lifeless face flashed across my mind like I was watching it on a movie screen, and I stared at him in desperation, wishing he could make it all go away.

But he couldn't.

"Why?" I managed to ask between gasps. "Why would God take that baby's momma away?"

"Maybe Mae's in a better place, Jessie."

"That's preacher talk! It don't help me understand God any." I waved my hand toward Mae's front door. "Mae was too young to die. She weren't but five years older than me, you know that? Someday that could be me lyin' there on the kitchen floor."

Luke took my face in his rough hands. "Stop talkin' like that!"

The sound of footsteps grabbed our attention, and we turned to see Nate Colby rushing up the walkway.

"What's goin' on?" His glassy eyes settled on me, and one look at my face told him more than enough. "Mae?" he shouted, leaping past me and Luke. "Mae!"

Luke's hands dropped from my face, but I grabbed them hard and held them tightly. We sat motionless, frozen by the cries of terror coming from the Colby house. We must have heard Nate call his wife's name at least a dozen times, and each time was like a knife plunging into my heart.

"Let's go away from here," Luke finally said. "We can't help now. I'll take you home."

Despite the ninety-degree weather, my teeth chattered, and as much as I wanted to stop hearing Nate Colby's sobs, I couldn't make myself move.

Luke gently tugged at my hands. "Come on, Jessie. Let's go home."

His voice sounded distant to me, and my mind was clouded with images I couldn't wish away—images of Callie's body lying broken by the roadside, of Mae's blank, staring eyes and Nate's terror-stricken face.

And of Joel Hadley.

My despair began to turn to rage in the instant that I

thought of him. It was Joel who had stolen Callie from us, who had bewitched and betrayed Gemma, who had ripped away Mae Colby's will to live. The hate that welled up within me was terrifying and satisfying all at once, and in my state, I had no sense of reason in me.

With sudden ferocity, I looked at Luke and said through tightly clenched teeth, "I'm goin' to kill him."

Luke's eyes narrowed in confusion. "What're you talkin' about? You're goin' to kill who?"

I ignored him and just said again, with even more conviction, "I'm goin' to kill him!"

My fury increased until I was shaking in near convulsions, and I felt like my blood would boil to a point that I'd explode.

Luke's face reflected intense worry, and he took me by my shoulders and shook me a little. "Jessilyn, what's wrong?"

I stared back at him, my breathing becoming almost a moan, and as much as I wanted to ease his desperate anxiety, I couldn't think well enough to speak rationally. For all I tried, I couldn't get Mae's face out of my mind, and it only fueled the angry fire that burned in my very soul.

"Jessilyn!" Luke cried, his voice rising in panic. "Stop! Stop shakin' and breathe. You're scarin' me. What's wrong?"

I got up suddenly, wrenching free from his grasp, and ran. It was the only thing I could think to do. My mind was so overwhelmed that my body was taken over by nervous tension. Sitting still was too much to bear, and I knew where I was going—to the Hadleys.

It was hot and humid, and the air was suffocating, perfectly still and smelling of clover and cut grass, but I kept running though my lungs felt heavy and overworked.

I ran through the trees and brush, hardly hearing the cries of Luke behind me, until I reached a small, mostly dry creek. The muddy bottom caught at my feet and forced me to slow down until I dropped to my knees in sheer exhaustion. My breaths were nothing but wheezes, and I tucked my head down over my knees, gasping for air.

Luke came up behind me and caught me by the shoulders, turning me a little so I could face him.

My eyes were filmed over with tears, but I could still see the abject terror in his eyes, and I was filled with pity for him. I knew I was putting him through a little piece of hell, but I didn't know how to say aloud how I felt.

He put his hands to my face and said, "Jessilyn, I don't know what's goin' on, but I got to help. That's the only thing I know how to do, and you got to let me do it." There were tears in his own eyes now, and I knew in another more lucid moment, he'd be ashamed for me to see them. "Who is it you're so mad at to kill?"

I ducked my head to gather in a few more breaths, steadied myself for a moment, and looked back up into his eyes. Then, as though his name were poison, I hissed, "Joel Hadley." Just saying his name aloud built up my strength, and I sat up straight and confident, opening my eyes full wide. "Joel Hadley," I repeated with more surety. "It's Joel Hadley I'm talkin' about, and I'm goin' to kill him for what he's done."

Luke had never liked Joel Hadley, and I could see right away that my mention of his name put fire in his eyes.

"What'd he do to you?" he demanded, his grip on my arms now almost painful. "Did he hurt you?"

I shook my head. "Not like you think he did."

"Then how?"

I no longer cared about my vow to Gemma. Witnessing death had destroyed any sense of loyalty I'd held to that promise, and I pointed back in the general direction of Mae's house before saying, "He killed Mae's girl. He killed Callie."

"What d'you mean he killed Callie? You mean he was drivin' that car?"

I nodded eagerly, willing myself to breathe in a steady fashion. "He killed Callie, he betrayed Gemma, he threatened me, he threatened my daddy, and now Mae's gone because of what he did. I swear to the heavens, Luke, I'm goin' to kill him!"

Luke looked like he was going to kill someone himself just then, and I backed away from him even though I knew he'd never lay a hurtful hand on me. He got up onto his feet and moved away from me, his hands balled into fists. He swore loudly, the first time he'd ever spoken disrespectfully right in front of me, and then he turned my way again.

"You should've told me this right away," he argued, taking his frustrations out on me. "Why don't you never remember that you can't take care of everythin' yourself? I done told you before that anytime anyone gives you trouble, you're to tell me."

I might have normally given him grief right back, but this time all I could do was stare at him. Deep down, I knew he was just lashing out because of his concern for me, but I backed farther away when his voice rose even more.

"You ain't never got reason to talk to trash like Joel Hadley, you hear? You leave him to me. I'll take care of Joel Hadley."

He swore again, and my discomfort must have shown on my face because his own expression suddenly softened into shame.

"Jessie," he said meekly, taking two long strides to stand in front of me. He took my face in his hands. "I'm sorry. I didn't mean to scare you."

I shook my head while it rested between his strong hands and said, "It's all right. You didn't really scare me."

He kept talking like he'd never heard me say anything. "Your daddy would kill me if he heard me talkin' like that in front of you. I'm sorry, Jessie. I shouldn't have said things like that."

"It's okay."

And it really was okay. Watching him vent his own anger had somehow helped ease mine, and I actually managed to turn one corner of my mouth up into a stiff smile. "I won't tell Daddy," I murmured.

He managed a small smile of his own and tipped his forehead down to rest it against mine. "We'll be all right, Jessie," he whispered. "You ain't goin' to kill anyone, and I ain't goin' to kill anyone. But we'll be all right. It'll all come out right."

Despite all that I'd been through, I believed him. There, with his hands supporting me, his heart beating so closely to my own, I believed we could get through the fires of hell.

As long as we did it together.

Chapter 17

There was blood on my hands, and I stared down, watching the tears drip onto the crimson splotches. "It's Mae's," I murmured.

Luke took his arm from my shoulders and pulled out a handkerchief. He dipped it into the one small pool of water in the creek bed and used it to scrub my hands. Once they were clean, he took them in his hands and spread my palms out, running his thumbs over them.

"There," he said. "It's gone."

I looked up into his face with no expression. "So's Mae."

He didn't say a word. He just watched me as I slowly took to my feet. I looked into his eyes and said with fierce determination, "I'm goin' to the Hadleys'."

Luke stepped back and folded his arms, blocking my way like a sentry. "No you ain't!"

"I ain't goin' to do nothin' stupid. I just want to see his face when I tell him what happened."

"Jessie, he ain't goin' to care any more than he cared about killin' Callie. That boy don't think about nothin' or no one except himself."

"Then maybe we best make him."

I got up and trudged off through the woods with a mission. I knew where I'd find Joel Hadley. He'd be home in that big house of his, wasting time like always.

Luke was behind me quick as a flash, and he swung me around by one arm to face him. "I'm a lot bigger'n you, Jessilyn. I got ways to keep you from goin'."

"You ain't never manhandled me before, Luke Talley, and you ain't goin' to start now." I shook my arm free of his grasp. "I'm goin' to the Hadleys'. You can either come with me or stay behind, but I'm goin'."

His glare was almost painful, but I knew I couldn't rest until I saw Joel Hadley face-to-face. It was suddenly like an obsession for me.

And Luke knew it.

He took me by the arm, wordlessly and much more calmly this time, and steered me through the brush. We said nothing to each other as we walked. The breeze we had become so accustomed to this summer stirred my hair and whispered things in my ears. *Joel Hadley,* it said. *It was Joel Hadley who killed Callie and Mae.*

I didn't need the breeze to tell me that. I already knew. And I was going to tell him so.

We reached the Hadleys' property from the back side, and my heart started to pound in anticipation as we walked through their meadow.

Joel Hadley hadn't fired Gemma, even after my words with him, so I knew I'd find her there. I had it in my mind that he was just keeping her around to make sure he could keep her quiet, and the very thought stirred my blood even more.

We found Gemma outside hanging laundry, and I cringed at the sight of her pinning up britches for a family like them. She glanced over her shoulder at the sound of us coming, and though most of her manners toward me of late had been harsh, one look at us as we were then made her drop the clean laundry on the grass. "What's happened?" she asked, her face creased with worry.

I couldn't say what I wanted to tell her. I was still focused on one thing. "Where's Joel?"

She watched my eyes closely and then raised a finger toward the far side of the property. "He's in the barn puttin' his horse away." She didn't try to stop us when we continued on to find him. She only followed behind, anxious to know what had sent Luke and me on our journey to find Joel Hadley.

Joel turned quickly when we entered the barn, mostly because Luke had thrown the door open so viciously, it shook the whole structure. There was a colored boy in the barn, taking the reins from Joel, and he jumped a mile with the noise.

Joel's face was livid, his temperature rising faster than Calloway's on an August morning. "Gemma!" he called once he caught sight of her. "What in tarnation is goin' on?"

She stood by without words, her face stricken.

"You ain't got no call to come bargin' in here," Joel said to Luke, but he backed away after seeing his face. "This here's Hadley property, after all," he added weakly.

"Jessie's got somethin' to say to you," Luke told him, leaving no room for Joel to reject me.

The boy who held the reins walked backward slowly, looking like he was planning to escape before trouble started.

"You see the blood here?" I asked, pulling my skirt out to display the remnants of Mae's tragedy. "You see that?"

At the mention of blood, Gemma gasped, but she didn't say a word.

Joel's eyes were wide but not so full of fear and dread as I might have wished, and I took a step closer to him. "This here blood's from the momma of that girl you killed. She done bled to death on her kitchen floor, and all because she lost hope that day you struck down her baby girl."

With that revelation, Gemma's sobs filled the barn, echoing in my ears, and I felt light-headed and suddenly too weary to stand. My knees buckled, and I felt Luke's arm go around my waist to hold me up.

I didn't have the strength to do any more, but I didn't have to. It was Gemma's turn.

Her face glistened with tears and her look reminded me of the one I'd seen in Mae's eyes not long ago, only Gemma's eyes were filled with fire. She lunged at Joel, pounding his chest with a sort of fury I'd never seen in her before.

Luke and I watched in shock until suddenly Joel grabbed Gemma by the arms and threw her to the ground.

That was all it took for Luke to lose any restraint he possessed. He let go of me and flew at Joel, punching him in the face once, only to pull him back and hit him again.

Joel Hadley had seemed very cavalier when he'd thrown Gemma down, but in the presence of Luke's fists, he was no more than the perfect picture of the coward I'd always known him to be. I dropped to Gemma's side and held her while we watched Luke rear back for another blow, but Joel threw his hands to his bloody face, pleading for mercy. He rested on his knees, his upper half held up by Luke's grasp on his shirt, and moaned in desperation, begging Luke to stop.

I could see Luke wanted nothing more than to hit him a few more times, but he thought better of it and let go of Joel's shirt, letting him drop with a thud. Joel scooted away quickly and ended up cowering in a corner, his clothes covered with hay.

Luke stood, glaring at him and shaking his sore hand; then he turned away and murmured, "Lousy coward."

Joel wasn't a man accustomed to humiliation, and he bristled at Luke's threatening tone. He narrowed his eyes in a failed attempt to cover his fear. "You best get off my land, Talley. Before I fetch my niggers to whip you up one side and down the other."

"That's right," Luke said, turning about with a smirk.

"You go on and get your hired boys to fight your battles for you. That's what you Hadleys have always done. Bunch of cowards!"

Then he gathered me and Gemma in his arms and walked us home. The little colored boy had left his hiding place and gave Luke a nod of respect when we passed him by. Outside the barn we discovered that a crowd of servants had assembled, and they all stood in a line, dipping their heads in a sort of deference to us. I took one more look behind me and saw Joel standing shakily in the doorway, his blood forming polka dots down his shirtfront.

"What're you lookin' at?" he screamed at the group of servants he'd threatened to send after Luke. It was clear by their expressions of scorn that he would never have managed to rally them against us in a month of Sundays. "Get back to work!"

The group slowly dispersed, shaking their heads but bound to do as they were told. Times were tough for finding work in Calloway, but they were tougher for colored folks, and I flashed them all a rueful glance because I knew that though we could walk away from the Hadleys and never look back, they had to stay or go hungry.

"Wish we were rich as Hadleys so we could hire them all," I murmured as we left them behind.

"We ain't rich, maybe," Gemma said, untying her apron and dropping it symbolically to the ground, "but we're a lot richer in the important things than them Hadleys could ever be."

I reached my arm behind Luke and tugged at Gemma's dress. She glanced at me and smiled the smile I'd missed so much in the past days.

I grinned back, and suddenly my weariness and sorrow didn't feel quite so heavy because I knew I didn't have to carry them by myself. I was surrounded by people who would help.

Chapter 18

We told Momma and Daddy the truth of it all that night, and Daddy was fit to be tied.

"There ain't no call for you girls to hold back somethin' like that just because you're worried for me," he argued. "Don't you never let anyone's cowardly threats make you suffer like that again, you hear?"

Gemma and I only had the strength to nod. I was sure he had more he wanted to say, but he could see we were sick inside, and he put his arms around both of us at the same time. "You get on to bed," he murmured. "A rest will be good for you."

Momma shuffled us off to bathe and then to bed, sniffling all the while, but neither Gemma nor I slept much that night.

The day after Luke had planted his fist into Joel Hadley's smug face, we all piled into the truck, even Luke, and headed into town to talk to the sheriff. Nate Colby was inconsolable and gave no mind to the baby, so Miss Cleta had taken her in for the time being, and some of our time in town would be spent gathering supplies for her to care for her new charge. She was nameless, that poor child, and as fatherless as she was motherless.

My momma had the looks of a headache about her eyes, as she had since the tragedy yesterday, and I knew the future of that baby weighed heavy on her mind. Everything laid heavy on our minds that day, and Luke, Gemma, and I were silent as we bumped along in the back of Daddy's truck.

I glanced over at Luke, who was lost in thought, his hand flexing in and out mindlessly at his side. "That hurt?" I murmured over the noise of the truck.

My words broke his reverie, and he peered at me from underneath his low-slung hat. "What's that?"

"Your hand," I said, nodding toward it. "It hurt? You keep bending it around like it hurts."

He shook his head. "Hadleys got hard heads, is all. Ain't nothin' that won't mend on its own."

"Maybe we should bind it up. Might make it feel better."

"The one thing that makes it feel better is rememberin' why it hurts." He grinned at me, one blue eye flashing me a wink from beneath his hat. "You ain't got to worry over me, Jessie. I'll be fine."

"Ain't never a day you're gonna convince me to not worry over you, Luke Talley. Besides, you're always worryin' over me."

"Well now, I figure I got me good reason to," he said, tugging my ponytail, "seein' as how you're an expert at gettin' into trouble and all."

I could have thought of a million ways to argue with him, but I was in no mood for belligerence that day. I rolled my eyes and let him have the last word. My right foot rested next to Gemma's leg, and I tipped it out to give her a nudge. She gave me her restless attention for a second, and we shared a wordless message with our faces. I could see she was feeling beat up with guilt just as much as she could see I was sorry for it. It was just that there were no words to say, and we shrugged at each other, both wishing we could wake up and find these last weeks had been nothing but a dream.

When the truck rolled into town, the three of us tumbled out of the back in silence, my only consolation of the day being when Luke took my waist in his fine strong hands to lift me from the truck. Being a gentleman, he did the same for Gemma, but I knew that his hands said more when they held me. Tragedy or no, I was still alive enough inside to see things were changing between him and me, and I let it be the one thing that kept my head above the troubled waters that surrounded us.

The sheriff wasn't in when we got there, and Daddy gave the deputy who told us so a long sigh.

"Ain't that man ever around when a body needs him?" he muttered.

"He'll be back soon, I reckon."

"Well, I reckon we'll be back here soon too. We got

important business to discuss with him, so you make good and sure he don't leave again before we see him, you hear?"

The deputy nodded, but I could see Daddy didn't trust him more than he trusted a snake, so he told us he'd wait in the jailhouse for the sheriff.

"You may as well go and get things for the baby while I wait," he told us.

So Momma, Gemma, Luke, and I scattered out, each with items to find. It was my job to pick out some fabric so Momma could sew some clothes for the Colby baby.

It was a sad task, and Mrs. Noble didn't do much to help my troubles as she was filling my order. "Seems a real shame havin' Mae pass on like that," she murmured while her scissors worked. "A right shame at that. Makes a body wonder what Nate Colby will do, raisin' a girl all on his lonesome. A baby ought to have her momma around; that's what I say."

I ignored her and let my eyes wander around the store. After all, she talked on no matter if she had an audience or not. There was a blue dress in the front window that had caught my eye, and I wondered if Momma could make me one like it. I left Mrs. Noble to her mourning and scissors and walked to the window, fingering the soft fabric while I made a memory of the dress in my head for telling Momma later.

As I stood there, a voice I knew as well as my own carried in from outside, overshadowing the drone of Mrs. Noble's endless chatter. My eyes flicked up and saw Luke standing on the sidewalk, a look of pure frustration painted across his face. Sheriff Clancy was in front of him, a finger pointed toward Luke's chest.

"I ain't sayin' I ain't done it," Luke argued. "What I'm sayin' is he had it comin'."

The sight of Joel Hadley standing next to the sheriff told me there was trouble sure enough, and I forgot about the dress fabric and Mrs. Noble's conversation and ran out the door in a flash.

"What's goin' on?" I demanded. "Sheriff givin' you some kind of trouble, Luke?"

"Not so much trouble as he gave Joel Hadley yesterday," the sheriff muttered without taking his eyes from Luke's face. "Now you gonna come with me peaceful-like or do I have to get official with you?"

"Come with you where?" I wedged my body into the small space that separated the three men and squared up eye level with the sheriff. "To jail? You makin' a habit of arrestin' law-abidin' folks?"

"Don't you start with me now, Jessilyn. I got me a job to do and I aim to do it whether you're standin' in my way or not."

"Jessilyn," Luke said behind me, "I ain't got to have you fightin' my battles for me."

"I ain't fightin' no battle. I'm just tryin' to tell the sheriff here if he's determined to go arrestin' people, then he best look to his left and hook himself a real lawbreaker for a change."

My arrogant tone did nothing to ease my standing with Sheriff Clancy, but it felt good to me all the same, and I met his challenging stare until he relented out of curiosity.

"All right, then, Jessilyn. Let's just say . . ." He took his cigarette from his mouth and blew a bit of smoke into the wind, taking a nervous glance at the gathering crowd of curious onlookers. "Let's just say that you got some truth to tell me."

"Let's just say I do. You want to hear it or don't you?"

He dropped a few ashes at my feet, and I kicked a bit of dust over them with a flick of my shoe. "Well, do you?"

"I ain't got me much time, so why don't you come out with it so's I can get back to work. I know you ain't gonna give me no rest till I hear it anyhow. What is it you got to tell me about this here Hadley boy?"

"She ain't got nothin' to tell," Joel interjected. "She's just tryin' to protect her boyfriend, is all."

Luke and I each flashed our own angry glare Joel's way, but we didn't get a chance to say a word before a voice told what I was prepared to say.

"Joel Hadley's the one who struck down Callie Colby."

The voice didn't come from any of our crowd but from behind Sheriff Clancy, and though every eye in our party turned to look at the speaker, I kept my eyes on Joel Hadley because I knew who it was that had called him out.

Sheriff Clancy turned and laid a squinty eye on Gemma. "What's that you say, girl?"

I took a glance at her and could see by her face she was nothing but a bundle of nerves, but she was bound and determined to come out with it, I knew. And when Gemma was bound and determined to do-something, she did it.

"I said Joel Hadley did that killin'."

Joel's face was lit up like a Christmas tree, and I saw Luke take a step closer to him, his hand at the ready to hold him up if he tried to bolt. "That's nothin' but slander, Sheriff, and you know it. This here girl's just after me because she has her heart set on me." Joel looked at Gemma with an expression of gentility and said, "Gemma, I done told you there ain't no hope in it, so's you best take your crushes elsewhere and pick yourself a nice boy of your own kind."

Now, my momma had tried hard to raise her up a girl she could be proud of, but I wanted nothing more in that moment than to rip Joel Hadley's pretty head off and throw it in the river. Luke knew as much and put a hand on my back—a warning to be patient. There was never a day a calming hand from Luke Talley didn't do its trick on me, and I backed down a bit, casting Gemma a glance that told her she'd best stand up to Joel Hadley once and for good, especially here in public.

She didn't let me down.

"There ain't no *kinds* in this world but good kinds and bad kinds," she spat back. "And far as I see it, you ain't nothin' near the good kind. Ain't no sensible day I ever wanted to be sweet with a boy who ain't got a decent sense of respect and responsibility." She stepped right up close to Sheriff Clancy. "It was Joel Hadley who took Mr. Poe's car that night. It was Joel Hadley, tipsy from the drink, who ran down Callie Colby and said it must have been some old deer or somethin'. And it was Joel Hadley who found out what happened to Callie and told me I best keep my mouth shut about it lest

I wanted ruin to come to Jessilyn's daddy. And I know all this because . . . I was there."

A moment of panic creased Joel's face, but he quickly brought it under control with practiced ease, slipping into the part of a righteous white master who felt sorry for his slave. He reached out a hand to tip Gemma's face up so she could look at his. "Now, Gemma, I understand you feel slighted. But you can't let your feelin's get the better of you or I might just end up in real trouble. Why don't you go on with your business and stop all this nonsense."

"She ain't doin' no such thing as lyin'," I argued. Luke's hand moved to my shoulder, but my dander was up too far to be restrained completely. "Joel Hadley's the cause of all this trouble, drivin' under the drink and stealin' Mr. Poe's car. Go ask the Hadleys' servants if you don't believe us—one of them probably had to go help him push his own car back. And now he's lettin' Mr. Poe suffer for his crime and callin' Gemma a liar."

Joel raised an eyebrow and dug an elbow into Sheriff Clancy's ribs. "The way she threw herself at me, she's lucky I don't call her more than that."

At that remark, Luke's other hand flew out to catch Joel Hadley by the collar, but he stopped short of violence when the sheriff called out his name.

"Don't make me add charges to the list, son," Sheriff Clancy warned.

"You still want to charge Luke when you just heard all you

heard?" I asked. "Just what'd this town elect you for? Sittin' on the stoop watchin' the world go by?"

"All right, that's it!" Sheriff Clancy flicked his cigarette into the dirt and gripped my arm. "You head on out of here, Jessilyn, before I stick you in that cell with Mr. Poe, seein' as how you're so anxious about him anyways."

"You can't make her go anywhere," Gemma said, pushing her way to my side. "She ain't done nothin' but question the job you're doin'. There ain't no crime in that."

"There is when she's impedin' an investigation."

"Don't seem likely there's too much investigatin' happenin' here." Daddy walked up to us and firmly removed Sheriff Clancy's hand from my arm. "Looks more like a good old-fashioned argument to me. Now, why don't somebody tell me what's goin' on?"

"Your girls say this here boy's the one who ran down Callie Colby, but they ain't been able to offer up nothin' even close to proof."

"Seems to me you ain't given them any chance," Luke said.

I looked pleadingly at my daddy. "All he's set on is arrestin' Luke for doin' what somebody should've done long ago."

"What's that?"

"Punchin' Joel Hadley in the face."

Daddy took a look at Joel and stifled a proud grin when he saw Luke's handiwork. "Can't two boys have an honest disagreement in this town no more, Charlie? Seems to me I remember you in a scuffle or two at their age."

"This weren't no scuffle, Harley. Talley here got in the only shots, so I hear it."

"So I *see* it," Daddy agreed. "But you can't arrest a man for havin' a good right hook."

"All right, now it still stands that these girls don't have any good proof to back up their story."

"They say it. Ain't that enough for you to look into it?"

"Harley, I ain't got time to go chasin' after ghost rabbits. Your girl here's been tellin' me every chance she gets that I ain't doin' my job right. I ain't got time today to listen to her crazy ideas. What I do have proof of is this boy's face bein' black-and-blue from that boy's fist."

"No you don't," I cried. "Lest you got yourself a photo-graph or knuckle marks that match up to Luke, you ain't got nothin' but the word of Joel Hadley. And that ain't sayin' much."

Joel let out a snide laugh. "You talk a big talk, girl, but you ain't never been nothin' but a nigger-lovin' brat."

Luke ripped off his hat and threw it into the road, his eyes lit up with the fire of revenge. "If I'm goin' to go to jail anyways, I may as well make it worth my while."

Daddy caught Luke's arm before it had a chance to come forward into Joel's jaw, and he stepped square in front of Joel, his large frame casting a shadow over him. "You listen here, boy, and you listen good. You keep away from my family, and you keep away from my home, and you sit at the ready. Because if there's truth out there about you, I aim to make sure it comes out. You hear?"

The crowd around us was so silent we could have heard a pin drop, and I reveled in the fear that sped across Joel Hadley's face.

"You just wait," Joel said with a wobbly voice. "You'll get what's comin' to you."

Daddy stepped an inch closer to Joel and stood three inches above him. "What's that you say, boy?"

Joel didn't say another word. He just stared at my daddy with a look that told us words he wouldn't voice in front of the sheriff.

It was a rare day that I'd seen my daddy this angry, and I took hold of Luke's arm, worried about what might come next.

But Daddy did nothing. He just stared at Joel and said, "Sheriff, you be sure to look into what these girls said. And until you got more than that Hadley boy's face that says Luke committed a crime, he's comin' home with us." Then he stepped away, took me and Gemma by the arms, and steered us all back to the truck.

Nothing more was said by anyone for the rest of the trip. Nothing needed to be said. There were enough worries around for everyone to share, and we all knew full well what they meant. Mr. Poe was still in jail, Nate Colby was still consumed by grief and could come gunning for revenge again, and Daddy's mortgage was likely nothing but a memory.

Daddy's pockets were as empty as Joel Hadley's soul, and there wasn't a one of us who wanted to voice that out loud. The only sound in the truck on the way home was when Momma's silent prayers broke out in an occasional whisper.

I whispered a feeble one of my own. After all, I figured it was the only thing we had left.

Chapter 19

Now that the truth of everything had come out, so did Gemma's true feelings, and she was a mix of guilt and tears nearly every minute. Momma was in the business of making people feel better, and as soon as we got home, she went to work trying to feed Gemma back to her old self. But Gemma wasn't interested in food. She was only interested in freeing Mr. Poe. I was racking my brain, but I saw no way out for poor Mr. Poe. In my book he had no chance against a respected and powerful family like the Hadleys.

Late that afternoon I found Luke out on the front porch gobbling up some of the "medicine" my momma had fixed for Gemma. I sighed and plopped down next to him on the porch swing.

"Whoa there, Jessie," he said, checking his shirt front. "You about made me spill your momma's fruit salad."

"It'd serve you right."

He forked the last piece of watermelon into his mouth, nearly swallowing it whole, and glanced at me with wide eyes. "What'd I do?"

"Just look at you. The whole world's fallin' to pieces, and you're sittin' here like a dog with table scraps."

"Your momma offered me some."

"That ain't the only thing you've eaten, Luke Talley. Everythin' my momma's meant for Gemma ended up in your stomach."

"That's because Gemma didn't want it. What'd you expect me to do, let it go bad?"

"Fried chicken, ham biscuits . . ."

"Gemma didn't want them."

"Boiled eggs . . ."

"Jessilyn!" Luke said in such exasperation I couldn't help but manage a smile. "You plan on keepin' an eye on everythin' I put in my stomach for the rest of my life?"

I tipped my head sideways and smiled at him. "Long as you stay around, I expect."

He calmed down when he caught sight of my smile. "I ain't got plans of goin' nowhere."

"You best not. I got me enough troubles as it is. Last thing I need is you walkin' out on me."

There was a serious look in his eyes, one that I wasn't used to seeing, and I couldn't have pulled my gaze away if I'd wanted to. "I ain't ever goin' to walk out on you, Jessilyn."

The sound of my daddy clearing his throat broke the spell, and Luke jumped out of the swing like he'd been fingered by the law. The swing joggled to and fro when he hopped out, making me smack my head on it. I rubbed the sore spot and examined Daddy's face for his reaction. He had one hand on his hip, the other leaning against the doorjamb, and he closed his eyes briefly like he needed a minute to get his thoughts together. "Son, didn't I hear you say you were goin' to take Miss Cleta's supplies over to her?"

Luke slapped his hat back on his head but almost knocked it off right away with an emphatic nod. "Yes'r. That's right."

He grabbed the sacks that were sitting on the porch and made his way down the steps like a scolded animal, never even giving me a second look, and I watched him run out of the yard and onto the road. He turned right, hurried off about thirty feet, and then stopped dead. I couldn't help but smile when he turned back around and headed in the opposite direction.

"Seems that boy done forgot how to get around these parts," Daddy murmured. Then he looked at me and said, "Jessilyn, ain't you got somethin' to do with your time?"

"Yes'r."

"Then you best up and do it."

"Yes'r."

I got up and followed Luke's hasty path down the steps. "I'll go get the laundry off the line."

Daddy nodded and, with a loud sigh, made his way back into the house. When I was turning the corner by the kitchen, his voice floated out to me even though he was trying to be quiet.

"Sadie, I done thought I had me a few more years before I had to worry about them two takin' a shine to each other."

I skidded to a stop and leaned back against the house to listen.

"Now, Harley, either you're blind or you already know that girl of ours took a shine to him long ago."

"But she's just a girl!"

"She ain't no girl no more, and you know it."

"But that boy . . . he's . . . well . . ."

"He's what? He's a good man. And he won't go doin' nothin' we don't approve of."

"That right?" Daddy argued. "I just found those two on the swing makin' eyes at each other. What d'you say about that?"

"You ought to know a little somethin' about makin' eyes at a girl."

"You weren't no seventeen years old when I made eyes at you, Sadie."

"No, you're right." I heard Momma plunk something down onto the counter. "I was sixteen."

I smiled at Daddy's silence. He knew Momma had him over a barrel again, and I walked to the laundry line on clouds. I knew if my daddy saw something in Luke's way toward me, then there really was something there, and nothing short of pure calamity could ease my elation.

Gemma found me there a few minutes later, a clothespin in my mouth, Momma's good stockings hanging from my hand. "You daydreamin' or did a rattler get you?"

Her voice jarred away my pleasant thoughts like she'd shut a door in my face, and I frowned at her to express my displeasure. "Can't a girl have a little peace and quiet now and again?"

"It's finally fixin' to rain," she said simply, ignoring my complaint.

"Good. We need it."

"So . . . maybe instead of standin' here with your head in the clouds . . ." She gave a nod at the laundry basket.

"Oh." I looked at the sky, and the fat gray cloud above us plopped a raindrop in my eye just to prove Gemma right. I grabbed the laundry basket while Gemma pulled the things off the line. After a minute I said, "I didn't have my head in the clouds."

"I guess that's why I caught you standin' here all pie-eyed with no work done."

"If I'd had my head in the clouds, I'd've known it was about to rain, wouldn't I?" I flashed her a challenge with my eyes. "And I ain't never been pie-eyed in all my born days."

Gemma opened her mouth to say something, but whether it was my nasty glare or the sudden cloudburst that shut her up, she never uttered the words that had sat on the tip of her tongue.

I took off running as best I could with my arms full of the laundry basket and got beat by Gemma, narrowly squeezing through the door she let slam back at me.

Daddy was staring out the kitchen window, and he turned

to grin at us. "Got a couple drowned rats in here, Sadie. Best get out the traps."

"Land's sake, Jessilyn, I sent Gemma out to you so you *wouldn't* get caught in the rain." Momma dabbed at both of us with a dishcloth before realizing it was futile. "What were you daydreamin' for?"

"I wasn't daydreamin'," I repeated yet again, even though I was lying through my teeth. I let the basket drop at my feet with a thud. "I was just thinkin'."

"Thinkin' and daydreamin' are near about the same thing, ain't they?" Gemma asked just to get under my skin.

For days like this, Daddy had hung a line in the kitchen, letting one end lie free, coiled in a circle on the counter until we needed it. I picked up the loose end, strung it across to the far doorway, and wrapped the end around the hook that Daddy had put there. I slid the basket beneath the line and started hanging the wet things. "Near as I can figure, you'd be best off helpin' me string these up instead of comin' up with smart things to say."

Gemma sighed and grabbed a pair of dungarees and two clothespins. I heard the front door slam shut and glanced at Daddy. "Someone's here."

"Just me," Luke called. "Can't come all the way in 'cause I'm soaked through."

"Heavens, you've been caught in that gully washer?" Momma called back. She ducked under the line and peered around the corner, her mouth turning up when she caught a glance of Luke. "Well, you can't stay like that, for heaven's sake. You're a sight! Harley, get the boy some of your clothes."

"No, ma'am, I won't put you out like that," Luke said breathlessly. "I'll be fine."

"Ain't no man goin' to catch his death under my roof."

"Sadie, it's ninety-five degrees in here. I ain't figurin' a man can catch anythin' in this heat." Daddy took two strides out of the kitchen, paused for a look at Luke, and headed up the stairs. "Son, you can't stand there in a puddle till this rain stops. I'll get you some things."

"I'll dry up quick."

"In a month of Sundays. Now, you just stay put, and I'll find somethin' for you."

Momma took a look at me and Gemma and ordered us upstairs. "You too, girls. You're good and wet. Go get some dry things on, and I'll finish this laundry."

We slogged toward the stairs, pausing for our own look at Luke's dilemma. Miss Cleta's sacks sat at his feet, wet and soggy. His clothes were soaked through and his hat was weighed down with puddles, hanging over his eyes almost to the lashes.

"Don't you think you ought to take your hat off at least?" I asked.

"Can't without soakin' your momma's floor."

"You're already turning the front hall into a swimmin' pool," Gemma said. "May as well take off the hat."

I gave her a nudge and then walked over to Luke, reaching up to remove the soaking hat.

"It'll spill, Jessie," he argued.

"I'll be careful." I took the hat in hand, cautiously tipping the sides up, and kicked the door open at the same time as I grabbed the hat off his head, dumping the water on the porch. "See?" I stood next to him and studied his face. His hair was wet and starting to curl like it did when he sweat, and the ends of his lashes were tipped in water drops. He stared back at me for a few seconds before I reached up and pushed his hair away from his forehead. "Your hair's soaked."

Daddy came back downstairs in time to see my affectionate gesture and took the last three steps in one long leap, his boots pounding the floor so hard it made Momma's knick-knacks rattle. "All right, son, just take these clothes here and change. We'll give you privacy." He took my arm and fairly shoved me and Gemma toward the stairs. "You girls best get on upstairs and get yourselves dried off." His words came out fast and hurried, his cheeks lit up with flush. "And don't you come down here until Luke says he's done, you hear?"

Momma crossed her arms and loudly whispered, "Harley!"

Daddy looked at Momma sheepishly. "I'm just sayin' . . ."

She shook her head and rolled her eyes before coming behind me and Gemma. "Come on, girls. We'll get you good and dry and leave the men to themselves before your daddy has a heart attack."

We made our way upstairs with me pausing to mutter in a whisper, "I wasn't goin' to peek."

"Heaven knows you weren't, Jessilyn," she sighed. "Your daddy just thinks funny sometimes."

At the doorway to our room, Momma rubbed both of our wet heads and smiled. "Best get yourselves dried off and then I'll fix you somethin' to eat." She turned to leave but stopped short and said, "After Luke's done changin', of course." She left us with a wink and pulled our door shut behind her.

I peeled my clothes off and replaced them with a simple blue dress Momma had helped me make. "Can't believe Daddy," I mumbled.

"Daddys are careful about their girls, Jessie."

I tugged a comb through my hair twice and then stopped to look at Gemma with gleaming eyes. "He thinks Luke's sweet on me."

Gemma cocked her eyebrow at me. "He what?"

"I heard him talkin' to Momma today, and he's talkin' like he thinks Luke's sweet on me."

"Well, there's your answer. If he thinks that's true, then he's goin' to be extra strict with you."

I sat down on the bed and held the comb to my chest like I was cuddling a teddy bear. "What d'you think?"

"'Bout what?"

"'Bout me and Luke, of course. You think he's sweet on me?"

Gemma finished dressing and plopped down next to me, stealing the comb from my hands so she could finish straightening my knotted hair. "Know what I think? I think he's almost as sweet on you as you ever wanted him to be, but he don't know it. Reckon he's scared to know it. That's probably part of why he's stayin' away some of late."

My heart did a somersault into my throat, but I managed to say, "Why's he scared?"

"'Cause part of him remembers you as just little ol' Jessilyn, the girl he saved from the swimmin' hole years ago. It's got to be hard for him to stop seein' you as a girl and start seein' you as a woman."

My eyes drifted off into the corner where there was nothing but a cobweb, and I'm sure my face was painted with wonder. "Oh," I managed to murmur.

"'Course, besides that, he knows your daddy's like to shoot him if he so much as looks at you wrongly."

"But it ain't wrong to look at me sweetly."

"Depends on how your daddy sees it."

"Ouch!" I grabbed Gemma's hand as she tugged the comb through a particularly stubborn tangle. "That'll do. You're bound to yank my scalp off."

"Just one more tangle."

I grabbed a handful of sheets to withstand the pain and groaned. "I don't think my daddy should think that way about Luke. He's a gentleman, and he ain't like to step out of bounds with me."

"All depends on where your daddy sets the bounds. He's doin' the same thing Luke's doin', tryin' to see you as more'n his little girl."

"But it ain't my fault I'm growin' up. It ain't fair of Daddy to keep me and Luke apart just because he's nervous."

Thankfully Gemma finished pulling my hair out, and I took the comb from her to keep her from starting up again.

"I ain't sayin' it's fair. I'm just sayin' it's so."

"Well, he ain't bein' fair. I swear, Gemma, daddys ain't easy to understand."

Gemma took the comb from me and ran it through her hair, her eyes pointed at her skirt. "Least you got one."

I hated it when she did that. There I was having a good argument about what was wrong with my daddy, and she had to go and mention hers. Rest their souls, Gemma brought him or her momma up anytime I had complaints about my parents. "Least you got one," she'd say. "Least you know what it's like to have your momma get after you to keep the wrinkles out of your dresses." Or, "Least you have a daddy to scold you for leavin' the wheelbarrow out in the rain."

But it worked every time, and this time was no different. I took Gemma's free hand in my own and said what I always said. "Least you got us."

Gemma squeezed my hand in response.

Four rhythmic knocks on the door signaled the all clear, and I hopped up to peer at my reflection in the mirror. "Guess that means Luke's decent." I gathered I looked as best I could, considering my hair wouldn't be dry for an hour at best, and I tugged a lock of Gemma's hair. "You comin' down?"

"In a minute."

Every now and again Gemma would have spells of missing her parents, and now was one of them, I could tell. I kicked myself inside for having complained about my daddy and made her think of hers, and I planted a kiss on her cheek as reparation before heading downstairs.

"Lady comin' through," I called as I neared the stairway.

"You can come down," Luke called drearily. "I'm all dressed . . . sort of."

The minute I spotted him standing in the kitchen doorway, I dissolved into laughter. The scowl he pinned on me proved he knew what I was laughing at without any explanation.

My daddy was a solid, muscular six feet, compared to Luke's lithe six-feet-three, and Luke stood there in too-short pant legs and too-wide waistband. A leather belt cinched the pants in at the waist and though the shirt was on the short side, the shoulders and chest sagged. He was barefoot with his hands stuck in pockets that didn't sit at the right places, and it was all I could do to stand upright, I laughed so hard.

"You done yet?" Luke asked sharply after a minute.

"We got to get you photographed like that," I told him in a voice strained with amusement. I stood on my toes to peer over his shoulder. "Momma, did you see Luke?"

"Your momma and daddy are sittin' on the porch. And yes, they've gotten their laughs in at me, so you don't need to go gettin' them." He held his hands out in front of him, a smile starting to show up on his stern face. "You like this look so much, maybe I'll get me a whole closet full."

I tugged at the saggy middle of his shirt. "Don't matter to me none what you wear."

"Oh, and I guess you'd go into town with me lookin' like this."

I looked him in the eye and spoke as bluntly as always. "I'd go into town with you lookin' any which way."

Luke was so close to me our toes touched, and though there should have been thoughts racing through my head, I couldn't make any come together. I just stood there holding my breath, waiting for the moment to be broken.

A creak on the stairs warned of Gemma's descent, and I was certain she'd done it on purpose since she knew full well how to avoid the creaky step. Luke backed away from me, and Gemma pretended she didn't notice a thing and plopped onto the couch on her knees, staring outside at the rain. "Don't look likely to stop. Sure is a blessin' to see some rain."

Luke walked away from me and stood at the front door. "Hope it helps the crops some."

"I got to get into town tomorrow," Gemma said determinedly.

"What for?" I asked, joining her on the couch. "You got big plans?"

"I got to see Mr. Poe."

"Mr. Poe, he'll be fine," Luke reassured her. "Sheriff'll take care of things."

Gemma didn't have a chance to reply before a truck pulled up in a good hurry. Mr. Hanley, who owned the general store, hopped out and waved an arm frantically to get my daddy's attention. As if the mud-spewing stop he made in front of our house hadn't done the trick.

Daddy stood up from the porch swing. "Hey there, Harry."

His words were easygoing but his face was tight with anxious expectation. "What brings you out this way?"

"We got trouble in town, Harley. And I thought you ought to know about it since you're one of the few men who's got sense left in his head."

"What sort of trouble?" Momma asked.

"There's a riot in town. Joel Hadley's got them all stirred up, sayin' Gemma done accused him falselike and it was Elmer Poe who got her to do it. They's all excited, sayin' no half-wit and Negro are goin' to keep justice from takin' place. I swear, they's ready to string Elmer up first chance they get."

Gemma pushed herself off the couch and marched to the front door, squeezing past Luke to fling the door open. "That Joel Hadley will stop at nothin' to save his own neck. I knew this would happen."

Daddy put a hand on Gemma's neck to calm her down. "Now, Gemma, don't you worry none. We'll get things straightened out. Luke and I can go on into town and have a chat with the sheriff.

"I don't trust that sheriff one bit," she muttered. "Fact is, I think he's in the Hadleys' pocket. And if that's so, them Hadleys might get him to do something wrong to Mr. Poe."

I took my place in the doorway next to Luke. "We can't let them hurt him. Mr. Poe ain't never done an unlawful thing in his life."

"If Mr. Poe takes a fall for Joel Hadley, then Joel Hadley won't never have to take responsibility," Gemma said. "You can bet he wants this town to believe it's Mr. Poe's fault. Seein' Mr. Poe strung up will mean no one will ever point a finger his way again."

Momma was already crying quietly and wringing her hands so hard it's a wonder she still had any blood in them. But I didn't feel like I had much blood left in me either. I was cold all over, and I rubbed my arms to try to keep the chill away. Luke put an arm around my shoulders, and though I relaxed against him, there was no appreciation of his nearness. All I could think about was Mr. Poe's safety. There weren't that many people in this town who would stand up to the Hadleys, and with the chance the sheriff was against us too, I didn't figure on us having a good shot at protecting Mr. Poe from an angry mob.

Daddy trudged to the kitchen to get his rifle, and Gemma stalked off after him.

"I gotta go with you."

I stepped around the corner to watch my daddy's face, and what I saw there didn't surprise me one bit. "Now, Gemma, you ain't gonna do nothin' of the sort," he said with a hard shake of his head. "Don't even go thinkin' it."

"Ain't no one else who knows what I know. I told my side to some, but not to all. People got to hear it from my lips."

Daddy leaned his gun against the wall and put his hands on her shoulders. "Now listen here. Them people, they ain't thinkin' straight. They don't want to hear reason from nobody just now, and they sure won't go hearin' any from . . ." Daddy stopped short, but Gemma finished for him.

"From a colored girl. That what you were goin' to say?"

Daddy's face dropped. "Gemma, it sounds a sight, I know it. But it's the truth. I don't want you takin' a chance at gettin' hurt, especially not for nothin'."

"But I've got to go." Gemma was desperate, and her voice rose uncharacteristically. "Mr. Poe needs me to stand up for him."

But my daddy was firm, and he gently moved her aside, grabbed his rifle, and walked past her. Gemma looked at me with eyes that begged, and I stepped forward to catch my daddy's arm.

"Don't you start too, Jessilyn," he said firmly.

"But, Daddy, you don't understand. Gemma and me, we carried our secret about Joel Hadley all the time Mr. Poe sat in that jail cell. We did it all for fear of what them Hadleys would do to us, Daddy, and we're both carryin' guilt over Mr. Poe spendin' all this time in jail. Now it's bad enough that he might get hurt, and we've got to go do our part." My grip on his arm tightened like I was slipping off a cliff and he was my only lifeline. But then, at that moment, I felt like he was. "Daddy, please!"

Daddy looked down at the floor and squeezed the back of his neck with his free hand. Gemma and I watched him anxiously, fearing we would be left behind to wonder and wait, but our help came from an unexpected source.

Momma.

She took my daddy's arm from me and and held it in both

of hers. "Let them go, Harley. You can see on their faces, they won't be at peace unless they do this."

"Sadie, there'll be violent men there." He still held his rifle, and he nodded toward it. "Violent men with guns will be there."

"But so will our Lord."

There was a hush that settled over all of us following those words, and I instinctively reached out a hand for Gemma. I knew then without even looking at my daddy that we'd be going with him.

The sight we saw when our truck pulled into town was one that made my heart leap. Dusk had settled in, and the crowd of men equipped with torches and guns pounded hard against the front door of the jailhouse. There were no men in uniform to be seen, and I pictured them all inside settling their weight against the doors to keep the mob out.

As soon as I hopped out onto the sidewalk, I saw a hand squeeze through the bars in the front window and heard three shots pop out of a pistol. I jumped a mile and grabbed onto Luke's shirt for safety. He shoved me and Gemma behind him, but I peered around him and saw the pistol pointing through the window, smoke from the barrel making a gray cloud against the damp darkness. The rain had slowed, but a fine mist dusted our faces as we watched the crowd back down a bit in the aftermath of gunshots.

"Now everyone clear off," Sheriff Clancy shouted. "And I mean now!"

"You ain't got the right to keep us out, Sheriff," Joel Hadley cried. "These here men have a right to justice and this here's a public building."

"Son, don't be an idiot," Sheriff Clancy called back. "You boys ain't got no right to vigilante justice, and you know it. Now just back away while you still got the chance. I done called the sheriff in from Richmond, and he's sendin' some men out, so you best leave before they come in with their fancy rifles and whatnot. You know how these big-town boys like their guns."

"Sheriff's tryin' to run 'em off at least," I whispered to Gemma.

"Probably just tryin' to save his own hide from bein' trampled," she muttered.

"Don't matter none why he's tryin' to run 'em off long as he does it." I stood on my toes to whisper in Luke's ear, "We got to get to Mr. Poe."

"Jessie, you ain't goin' nowhere near that jailhouse."

"But Mr. Poe's got to be scared to death."

He turned around and put his face right up close to mine. "You step foot near that jailhouse over my dead body, Jessilyn."

Every muscle in my body flexed at his command, and I reared further up on my toes. There wasn't much more a body could do to rile me than to tell me I wasn't allowed to do something. I'd had enough whippings in my day to prove it. Amid the potential tragedy that surrounded us and the angry voices of senseless men, I found the time to let my pride swallow me whole.

"Don't you go tellin' me what I can and cannot do, Luke Talley. I ain't goin' to let Mr. Poe sit in there and rot, and you ain't got no right to tell me I am."

Daddy came around the front of the truck and separated the two of us by grasping each of us by a shoulder. "Dang it all, if I ain't got to spend most of my time breakin' up fights between the two of you."

"He's tryin' to tell me what to do, Daddy," I argued without taking my angry eyes from Luke's. "He thinks he knows all."

"I ain't said I know all," Luke returned. "I said I ain't goin' to let you get yourself killed."

"All right, now, that's enough." Daddy put both hands on my shoulders and pushed me back down to flat feet. "This ain't no time for you to be on your high horse, Jessilyn. We got bigger fish to fry."

"I ain't on a high horse. It's Luke who is. He done told me I can't go nowhere near Mr. Poe, and I say Mr. Poe needs us."

"Well, you're right, Jessilyn. He does need us."

I crossed my arms and flashed Luke a strong gaze of satisfaction.

"But he's right too. You ain't goin' nowhere near that jailhouse."

My satisfied smirk settled into an angry pout in two seconds flat. "Daddy!"

"Now, Jessilyn, you get back in this truck and stay there until I say you can leave." He lifted me so my feet left the ground by an inch and steered me into the truck. "You stay there until I say otherwise, you hear?" He pointed a finger at me and flashed me that look that said, "You listen up or be sorry."

"But, Daddy . . ."

The finger came a little closer to my face. "Stay!"

I flopped down onto the seat, fully aware that I'd lost this battle, and when you'd lost a battle with Daddy, you'd good and lost, plain and simple. Daddy opened the door wider for Gemma, and she hopped in beside me, though reluctantly.

I kept my head down in embarrassed defeat, but I angled my eyes upward to see Daddy and Luke head slowly toward the jail. My feelings were a mixture of anger and fear as I watched the two most important men in my life saunter off into danger while I was stuck cowering in the car like a scared rabbit.

"We got to get to Mr. Poe," Gemma whispered. "Them men'll kill him. Ain't nothin' your daddy and Luke can do to stop a whole mob like that."

I pulled my knees up to my chin and wrapped my arms around them. "Daddy says stay put. Ain't nothin' we can do."

"Oh, there's somethin' we can do all right."

I turned my head toward her, resting my cheek on my knee. "What've you got goin' on in your head?" She didn't say anything, but I could nearly see the wheels turning in her head by looking into her eyes. "Gemma! What're you thinkin'?"

"I'm thinkin' we're goin' to get Mr. Poe out of here."

"That's stupid! A jailbreak? You been readin' Jesse James stories or somethin'?"

"I ain't talkin' jailbreak."

"You near about are if you think we're gettin' Mr. Poe away from here. It ain't like you can sweet-talk the sheriff into lettin' him go."

"Well, we're goin' to find a way. That's all there is to it."

"But that don't make no sense. We can't just amble on up, unlock the doors, and let him out."

Gemma dug her elbow into my thigh. "If you'd just shut up for a while, I'd be able to think of somethin'."

"Yes, ma'am," I muttered, elongating each syllable. "You ain't got to shout."

Gemma's long sigh indicated her dissatisfaction that I had to get the last word in, but she said nothing else, and I knew deep down she'd figure out some way to extract Mr. Poe, no matter how impossible it seemed.

My heart fluttered like bird wings, and I gripped my knees, fearful the rioting would get out of control. I was fearful that *everything* would get out of control.

And I was afraid that Gemma would find a way to make it happen.

The tug on my arm told me I was right. I had every intention of arguing, and I turned toward her to do so. But the look on her face made me think twice. We looked at each other long and hard until I finally let out a sigh.

"Daddy's gonna kill us."

"Not in the same way that mob's gonna kill Mr. Poe."

I gave her a nudge. "Best get on out now while Daddy ain't lookin'."

Gemma opened the door and slid out first, keeping her eyes peeled in Daddy's direction. But the crowd was overwhelming, and Daddy had his hands full.

"You go ahead," I whispered, giving Gemma a shove. "I'll keep watch to make sure no one follows you, and then I'll come along in a few minutes."

We locked eyes in silent agreement; then Gemma took off across the muddy road. My gaze ran back to Daddy, and I saw him with his arms folded, shaking his head in disgust. Sheriff Clancy was on the porch now, trying to make them see reason, but reason wasn't on anyone's mind then.

The sky was aptly moonless since no light could possibly have been found in the evil that went on outside that jailhouse, and the torches cast an eerie glow. I had a sudden flashback to the cross that had burned in our front yard only four years earlier.

It always amazed me the evil men did at night. It was as though they felt the darkness hid their misdeeds, but my momma always said God had the only pair of perfect eyes in the world, and there wasn't any amount of darkness that He couldn't see through. I pictured Him just then looking down on us, seeing every bit of evil that colored every heart in that mob, and I hoped He had a mind to do something about it.

Chapter 20

Once a couple of minutes had passed, I began my own trek across the road toward the back of the jailhouse. I took a quick look around for Luke, but I couldn't pick him out, and that got me nervous since I could usually pick him out anywhere. He stood a good head taller than most, but he was nowhere to be seen. I wondered if he had spotted Gemma.

I had only traveled several yards down the road when something grabbed at my shirt, tugging me to an unexpected stop. Instinctively I cried out, but a hand slapped over my mouth.

"Dang it, Jessie, you're goin' to wake the dead."

Luke's whisper in my ear did nothing to allay my fear, and I ripped his hand from my mouth angrily. "Don't you go gettin' sharp with me," I whispered, twirling around to face him. "You're the one's sneakin' around. What were you thinkin' grabbin' me like that? You scared me to death!"

"Weren't no other way to get your attention. I've been whisperin' your name since you came around the corner."

I put my hands on my hips and stared him down. "What were you doin' hangin' around here anyways? You spyin' on me?"

"Just savin' you from yourself, is all. I knew you'd go and do somethin' stupid, so I kept an eye out."

I ignored his comment and grabbed his hand. "Come on. We need to find Gemma."

"Wait a minute," he said, yanking me to a stop. "I ain't goin' nowhere with you when your daddy said to stay put in that truck. Your daddy'll skin me alive and bury me on his back hill."

"Well, I ain't stayin', so you best let me go."

"I ain't lettin' you go, Jessie. You think I'm crazy?"

I rolled my eyes and sighed. "Luke, I ain't got time to waste standin' out here arguin'. Gemma's out there by herself, and I got to go find her."

"Then let's get your daddy."

"So you're worried more about your hide than Gemma's? 'Cause he'll light into her like a rabid squirrel if he finds out she went against him."

"No, I'm thinkin' about Gemma. She needs someone with her."

"That's right," I said, tugging his arm again. "So let's go."

"Jessie!" He drew my name out like it had ten syllables. "Your daddy's goin' to kill us both!"

"Best we go down dyin' for Gemma and Mr. Poe."

I could see his better judgment told him to get my daddy, but I could also see that better judgment fade in the light of my pleading. My last tug at his arm did the trick, and I dragged a resigned but anxious Luke Talley toward the jail.

Luke kept one hand on me and one hand on his waistband, which I knew meant he was ready to draw his pistol at a moment's notice. My mind reeled, grasping for ideas, but it found nothing but hopelessness. We couldn't manage to hold up against so many men with poisoned minds and a determined mission. I'd heard a story in Sunday school once about a man who had sinned and been swallowed up whole by the ground, but I hadn't heard of God doing any such thing lately, and I wasn't about to depend on that now. I was just about to yank away from Luke when I spotted movement toward the back of the jailhouse.

"Gemma!" I whispered loudly.

"Jessie! You done scared me to death."

"Well, you're scarin' me to death with all this craziness. We're even."

"Gemma, what're you plannin' to do?" Luke asked. "Break the man out?"

"I don't know what I'm goin' to do. I've been prayin' for help since we left the house. All I know is I've got to do somethin', and the Lord's goin' to help me do it. He told me so."

I squinted at her and shook my head. "And just how'd He do that? You got a burnin' bush somewheres I don't know about?"

Gemma's face lit up in anger so fiercely I could see it even in the dark, and I swallowed hard under her gaze.

"Jessilyn Lassiter, just 'cause you don't claim no belief in my Jesus ain't no reason for you to scoff at Him, you hear? I got me a certain feelin', and I got to believe in that feelin' no matter what you think."

Shame crept up into my cheeks, seeped out of my pores, and I stepped back a bit to lean against Luke so my shaky knees wouldn't show.

"Now, either you're here to help me or you're leavin'," Gemma continued. "Plain and simple. You got no different choices. But I got me a God to rely on, and I'm goin' to do just that."

I nodded at her slow and steady because I needed time to get my voice to work. Then I said, "I'm here to help you, Gemma," even though it came out in a squeak.

Gemma set off to the barred window of Mr. Poe's cell. I watched her go, and Luke gave me a pat on my back to reassure me. "It'll be okay, Jessie. Gemma's got good sense."

We followed her and found Mr. Poe curled up on the floor, his body bobbing rhythmically from one side to the other. It was an odd movement that I feared told a story of his deteriorating mental condition, but when he turned his head to answer Gemma's whispered call to him, there was a smile on his face.

"You okay, Mr. Poe?" Gemma whispered.

"Jes' fine, Miss Gemma. Jes' enjoyin' God's music."

I eyed Luke nervously, fearing Mr. Poe was near to insanity. "What music's that, Mr. Poe?"

"God's music, Miss Jessilyn. Ain't you hearin' it?"

We all sat for a moment straining to hear God's music, but all I heard was the chaotic buzz of angry voices in the distance and the sporadic pop of fiery torches.

"What sort of music is it?" Gemma asked.

"Night music. God's got Him some frogs and crickets, buzzin' cicadas. He got the whole symphony lightin' up the night. Makes me feel like dancin'."

"Well, Mr. Poe," Gemma said, a smile gracing her tearstained face, "we got plenty of that music out here in the open. So we come to take you out to hear it with us."

"But ah cain't come out. Sheriff says ah cain't."

"There's some trouble out front, and we got to get you away from it, you hear?"

"Sheriff wouldn't like it."

Gemma lay down flat in front of the window and grabbed onto the bars with both hands. "Lord's tellin' me to take you away from here, Mr. Poe, and I got to do what He says."

Mr. Poe stopped dancing to God's music. "That so, Miss Gemma?"

"Yes'r. I believe with my heart He means for us to take you away from here."

I squatted down and peered into Mr. Poe's dimly lit cell. He stood up slowly with bones that were weary and stiff and went to his cot to lift his worn Bible from it. "This is all ah got with me that counts," he said without a hint of doubt on his face. "Ah reckon it's all ah need to go with you."

I was heartsick to see the faith in his expression because I saw no way at all that we'd be able to help him get out. Gemma had all kinds of faith, I knew that for certain, but I didn't see any way that faith could remove bars from windows or unlock jailhouse doors.

I didn't know much about faith then, and I certainly didn't know that God could use a man who was mostly low-down to honor someone's faith. But He did.

We all watched, awestruck, as Mr. Poe's cell door swung open, and for a minute I thought it must have been done by an angel. Well, maybe it was. Because the way I figured it, it would take a mighty big, convincing angel to make Sheriff Clancy open that jail door so we could take away his prisoner. But that's exactly what happened. Without a word he looked at the three of us, jerked his head sideways toward the back entrance of the jail, and then disappeared.

Mr. Poe peered at the ceiling, said a word of thanks to God, and shuffled out of his cell. We all took off like squirrels to the back door, with Gemma reaching it first. She yanked on the door, which opened with ease, and ran inside. Luke and I waited on the worn patch of grass until the two of them came out together, and then we all made off into the woods behind the jail as fast as Mr. Poe's shaky legs could carry him.

The rain opened up on us again, and we trudged along with clothes that stuck to our skin like paste. Poor Luke was ill equipped for it in Daddy's old shirt and pants, and my heart warmed toward him even more for never letting me down. As we walked, heavy with the burden of uncertainty, Mr. Poe, broken down as his body was, kept his head held high, listening to more of God's music, I supposed. I marveled at his peace and wondered how a body could find such a thing.

There was a stiff wind along with the rain, and at times it pricked our faces like bee stings.

"Where are we goin'?" I asked Luke. "Ain't many places to hide out those men won't know about."

"Gemma seems to know where she's goin'." He nodded at her as she led the way. "Best follow her since she's been right so far tonight. I reckon God really is talkin' to her."

"You believe God talks to people, Luke? Right up talks to them?"

"Can't say as I've seen anythin' like it, but you can't rightly say this here happened by chance, now can you?" He looked at me from beneath his soggy hat. "You and I, we've seen enough over the years to get us thinkin', don't you reckon?" He stuck his hands in his pockets, shrugged, and lowered his head to concentrate on making his legs move.

We'd been walking for what must have been a solid hour when Gemma motioned toward an old shack that was nestled amid a mass of trees and shrubs. In the dark it looked unfamiliar, but once Gemma unlocked the door, I realized where we were.

"Gemma and I used to play here when we were younger," I said to Luke.

"This old shack?"

The shutters were falling off, rusty hinges held the door on by threads, and it looked haunted by bad memories if not by ghosts. But for me it held only good memories, and a weary smile settled on my lips. "It wasn't a shack to us."

I entered the house on legs that were beginning to revolt, and before I could even find a spot to rest, Gemma had lit strategically placed lamps with a box of matches, popped another match into a stocked woodstove, and arranged chairs for all of us to settle into.

I watched her in awe, and she caught the question in my eyes right off the bat.

"Been plannin' for a while now" was all she said in reply. "We got all we need for a spell."

Luke helped Mr. Poe into a chair, and I followed Gemma into the cramped space that served as a kitchen. There were stacks of canned goods, a sack of biscuits, and containers of well water crowding the countertops.

She no doubt saw the expression of wonder on my face, but she ignored it and busied herself by putting some stew in a pot on the woodstove. "Made this yesterday. I bought the goods with my own money so as not to steal from your momma."

"My momma would've welcomed you to use her things," I whispered. "Gemma . . ."

"Don't say nothin', Jessie. I'm just glad you're here."

Gemma hadn't forgotten a thing, and I noticed every detail of a plan she must have been keeping from me for days. She'd even brought some clothes along for me since she knew me well enough that there was no doubt in her I'd follow her here. After all, I'd always followed her everywhere.

We had enough to hide out for at least a week, but beyond that I couldn't see what we'd do. We couldn't all live here forever like some mishmashed family. But I wouldn't say as much to her. She'd done all she could, and besides, she said God had led her to do it all. Questioning God was something I'd done plenty in my life, but I didn't think Gemma would like it if I did it to her face.

By the time I'd changed into fresh clothes, Mr. Poe had fallen asleep on the dusty old sofa in the main room. The ratty thing was broken on one side, and it slanted so much I worried Mr. Poe might slip off onto his head. There was a wool blanket over him that I recognized as the one Momma kept in the truck for her legs.

"Got moth-eaten," Gemma said, noticing my gaze. She poked a finger through a frayed hole in the cover near Mr. Poe's feet. "Your momma sent me off with it to the poor closet at church."

"Daddy's shirt," I murmured, seeing Daddy's old plaid keeping Mr. Poe warm.

"Your momma gave me a whole bag that day for the poor closet."

Gemma left for the kitchen, but I leaned over and studied Mr. Poe to make sure he was breathing okay, he was so still.

Once I heard evidence that he was still with us, I straightened up and tucked the blanket in at his sides to keep the draft off. I took one quick look at his feet on my way out of the room and smiled. He wore Daddy's old work boots with the patched-up sole.

I guess God found another way to clothe the poor that month.

"Where's Luke?" I asked as I started helping Gemma dish out stew.

"Gettin' more wood."

"But I saw some by the fireplace."

"I put some there, but he says we may need more, and he'd best collect it now so it has time to dry up before we need it."

"He'll be soaked."

"He can use some of the things I brought for Mr. Poe."

The thought of Luke in more of Daddy's castoffs made me grin. I sat down opposite Gemma at a wooden table littered with splinters, eager for some food. But before I could get the first spoonful into my mouth, Gemma grabbed my hand.

"We gotta pray first," she said adamantly.

We'd said a prayer before every meal all my life, but there was more in this prayer of hers than a usual supper prayer. It was more like what I'd heard Daddy pray so many times when he and Momma were talking over the troubles of life. It was a prayer filled with pleading, and I almost felt like I was intruding in this conversation between Gemma and God.

My first bite went down slowly since I could see Gemma had a tear in her eye, and we sat together in silence until I'd gotten to the middle of my bowl.

I put down my spoon and reached across the table to grab Gemma's free hand. She dropped a wedge of potato out of her spoon back into her bowl and leveled her misty gaze on me. I could see she was starting to wonder, having one of those "tests of faith" I'd heard my daddy talk about many a time, and all I wanted to do was make her feel better.

So I smiled at her and said the only thing I could come up with. "You done good, Gemma. Real good."

The crease that I'd started to think might make a permanent home on her forehead got a lot smaller, and she managed to turn one corner of her mouth up. She took both of my hands in hers and laid her head down on the table, fatigue hitting her like a punch. I sat there for a few minutes until I heard her rhythmic sleeping breaths, and then I let go of her hands and took a blanket from the small stack Gemma had laid in the corner of the kitchen. I covered her as best I could and then sneaked away to wait on the porch for Luke to come back.

The sky was black and filled with pouring rain, and I peered upward searching for God in the place my momma always looked.

"I don't see nothin'," I said aloud. "But I sure hope You're there, anyways."

Chapter 21

It may have been the middle of summer, but I woke up that first morning in the cabin with a chill in my bones. Gemma was next to me on our makeshift bed on the floor, and I opened my eyes to see her face nose to nose with mine. I hated to wake her, so I slid away from her slowly and took a good three minutes to dress, I was being so careful. On my way from the room, the floorboards creaked, and I stopped on my toes and turned an eye to Gemma. She snorted once and rolled over, slipping quickly back into steady breathing.

I found Mr. Poe sound asleep, his toes up in the air, his head slipping off to one side of the couch. But Luke was absent, and when I peeked out the front window, I could see him standing on the porch, just staring at the leaden sky. Rain was falling by buckets, and I figured he was calculating how long it might stay with us, but when I pressed my face closer to the windowpane, I could see that wasn't it.

There was something about his face that wasn't like any expression I'd ever seen there before. He was staring out at nothing in particular. Not the rain. Not the sky. It was like he'd spotted something I didn't.

Part of me felt I shouldn't disturb him, but the other part of me—the stubborn, self-centered part—was too curious not to find out what was going on. The door squeaked when I opened it, but Luke never even budged.

I crept softly across the porch. "Luke?" I whispered, and then when he didn't answer, I said again, "Luke. You all right?"

He blinked twice and turned at the sound of my voice. His cheeks turned a splotchy pink when he saw me there, and he didn't quite look me in the eye when he murmured, "Mornin', Jessie."

"You worried about somethin'?"

"Nah, I ain't worried. Everythin's goin' to be okay."

But the way he leaned heavily on the porch rail told me differently, and I went to lean on it next to him.

"Seems there's somethin' on your mind."

"Just life, is all. Gives you plenty to think about."

There wasn't much I could say to that, so I stood silently with him for a few more minutes. "Mr. Poe's sleepin' sound."

"Yeah, we were up in the middle of the night, so he's likely tired."

"What were you doin'?"

"He wanted some water, and I heard him, so I got up to

help. He don't get around so well these days, especially after all that walkin' we made him do." He rubbed the back of his neck hard. I knew there was something he wanted to say. I could always tell when he had something on the tip of his tongue but wasn't comfortable saying it. So I just waited with a patience that I didn't usually possess. It was a long time of watching the rain splatter against the mud puddle outside the porch before he finally spoke.

"That Mr. Poe, he knows his Bible."

"He was raised on it, I guess."

He looked at me quickly. "So were you."

"So?"

"So, you don't know your Bible like he does. Seems he's got somethin' in his knowin' of it that most people don't have, you know? Somethin' special."

"Like what?"

"Don't know." He turned and put his back against the rail and looked at the house like he was watching Mr. Poe even though he couldn't see him from where we stood. "That man in there, he's what? Almost seventy? He's lost all his kin, got nobody to take care of him, and he's been wrongly accused and thrown in jail for somethin' he ain't never done. Now we got him on the run now like some murderin' convict. And you know what? He ain't the least scared." He looked at me with a sort of surprise in his eyes. "Not in the least," he confirmed. "What makes a man like that?"

"Well, Momma always said there's somethin' off about Mr. Poe. He's slow, they like to say."

"That ain't it. Not this time, anyways. There's somethin' else. Ain't you seen it?"

"I reckon. Maybe I just ain't thought about it like you have."

There were another few minutes of silence before Luke said in a voice I could barely hear, "Mr. Poe says it's God."

"Doin' what?"

"Givin' him peace, he says. He says he has faith God'll take care of him, so he don't worry about things."

For the first time in our conversation I recognized the look on his face as one I was sure to have worn many times in my life. I could guess what was going on in his mind now as sure as I'd known it to go through my own time and time again. It was the look of someone who knows there's something important to pay attention to but doesn't know how.

"That's what my daddy says," I fairly whispered. "Heard it every other day, near about."

"What do you think about it?"

It nearly broke my heart to say it, since it meant I was likely the most selfish, sinful girl in the world, but I told him the truth. "Guess I don't think about it much at all. Leastways, not serious-like."

"Uh-huh." He nodded and turned back around to look at the rain that now fell in sheets and made it hard to hear anything else. "But I reckon I got to think about it sometime."

We didn't say anything more about it then. And we didn't say anything more about it all that dreary, rain-filled day. Mr. Poe had plenty of stories to tell—even though his tongue seemed heavy and he tripped over words a lot—and most of his stories brought the Lord into it. It was as natural as a sunset for him to do that. He got under my skin enough that I started praying almost every hour, prayers that I figured might not mean much coming from me. But I prayed the Lord would take care of Mr. Poe, no matter what. He was such a good soul, I figured God would hear prayers about him from someone who wasn't sure she even believed they made a difference.

Hours went by with nothing but rain and more rain. And hours went by with worries and more worries. I thought of Momma and Daddy and knew they'd be worried stiff. My mind wandered to the scenes that were likely taking place just out of our reach—an anxious Momma and Daddy, an overwhelmed sheriff, and rioting townspeople played around in my thoughts.

We were all about as quiet as mice that day, full of thoughts that made words hard. Mr. Poe was worn and often mumbled things under his breath that didn't make any sense to the rest of us. Any time I asked him how he was, he'd nod his head and say, "Jes' fine, Miss Jessie. The good Lord provides."

It was late afternoon, and I longed to see the sun dipping down, but it kept its place behind the clouds. I sat in front of the window, my face so close to it my breath clouded the glass. Gemma had dozed off in the bedroom, and Mr. Poe slept noiselessly behind me on the couch.

Luke came over and made his own clouds on the glass several inches above my head. "Rain's slowed."

I nodded, but I didn't feel there was anything to say. We sat quietly on that windowsill for so long, I drifted off, but I awoke with a start, banging my head against the windowpane. Luke was at the front door, his head stuck outside.

"Luke?"

He shushed me with a wave of his hand, and I sat by waiting impatiently to find out what was happening. It didn't take me long to guess. I could hear a whine in the distance, an eerie, disconnected sound that gave me a chill.

In no time I was standing next to Luke, my head out the door like his. Seconds passed before it became clear what we were hearing.

"Dogs!" we whispered to each other.

The flurry of activity that followed was a blur. We gathered up Mr. Poe, bleary-eyed as he was. Gemma was alert in a flash, and she immediately started gathering supplies the minute I told her what was happening. I helped her pack as many things as we could carry, and we met Luke and Mr. Poe at the door.

Luke's pistol was very evidently sitting at his waistband, and I worried he might have cause to use it. He caught my gaze and held it for a moment, a look that told me just how serious our situation was.

"Sounds like a lot of them," I murmured to him.

"We should head for Rocky Creek," he said. "They'll have a hard time trackin' if we cross it."

"If it's been rainin' this hard up the hill, that creek'll be flooded by now. It's always spillin' over."

Gemma came up behind us and hung a bag of supplies on my arm. "We'll just have to hope it ain't."

Luke turned to help Mr. Poe down the steps, and I reached out to grab Gemma's hand for support.

And then we set off into the mud.

After half an hour, we had walked only half of the distance we might have covered in better conditions, and we were all worn thin.

In the distance, the howling kept pace with us, and I was beginning to feel hunted like a mangy fox. I sidled up next to Luke and tugged at his shirt to get his attention. "They're gettin' closer. I don't think Mr. Poe can make it fast enough."

The uncertainty on Luke's face said everything I was thinking, and it made me shiver inside even more knowing he had as little hope as I did. We continued on wordlessly, with Gemma in the lead, and as we went, I prayed as many things as I could think of to pray.

The dogs were so loud, I wondered if God could even hear my whispered prayers, and the gray skies were nothing but dampers to our spirits. With the eerie cries of the dogs in the distance, fear seemed to be chasing us right along with the posse behind us. And both were gaining on us.

Another half hour went by and we were managing less and less distance on our wobbly, worn-out legs. The howls were echoing behind us now, and Luke was fairly dragging Mr. Poe along as he had lost strength altogether.

I was losing any faith in prayer, and the words that I sent

heavenward were expressing more and more doubt that He was even listening.

By the time the dogs were within seeing distance, we had reached the creek, and the rumble we heard through the trees told us it had flooded as I'd feared.

"Creek's up, all right," I called to Luke.

Luke pulled up short of where the water roiled below us and let Mr. Poe lean against him. He turned to gaze behind us, fatigue written all over his face. But there was determination there too, and he shielded Mr. Poe's body as though he could keep anyone from touching him. And that's what Gemma and I did as well.

We all knew we were only minutes from being discovered, and there simply was nowhere to go. If we'd only been able to cross the creek, we were just minutes from our farm, and I was sick at heart to be so close to home but so far from the security it offered.

I crept as close to Mr. Poe as I could and said, "I'm sorry, Mr. Poe. We ain't caused you nothin' but trouble."

With an energy that belied his age and situation, he stood up tall and put one shaking hand under my chin. "Miss Jessie, ain't nuthin' you done fer me but help and care. Ain't nuthin' anyone's done that God ain't in control over, neither."

"But I've been prayin', Mr. Poe. I've been prayin' and them dogs are still on our heels, and them men still want you to pay for somethin' you ain't done. I tried to help, but God ain't hearin' me. I don't think He cares much."

"Oh, He cares, Miss Jessie. It's jes' sometimes His plans'r plans only He understands. That's sure 'nough."

"But that ain't fair!"

"Aw, Miss Jessie," he said with a shake of his head. "But He's God."

For the first time in my life I saw a completely coherent Mr. Poe. There was no dreaminess about him, no rambling speech. He was more focused and in control now than any man with all his wits about him, and I couldn't stop the tears that spilled down my cheeks.

And as we stood there in a circle around Mr. Poe, the only blockade to the dogs and angry men that were fast gaining on us, Mr. Poe was the one who stood strong among us.

He swiped two thumbs across my cheeks, wiping at the tears. "Don't you cry, Miss Jessie. Muh God's got a place for me."

I stared into his eyes and saw nothing but peace. Luke looked at us both and put one strong hand on Mr. Poe's shoulder and one on my arm. The two of us exchanged a desperate glance.

And then they were upon us.

Gemma had her arms spread out in front of our group like a shield, and all I could hear was my heartbeat. The dogs seemed to bark soundlessly in slow motion, and I watched as we were circled by men with shotguns at the ready. I was filled with indescribable hatred as Joel Hadley made his way to the front of the pack, a rope coiled around his shoulder.

Instinctively I jumped in front of Gemma so Joel couldn't

lay one of his filthy hands on her, but he didn't care much who he manhandled. The fact of the matter was, his life was on the line if the truth ever came out, and the fear of that happening was written on his face, coloring it with determination.

"Best get out of my way, Jessie," he growled. "I ain't got me a lot of patience today, and I've had a hankerin' to teach you a lesson a long time now."

Luke catapulted forward and dragged me behind him, every muscle in his torso tensed for a fight. "Get on outta here, Hadley," he said through clenched teeth. "None of this is your say."

Joel's smirk spoke a million words, and all I wanted to do was slap it off, but Luke's hold on me wouldn't let me budge. I could only stand on my toes to peer over his shoulder.

"Way you're holdin' that girl makes me think things ain't as innocent as you pretend they are," Joel said loudly enough so the crowd could hear. "Her daddy know what's goin' on between you two when he ain't around?"

I could have sworn Joel was begging for some broken bones, and I lowered down onto flat feet just in time for Luke to leave me behind and plant his fist in Joel's jaw. When Joel steadied himself, there was enough blood dripping down his chin that I wondered if he'd bitten his tongue off.

"He broke my jaw!" he yelled incredulously, blood spitting out with every painful syllable.

I was surprised by his shock since he'd deliberately egged Luke on, but I was more surprised by the gunshot that brought all of us to attention.

Sheriff Clancy stood there at the back of the crowd, pistol in the air. Next to him was my daddy, and for the first time in my life I wished he weren't there. Angry men with guns didn't add up to much good most times, and I had enough worry about Mr. Poe, Luke, and Gemma. I didn't want to worry about my daddy too.

"You all right, Jessilyn?" he called out in a voice that mixed rage and fear together.

"Yes'r," I called back. "Just now, anyways."

"Gemma, Luke?"

"Yes'r," they hollered back.

Sheriff Clancy took one almost-imperceptible step forward. "All you boys are in danger of breakin' the law, here," he called out in a tone that bordered on laziness. His expression was far from lazy, though; I could see he was trying to play down just how dangerous the situation was. Even with the help he'd called in from Richmond, he and his deputies were outnumbered by a dozen. "Now, this here ain't your job. It's mine. I'll just take the prisoner back into custody, and things'll all get worked out. You boys can get on your way now I'm here."

"Now you're here, why don't you do your job and arrest Talley?" Joel said, his words jumbled by his already-swollen jaw. "He broke my jaw!"

The sheriff made his way to the front, his pistol still at the ready. "You got proof he did it?"

"'Course I got proof," Joel argued. "Got seventeen witnesses!"

Sheriff Clancy let his eyes roam over the vigilantes. "Well now, all I see is a posse. Since they's likely breakin' the law somehow, I reckon they ain't such fine witnesses." The sheriff was clearly willing to ignore the red knuckles Luke was flexing repeatedly, and the look he flashed me promised an ally in a place I had never expected to find one.

But we were still overwhelmed in number and passion, encircled as we were by such angry men, and I took a handful of Luke's shirt for support. The creek behind us continued to roar, but there was a moment of silence amid our weary group. We were pensive, all of us with eyes that roamed about trying to determine who would make the first move.

It was Nate Colby who made it, and my heart withered at the sight of him, his whole body wrapped up in hate. His rifle stuck out like an extension of his arm and pointed straight at Luke, who still stood guard in front of me, Gemma, and Mr. Poe. His movements were mirrored by the men behind him, and I clung to Luke with both hands, so fearful for his life I couldn't breathe.

Sheriff Clancy lowered his gun to appease the men who'd trained their guns on Luke. "Nate, don't you go doin' somethin' we'll both regret. This here ain't your fight."

"That's where you're wrong. This here's more my fight than anyone's." Nate took two more steps and jabbed the barrel of his gun into Luke's stomach. "Now get out of my way, boy. I don't want to hurt you, but I will."

Joel waved a hand at two men, and they scurried over to

the lawmen to remove their weapons. Luke's gun was in his waistband, and I watched hopelessly as it was stolen away.

Then Mr. Poe moved forward, his body weary but a lightness touching his face. Gemma reached out to stop him, but he shook his head and patted her hand gently. "It's okay, Miss Gemma. Ah got tuh do it, is all. Don't you worry none."

"Mr. Poe," I said in what came out as a frightened wail. "No."

But there was nothing we could do to stop him. He turned to look at me and smiled. "A body don't never say no tuh his God, Miss Jessie." And then he left us and stood in front of Nate. It took only a second for Nate to switch his gun from Luke's gut to Mr. Poe's. I felt Luke take a long inhale, filling lungs that had been starved for air while he'd held his breath in expectation.

Tears spilled down my cheeks, and though Luke's limbs were shaky, he found the strength to wrap an arm around me. "They're gonna kill him," I cried out to Sheriff Clancy. "Do somethin'!"

But I knew as well as anyone there was nothing we could do. We were unarmed and outmanned, and we all stood helplessly by as Joel tossed the rope to Cole Mundy and ordered him to string up Mr. Poe.

"Can't do it yourself, can you?" Luke spat out. "Coward!"

"You won't get away with this, Joel," Sheriff Clancy yelled before someone jabbed a rifle in his gut to take his breath away. He bent over, gasping for air.

Gemma was behind us crying out, but she wasn't

demanding justice, she was praying in a voice that shook with emotion.

They dragged Mr. Poe to the cottonwood tree that spread out over the creek and stood him up beneath a sturdy branch. Mr. Poe had his eyes closed, a sweet smile on his face, and I couldn't decide if I should hide my face to spare myself the memory of what was to happen or keep my eyes on Mr. Poe in honor of his courage. Luke decided for me and tucked my face into his chest. But it took only moments for me to lift my head again. Not knowing was worse than seeing it with my own eyes.

It all seemed to come too slowly, Cole's stubby fingers muddling through the job of tying a suitable noose. A thought rambled through my mind that a Klansman such as Cole should have been an expert at it. The men around us had their guns and eyes trained on all of us, sneaking occasional glances at Cole's progress.

Gemma's prayers got louder by the second, and I hoped if God wouldn't hear her, maybe the men would and it would prick their consciences. But there was no movement of surrender, only the painstaking inadequacy of Cole's fingers. I could hear Luke's breaths coming in ragged gasps, and it sparked such fear in me to know his desperation that I turned my head to dull the sound.

Joel tired of waiting for Cole and grabbed the rope from him. "Ain't you ever tied a knot before?"

It was then that I caught a sudden movement by Sheriff Clancy, pulling something from beneath his pant leg.

The sound of the shot that followed rang off the trees and echoed in my ears. Startled men ducked and threw themselves out of the way, but none of them effected the tragedy that Joel Hadley did.

Sheriff Clancy's aim had missed Joel but startled him, and as he toppled sideways toward the angry waters, his hands grasped for something to hold on to.

The only thing he found was Mr. Poe.

I watched in disbelief as the two tumbled over the side together, disappearing into the muddy rapids. My screams seemed to come out all on their own, but they mingled with the shouts from everyone else. Gemma, Luke, and I all ran to the creekside, but the foaming water looked like prisms through my tears, and I squeezed my eyes shut for a second to force them out. Luke was on his stomach in the mud, reaching over the side, and I did the same to see what he was seeing.

There beneath us was Joel Hadley, his hand wrapped tightly around a bush that grew from the side of the bank. The water licked at his legs ferociously, and it was all he could do to hang on.

His was the last face I'd wanted to see. I'd only wanted to see Mr. Poe, and for my thinking, Joel Hadley could be washed downstream and I wouldn't shed a tear.

But Gemma was crying out next to me, words that sounded more hopeful than devastated, and I peered further over to see that Mr. Poe had a desperate grip on Joel's leg.

Luke reached out and gripped Joel's wrist, straining to lift his weight. I grabbed on to Luke's waist, for all the good that would do, and hung on to him with every bit of strength I had. Gemma joined me, fairly laying her whole body across his legs.

Daddy tried to help, but there was nothing to hold on to but Joel's slippery, wet arm. I could tell Luke was barely able to breathe, he strained so hard to hang on.

"I can't get them up."

"Too much weight with the two of 'em," Daddy called back.

Gemma wriggled up beside Luke to see over the edge. "Mr. Poe!" she screamed. "Hold on!"

The men tossed out the rope they had almost used to hang Mr. Poe in hopes that it would now save him, but it was repeatedly swept away with the current.

Then I saw Mr. Poe's eyes find Gemma's, and for a few seconds, he held her gaze in a way that went far beyond any words he could ever manage to speak. Gemma stopped screaming and lay still, and then I saw her nod slowly, tears starting to stream down her face.

They may have come to an unspoken agreement, but I hadn't, and I threw my arms over the edge, crying out with every bit of breath I had left.

I was only in time to watch Mr. Poe let go of Joel's leg and slip beneath the water.

What happened next was a blur of grief and chaos. Without the weight of Mr. Poe, Luke managed to pull Joel back to solid ground, and then his arms were around me and he was whispering to me to calm down. Gemma knelt at my feet, telling me through her tears that it would be okay.

But Mr. Poe was gone. And Joel Hadley was still here.

Some of the men ran downstream, calling out for Mr. Poe, but I instinctively knew as I sat there by the swollen creek that it had claimed his life. Joel sat on the ground only feet from me, and worn through as I was, I still found the strength to push Luke and Gemma away and lunge for him. He put his arms up to shield himself from the fists I threw at him, but he took everything I gave him. There was a resignation in him I hadn't expected.

I sat back on my heels to stare at his face. "You killed him," I spat. "Just as much as if you'd hung him from that tree, you killed him!"

Daddy came behind me and wrapped me up. "That's all, Jessie," he murmured. "That's all."

Joel's face was blank, and he sat with his shoulders humped, shivering.

Not one man spoke a word. No one moved except Nate Colby, who had dropped to his knees at the side of the creek. "What'd we do?" he cried out suddenly. "We killed the man."

I gently peeled Daddy's arms away and stumbled over to him, kneeling beside his crumpled body. "It weren't your fault, Nate." I put one hand on his back awkwardly. "You're just all beat up inside. You didn't know what you were doin'."

"He was a good man," he said, his shoulders heaving with regretful sobs.

I looked helplessly at the sheriff, and he and his deputies came together to lift Nate to his feet.

I sat back on my heels, and Gemma knelt beside me, taking my hand in hers. "It's all right, Jessie," she whispered tearfully. "Mr. Poe's with Jesus."

I shook my head vehemently. "He didn't listen, your Jesus. I prayed, and He didn't listen."

"He listened, Jessie. He just didn't want the same thing you wanted."

"Then what good is He? What good's a God who don't care about people He created?"

"'Course He cares. It's just He knows more'n we do. Sometimes what we want ain't really best."

"So takin' Mr. Poe away's best?" I argued. "How's that best for us?"

She gave me one of those looks that said I was a selfish girl, and I steeled myself against it, determined not to let her make me feel guilty. "Maybe it's best for Mr. Poe," she finished.

I gritted my teeth to keep from saying what was on my mind because I knew Daddy would hear. And I knew it would break his heart to know what I was thinking just then. Amid the sound of Nate Colby's cries and the rushing waters that had taken Mr. Poe's life, I sat in silence, watching the current cut new boundaries.

Raising my eyes to the rainy heavens, I silently disavowed

the God who had ignored my pleas. A clap of thunder broke the silence as though He were speaking just to me, but my ears were closed to His voice.

Just like I figured His were to mine.

Chapter 22

Mr. Poe washed up downstream a day later. Sheriff Clancy came by our place to tell us personally, but I knew what he was there to say the minute he drove up, and I wouldn't go to the door to hear him say it.

Momma hadn't stopped crying since Daddy dragged Luke, Gemma, and me from his truck, muddied and exhausted. She'd kept vigil over us that whole evening, offering up soup, warmer clothes, and prayers. Gemma and Luke managed to sleep, but I lay awake in my bed, staring at the ceiling, bitter thoughts eating away at my insides.

Joel Hadley disappeared that very day we lost Mr. Poe. His feet had left guilty prints all the way out of Calloway, and there wasn't a single soul who didn't believe Gemma's story after he ran like a coward.

But being rid of Joel didn't help everything. There were still money problems, lives in need of healing, and all sorts of feelings for me to work through. Most of all, there was a hole in my heart the size of the hope I'd had that someday I'd be able to believe what my momma and daddy did, what Gemma did. It was the one thing that had always divided us, and I'd secretly hoped I'd someday find that thing that was missing between us.

But all my hope died the day Mr. Poe's fingers slipped from Joel Hadley.

We buried him two days after he was found, and though I heard the prayers and the kind words, I spent the time scanning the faces of all who stood by Mr. Poe's grave daring to lift up a man they'd betrayed that painful summer. They were false people, the way I saw it, people who could condemn a man while he lived and praise him when he was dead.

Luke hovered around me from the day we arrived back home, but even his presence did little to lift my spirits. My whole world was off-balance, and it was more discouraging for me to discover that Luke Talley couldn't heal all my hurts.

And I desperately wanted healing. I hated walking around like a shell, living life without even noticing. But I feared there was nothing that could heal me now.

❧

Miss Cleta's teakettle whistled, an earsplitting noise that matched my mixed-up thoughts. Nothing was the same anymore. I'd been in this place before, this forced acceptance of things I never wanted any part of, and I was tired of life always having its say. I removed the kettle from the heat and joined Miss Cleta in the living room.

Nate Colby was sitting on Miss Cleta's sofa, doubting himself as I'd seen him do so many times of late. "She ain't takin' it, Miss Cleta," he moaned. "I'm tellin' you, she don't like me."

"You're gettin' all worked up over nothin'," she scolded, taking the bottle from Nate's hand and using it to tickle the baby's lips. "You just got to give her some hints, is all."

The baby's lips wriggled and then latched on, and Nate's smile broke out in a way I hadn't been sure it would ever manage to again.

All because a baby sipped some milk.

"There you go, you see?" Miss Cleta squeezed Nate's shoulder and looked away so he wouldn't spy the tears that glistened in her eyes. "That baby knows her daddy."

I reached out to touch the baby's tiny toes. "What're you goin' to call her?"

His face creased up, so that I immediately regretted my question. The look on his face reminded me of the one I'd possessed since that day at Rocky Creek. But he kept his eyes locked with those of his baby girl and managed to whisper hoarsely, "Grace."

"Oh, that's fittin'," Miss Cleta murmured. "Sure enough, ain't no name better."

The moment did nothing to cure my blues, and I crept away into the kitchen.

I heard Nate leave minutes later, and when Miss Cleta came into the kitchen, my face felt stiff from dried-up tears. I lifted my chin to keep any new tears from spotting Miss Cleta's tablecloth. "Feels like everybody's gone all at once, and I don't know why. There ain't no reason to any of it."

Miss Cleta poured the tea and then sat next to me, taking my shoulders in her aged hands. "Ain't nothin' without purpose, Jessilyn. Nothin'. God gives us kind people out of the goodness of His heart, and He takes them home when He's good and ready."

"But He always takes the good ones," I argued, anger ripping through my insides. "There's bad people walkin' this earth like a plague, but the good ones always get taken away! What sort of God does things like that?"

"We ain't got the right to argue with Him, Jessilyn Lassiter. The sooner you realize we ain't much more than God's creation, subject to the Master, the better off you'll be."

Her voice was firm and strong, and I swallowed hard under her stern gaze. "That's what Mr. Poe said, near about, just before he surrendered himself. He said, 'A body don't say no to his God.'"

Tears welled up in her eyes, but she leaned forward to wipe my own away with her thumbs. "People thought that boy had no sense, but he had more than all of us put together." She pulled a lace hankie from her sleeve and blew. "He knew what life was all about, and he knew what death was all about, and he didn't argue one bit when his Maker called him home. Don't you go lettin' bitterness sweep away your life, Jessilyn. I seen it enough, and it ain't nothin' but tragedy." She stuck that hankie back in her sleeve with decisiveness. "Those men you're hatin', Joel Hadley and the like, they get those hard hearts from bitterness. Don't you go becomin' like those people you're bitter against."

Her words struck hard, and I buried my head in my arms to keep her from seeing my shame.

She reached a hand out to ruffle my hair, and I heard her let out a long sigh. "And besides that, Mr. Poe ain't really gone. He's always in our hearts. All those things Mr. Poe said to you, they were special to your heart, weren't they?"

"Yes'm," I said, my reply muffled by my arms.

"Well, they're as special now as they were then. Don't matter none if he's gone." She sat back in her chair, and her face took on a wistful expression. "Heaven knows my Sully was taken earlier than I'd have liked. The day he left me, part of my heart crumbled into pieces. He was a good man, Sully was, and he always had a way of sayin' things that made me smile even when I didn't feel like it." Her eyes blinked three times fast to keep tears away and then focused on me. "Don't you know he's never gone from me, though? My memory of that man won't never leave me, no matter how old I get. That's God's gift to me. He didn't have to do that, you know. He didn't have to even give Sully to me at all. He could've left me alone all those years, but He didn't. And now I've got years of memories to keep me goin'."

I watched her through misty eyes as she got up from her chair arthritically slow and shuffled to the open kitchen window. "Hear that breeze?" She closed her eyes and a sweet smile spread out across her face. "It's like the breath of God washin' over me, stealin' away all my worries, whisperin' precious words."

But the tears still painted tracks down my cheeks, and Miss Cleta's face creased up into sadness on my behalf. Suddenly she took my hand and led me outside. "Ain't nothin' to heal a heart all at once," she said as we made our way down her back steps. "But there's balms to soothe it if you know where to look."

I was hiccuping in air as we walked, but the cool breeze was just what Miss Cleta said, a balm. It tossed my hair away from my face and dried the tears up into salty streaks. I felt peace tiptoe into all the nervous spots of my spirit and dropped to the ground with my head held up, eyes closed. Before I knew it, Miss Cleta was beside me, no matter her advanced age.

The trees around us swayed and rustled, a sound that blocked out all the worries that had been racing through my head for days.

"Those trees are talkin'," Miss Cleta said, and I opened my eyes in time to see her smile. "It's days like this I swear I can hear my Sully. Whisperin' on the breeze just like he was whisperin' in my ear." She leaned back on shaky arms and crossed her ankles. "There weren't nothin' my Sully loved more than sittin' on the porch on a beautiful day. 'Cleta my darlin',' he'd say, 'the good Lord favored us with a fine one today.' The man knew simple blessin's when he saw them."

"You say you hear his voice, Miss Cleta?"

"Not so much in my ears, mind you, but in my heart."

I lay back on the grass, the windblown blades tickling my ears, and stared at the cottony clouds that streaked the sky. "You think Mr. Poe's in heaven?"

"Oh, honey, that man knew my Jesus like nobody else I know. Folks around here thought he weren't given much since he didn't think like most people, but that ain't true at all." Like a young girl, Miss Cleta lay down beside me and searched the clouds. "Most people think too much about things that don't matter, but that weren't true with Elmer Poe. He didn't clutter his mind up with all that much, and that was a gift from God, sure enough, because it kept his mind free for higher things."

"You sayin' he was better off not bein' smart?"

"Smart's somethin' people come up with, not God. Who says what's smart? It's knowin' God and His Word that means somethin' to Him, not knowin' what people wrote in books. Elmer didn't know all the particulars about book learnin', but He knew as much as a body can about our God." She took my arm in her hand and gave it a squeeze. "Sure enough that man's in heaven now, sittin' at the feet of Jesus. Don't know of no one who loved our Lord more. And that's what Jesus asks of us, Jessilyn."

I wiped my nose with the back of my hand and kept my eyes on the sky, knowing full well her words were aimed at my unbelieving heart.

"He up and walked this earth, took our sins upon Him,

and died on that cross, just so He could rise again for you and me. There weren't no better gift than that, givin' up His life for ours. And all He wants is for us to believe, to let Him take us by the hand and help us walk through this life. Elmer knew that. That's why he was able to give up his own life, because he knew he was goin' somewhere so much better than here."

The clouds tumbled over the sun, so I didn't have to squint for a minute, and I took Miss Cleta's hand. "I don't know why I can't," I murmured.

"Why you can't what?"

"Believe."

Miss Cleta turned her head to look at me and let tears spill to the grass. "Oh, honey, just sayin' that tells me whose you are. You just don't know it yet. If you *want* to believe, some-day you will. You just wait. God'll open your heart when you least expect it, and He'll take that wide-open heart of yours and fill it up with believin' till there ain't no room left."

Her words soothed my anxiety, and I closed my eyes with a deep breath. There weren't any more words to be said, and the two of us lay there beneath the busy trees, close in spirit if not in age.

And we listened.

Chapter 23

Gemma and I visited the creekside two weeks after the tragedy. Daddy had come earlier to place a memorial cross under the cottonwood tree, but neither Gemma nor I could go with him. Our hearts had still been too raw. But this day we decided to go there, just the two of us, to pay our last respects, so to speak.

It was a warm and quiet day, but a breeze had begun to filter in as we walked, and by the time we got there, the creek was rippling in a steady wind. I found the spot beneath the cottonwood tree where I'd last seen Mr. Poe and settled on the ground, lifting my face to the heavens. Cool air rushed across my face, setting the leaves into a noisy flutter.

For the first time in days, I felt a sort of peace push its way into my angry heart. I thought of Miss Cleta and a smile crossed my face. "What's that you say, Mr. Poe?" I asked aloud.

Gemma turned her face into the breeze, her hair fluttering across her lips. "What'd you say?"

"It wasn't me. It was Mr. Poe."

She sat up sternly and shot me a worried glance. "What're you sayin', Jessilyn Lassiter? Mr. Poe can't talk no more, and you know it."

"It's not what he's sayin' now, Gemma. It's what he already said. If you listen close to the breeze, it sounds like he's whisperin'."

"That's foolish talk."

"No it ain't! Miss Cleta says she hears it sometimes. It's just rememberin', is all."

Gemma sat and stared at her toes for a minute before finally giving in to my notion. "What'd he say, then?"

"You remember that day some years ago when he took us to see that honeycomb out in back of his house?"

Gemma frowned at the memory. "That's the day I got my first bee sting."

"But you remember what he said when I said you were actin' like a baby over it?"

"No, but I remember you callin' me a baby." She put her arm up in front of my face. "I still got a scar from that bee sting right here, it got me so good. See?"

"Well, I ain't talkin' about that part," I said, pushing her arm down. But I didn't let go of her. "I'm talkin' about what Mr. Poe did. He tended to your arm in the best kind of way, and then he looked at me and said, 'Miss Jessie, ain't a body that don't need a good cry every now and again, 'specially when they're hurt. Besides, good friends look out for each other.'"

She smiled and looked at the creek that now ran so smoothly, no one would have believed its fury just weeks before.

"His words made me feel all sorts of guilty for days," I said. "Miss Cleta says even though he weren't book smart, he was smart in ways most men ain't."

"I reckon she's right."

"Well, I reckon he was right too. And he sure knew about friends." I grabbed her hand and held it in both of mine. "You always look out for me."

She let her head drop between heavy shoulders and sighed. "I tried to look out for Mr. Poe too, and now he's dead."

"You know better'n me you ain't in control of everythin', Gemma Teague." I tipped her chin up to make her look at me. "Don't you go takin' things on your shoulders like that. All this evil came from the likes of Joel Hadley. It ain't for you to be takin' responsibility."

I watched her tears trickle down and drop onto her lap. "Life's too hard," she managed to squeak out. "It hurts too much."

She was right, and I figured there wasn't much I could say to that. But the last thing I wanted to see was my Gemma weighted down by the problems of all the world. I squeezed her hand tight. "Then it's a good thing we have each other, ain't it?" The wind rustled the trees again, and I smiled upward. "There he goes again."

Gemma swept a hand across her wet cheeks and rolled her eyes. "I think you're goin' crazy or somethin', Jessilyn."

I closed my eyes and lifted my nose to catch the scent of honeysuckle. Then I pulled Gemma close with one arm. "Nope," I said with a defiant shake of my head. "For the first time in a while, I think I might just be fine."

❧

Luke wasn't himself after Mr. Poe died, like the rest of us, and I could tell that seeing Mr. Poe slip away like that had stuck with him. There wasn't a lot I could say to make him feel better, much like there wasn't a lot I could say to make Gemma feel better. Besides, a few whispering winds couldn't heal my heart all up; they were only that balm Miss Cleta had talked about.

But I started a new habit. Every time I started feeling sad about the events of the summer or about life in general, I thought up a new memory of Callie or Mae or Mr. Poe. I likely drove my family crazy talking about them so often, but it was my way of coping, and they knew it. Luke listened most of all, especially when I talked about Mr. Poe, and whenever I'd finish my story, he'd say, "He was an uncommon man, sure enough."

It was this uncommonness that was taunting Luke, I could tell. One day I found him flipping through Daddy's Bible, fingering the pages without reading a thing.

"You know anythin' about this Bible outside of church learnin'?" he asked.

I wasn't all the way over my unhappiness with God, even after Miss Cleta's strong talk, so I shrugged. "All's I know is the stories."

He didn't say anything. He just nodded slow.

Momma opened the noisy screen door with her hip and came onto the porch, balancing two large glass bowls. Luke jumped up to take them from her, causing the Bible to slip to the floor.

Momma glanced at it but looked away quickly as though she'd break some sort of spell if she let on she saw it. It was just like when she would come upon Gemma and me having a nice sisterly moment, and she'd stand real still to keep from making any noise to distract us.

Luke put the bowls onto the wooden table in the corner of the porch and then snatched the Bible up, embarrassed.

"Well, I got me here some corn to shuck and beans to snap," Momma said, pretending she didn't notice anything out of the ordinary. "You two can decide who does what."

On her way inside, she stopped in the doorway and peered back at us, a mist in her eyes. Luke had already grabbed the bowl of corn and let his head drop down to pay more attention to the contents than he needed to.

When the door slammed shut, I sat in silence, mindlessly snapping the beans. Luke sat as quietly as I did. And when Gemma came outside with an extra bowl of snaps, I scooted over to make room for her, and she sat as silently as the two of us.

But I didn't need talk just then, anyway. I decided not to think about life's scary parts and tried to think about the good parts. Sitting there between my best friend and the man I was determined to marry someday, I figured life wasn't always as tough as I thought.

In spite of all the hate and unhappiness and ignorance in the world, some things were just good no matter how you looked at it. For now, I had Gemma humming a hymn beside me, Luke tapping his toe in time . . .

And memories of loved ones whispering on the breeze.

Discussion Questions

1. Jessilyn and Gemma are sometimes at odds throughout the book. What factors do you think contribute to this? Have you experienced a similar situation in your own life?

2. What brings about Luke's change in attitude toward Jessilyn at the beginning of the story? Can you relate to Harley's reaction to Luke's birthday gift for her?

3. In Jessilyn's past she's faced violence, but finding Callie battered by the roadside impacts her very strongly. What fears do you think Jessie was forced to confront as she waited alone with her?

4. Gemma withdraws when she finds out about Callie. How does her reaction vary from Jessilyn's? How do the differing reactions exemplify their personalities and situations?

5. Gemma's normally logical outlook is challenged by Joel Hadley's flattery. Have you ever experienced a time when emotions blinded you to sensibility?

6. Gemma and Jessie can't clear Mr. Poe's name because Joel has threatened to foreclose on the family's farm and also because they are afraid they won't be believed. Would you have handled the situation any differently? How?

7. Harley's faith wanes during the drought. What do you think made his faith particularly shaky now? Do we tend to be more heavily impacted by repetitive hardships?

8. Mr. Poe's arrest leads the people of Calloway to condemn him without trial. Have you seen similar examples in our world today? in historic events?

9. Even though Jessilyn nearly died four years earlier, Mae's death seems to be her first true realization of her mortality. How can age and maturity color our experiences?

10. Mr. Poe's sacrifice has widespread impact. Who is affected and how? Do you agree with Jessilyn that some of the townspeople were hypocrites?

11. Miss Cleta encourages Jessilyn to hear the "whispers" of memories she has of Mr. Poe. Have you ever been touched by your own "whispers"?

12. Jessilyn's anger at God eases with time, but she still hasn't been able to find solid faith in Him. What do you think is holding her back?

Snyder Companies, Inc
1 N. High St.
Selinsgrove, PA 17870
(570) 374-7163

CP0128